THE BOY'S MARBLE

ESSENTIAL PROSE SERIES 199

Canadä

ONTARIO ARTS COUNCIL
CONSEIL DES ARTS DE L'ONTARIO

an Ontario government agency
un organisme du gouvernement de l'Ontario

Canada Council   Conseil des arts
for the Arts   du Canada

Guernica Editions Inc. acknowledges the support
f the Canada Council for the Arts and the Ontario Arts Council.
Ontario Arts Council is an agency of the Government of Ontario.
knowledge the financial support of the Government of Canada.

THE BOY'S MARBLE

Nataša Nuhanović

GUERNICA
EDITIONS

TORONTO • CHICAGO • BUFFALO • LANCASTER (U.K.)
2022

Guernica Founder: Antonio D'Alfonso

Michael Mirolla, general editor
Julie Roorda, editor
Interior and Cover design: Rafael Chimicatti
Cover image: Nick Marinkovich
Guernica Editions Inc.
287 Templemead Drive, Hamilton, ON L8W 2W4
2250 Military Road, Tonawanda, N.Y. 14150-6000 U.S.A.
www.guernicaeditions.com

Distributors:
Independent Publishers Group (IPG)
600 North Pulaski Road, Chicago IL 60624
University of Toronto Press Distribution (UTP)
5201 Dufferin Street, Toronto (ON), Canada M3H 5T8
Gazelle Book Services, White Cross Mills
High Town, Lancaster LA1 4XS U.K.

First edition.
Printed in Canada.

Legal Deposit—Third Quarter
Library of Congress Catalog Card Number: 2022932126
Library and Archives Canada Cataloguing in Publication
Title: The boy's marble / Nataša Nuhanović.
Names: Nuhanovic, Natasha, 1984- author.
Series: Essential prose series ; 199.
Description: Series statement: Essential prose series ; 199
Identifiers: Canadiana (print) 20220165599
Canadiana (ebook) 20220165637
ISBN 9781771837392 (softcover) | ISBN 9781771837408 (EPUB)
Classification: LCC PS8627.U43 B69 2022 | DDC C813/.6—dc23

13,952 People (Maybe More)

It is only fitting we met on February 29, a day that does not exist for most of the time. There have been only eight of those in my lifetime. I don't know that the first two even count, because I barely remember those. That leaves me with six. Even though there aren't very many in competition, I hope you will take it as a compliment that my second favourite is the one on which we met. My favourite one remains February 29, 1996, the end of the Sarajevo Siege. The beginning came on April 5, 1992 with the beginning of spring. I guess that year, life began to bloom in a very different way. The beginning exists every year and outnumbers the days marking the end. Sometimes I am afraid of that. It won't be long. It will be over soon, most of us thought. The siege lasted for 1,425 days. This day is the last one. Only today left.

Only today left. I wonder who will arrive first, you or your letter. One more night of sleeping until I see you again. This is the last sentence you wrote to me. When I read it, I started liking you just a little bit more for reasons I hope you don't find too entirely strange. During the war, many people wrote a sentence just like that. If you knew that this is what the boy said to me the last time I saw him, you might understand why I want to see you again without even knowing who you really are. I am not even fully sure I am ready to find out. The words in your sentence return to me in the voice of the boy: an innocent sound swerves through the dark air, rustles. One more night of sleeping until I see you again. The boy's sentence echoes in my mind one more time. This is what he said before he turned around. His hair curled up at his collar toward the stars and then he left. I wonder if at least one of the stars could see the exact wave of his hair, because your hair curls up like that, too. I hope at least one star could see that far. Maybe it could tell me then if your hair moves precisely the same.

I know it may seem strange that the boy would count when there was only supposed to be a single day left between the moment we parted and seeing me again. But we had already been counting a long time for the war to end, and we no longer wanted to wait. We decided it was time to start counting the days towards our escape. When he said that sentence, we knew tomorrow was the day to run away. Tomorrow, we would leave behind the city full of black clouds. I think I saw one dissipate the further away he went. I have not seen him since. The more time passes, the more I wonder whether the falling-apart cloud was the universe trying to reveal another star or two in an attempt to show in which direction it would be best to walk. I don't know, but I am still counting all the todays until I see the boy again.

Maybe today will be the last. Today, I am driving from Toronto to Montréal just to see you. Despite my excitement, I still can't help but continue the count. I know I should be looking straight ahead instead of down, but I can't. I need to keep track of all the little white lines separating the lanes. Maybe I need to slow down. I feel I may be missing some of them. I need to know exactly how many I passed. I know it is definitely more than 1,425 now. Everything is moving too fast. They are all blending into one white line that is getting too difficult to separate.

Back then I was not aware that more than two decades later, the broken-up lines on the highway would remind me of the streetcar tracks on Sniper Alley. It used to be just a street on which I played before it became something else. It ran all the way from the Old Town to the airport and encompassed two streets: Ulica Zmaja od Bosne (Dragon of Bosnia Street) and Meša Selimović Boulevard. Even a dragon and one of the most prolific Bosnian authors together could not stop the war. The main streetcar line passed through here until the war began. Every time the streetcar passed, a bell would resound through the air. It was very quiet now. The streetcar refused to come out. I wish they would have still kept the sound of the bell, despite everything else.

That's okay. I understand. I understand silence was more appropriate. Or maybe the person operating the bell had a more important task now. I think it was that. I think he had to write all the signs on the side of the road that said: Pazi! Snajper (Careful! Sniper). I know it was him. The handwriting on the signs had the same beauty and compassion as the sound of the bell, only with added sadness. I told myself then that I would stay. I am not going anywhere until I hear the bell again. Besides, I needed to stay and help with writing the signs. More and more snipers appeared at their posts every day. One person to write the warning signs is not enough. We need more. We need more.

I think if I tell the man who used to ring the bell that I am sorry I kept placing tiny rocks on the tracks even though he told me to stop, he would let me help. I don't even know if my handwriting is good enough, but maybe he will let me write some of the signs anyway.

Possibly he will forgive me even more when I give him a few of the rocks the streetcar drove over. He can make fire with them now if he grinds them against each other. He could use some now, I thought to myself then. There aren't that many matches and lighters left in the city. The new ones that come in from other places are becoming a little too expensive. I think the people from other countries who are sending them don't know how quiet it is here now. If they knew, I am sure they would come. They will. They will. Another day went by. No one came.

Another streetlight passes by outside the car window. The ease with which it deflects its light off the soft window glass disturbs me. It seems too careless, too certain of itself and that nothing will ever change. You don't seem like the kind of person to ask me one of the usual questions like how my drive went, but if you did, I wonder if I would tell you any of this.

Telling you nothing at all would maybe be best. It might come over me to mention that on my way to you, I thought a lot about the way your coat rested on your shoulders. One or two sizes too large, I thought. Just the way it should be. The boy liked to wear his coat that way, too. I need to grow up faster now, he said. I need to grow taller than the grownups, so that I can stretch my arms up into the air and move away the clouds. Once the grownups see the clear sky again, they might remember a different life and that where they are now is not where they were supposed to go. I need a bigger coat now, he said. I will grow taller soon, I know. With his arms down, only the tips of his fingers peered from the edge of his sleeves. Inside your sleeves, movements could happen without notice. Some might think that looks sloppy, but not at all; its fabric draped over the curves of your shoulders comfortably and without exposure. A dust speck was revealed here and there, depending on the way you moved. Three or four fell, floated through the air until they, too, found their hiding place.

Before we parted, you lifted your collar up to hide more of your neck. Somehow the instinct you had to do that made me feel you may understand what it is like to not know if you will arrive on the other side of the street alive. Little gestures like that make walking outside feel more safe.

The grownups with the snipers won't see me now, I told myself on one of the days. I pulled my hoodie over my head and went to check if the streetcar had come back. Even though it was winter, I did not have a coat on. It was just too warm. Orange-red broke through the colourless air while the growling sounds continued to make it tear. Smoke whirled around in an attempt to hide the horror. The smoke is still here, filling up my car. I can wave it away with my hand. I can wave it away. Behind the narrow gap my fingers make, entire buildings have aged by centuries. Age spots have appeared on the walls, freckles rest underneath shattered glass. Shoes are beating against the asphalt. My foot is pressing harder on the gas pedal. I can still hear them. The howls. The irregular echo of the unbearable: the sound of a child's single glove lost on the street, immovable. The air is tearing again. I can't hear anymore. I can't hear.

You told me that you can't hear so well on your left side. This reminds me of too many raindrops landing in the boy's ear. That day when the boy went home, the sky did not know where to put all that rain. There was too much of it even for the more experienced clouds, the ones that usually knew what to do. I remember the boy held an umbrella above my head as he told me where to meet him the next day. The drops started falling faster and faster. He leaned the umbrella towards me, closer and closer. I think I should have told him he needs to remember to protect himself, too. I think he forgot, because raindrops kept sliding from the umbrella into his left ear, one after the other. If only it had rained a little less, he may not have gotten wet, I keep thinking to myself, night after night. Too many drops fell. Too many for him to still be able to hear the same way as before that day. At least I think that may be the case. Maybe I am afraid to find out from you how long ago you stopped hearing so well. Maybe I can at least tell you that this makes me feel closer to you.

I cover both my ears as I drive. No one is holding the steering wheel for a moment. In that moment, I remember I placed my coat over the seat in front of me in the streetcar. Someone had written with a black pen on the back seat that they were here. I forgot my coat on the chair that day, but maybe it was for the best. Some shelter. I don't know if he is still there. I just don't know.

I just don't know if I am ready to ask you anything. I don't know if I am prepared to find out everything about the past. Everything I ever wrote to you about me, my life, or my past, still waits to hear the sound of that bell. Maybe I wrote too much. Maybe it is too early for all that. Maybe there are too many lives I don't know enough about. I am afraid you won't like some of mine. I am afraid I may find your hair does not move the same way the boy's does. I am afraid when he walked away that night, the clouds covered too many stars. I am not sure he could see the street properly. I am not sure I know how to tell you about a past I do not understand. I fear I am making it worse. I fear I am making it come back to life before I know what to do with it.

Normally, I probably would not feel comfortable speaking about any of this at all, but the way you lifted your coat again before you buttoned it, made me reconsider and think I might. The boy buttoned my coat just like that before he left. Today is a cold day, he said. I wonder if it was even colder that day, almost six months ago, when you and I first met. I had just landed in Canada. Not long after, a snowflake *landed* on your hat. I have not seen you since, but I remember very well you touched the tip of your ear and shook your head as if there was too much water inside. For a moment, you even looked like the boy. Though I can't be sure, because a snowflake was covering my eye. He must be alive. He must be alive. I need to find out.

THREE YEARS

One

I can hear a beeping sound. What happened to my eyelids? They are not working anymore. Regardless of my attempts to lift them up, they remain shut. Someone tell me what is going on. Endless streams of suitcases are arriving, but there are no passengers, only a body-less voice repeating unclaimed luggage will be destroyed. Where is this voice coming from? Who is saying these things without wondering where everyone went? Where am I? Why is the emergency light on all the luggage tracks flickering? A flash of an unknown wallpaper reveals itself to me for a second, before I am standing in front of the arrivals board. It says all the flights are delayed. No, that cannot be. They are lying. New arrival time: Unknown. I am here. I can see all the suitcases falling off the tracks. Why is the sound the same as someone knocking on my door? What is this fluttering in my pocket? Sarajevo – Montréal: My boarding pass with no travel date. It floats on my palm like a sea mattress before folding itself into a bird. One of its wings traces a line on my palm, the other wing moves slowly in the air. This wing is torn on its side. The airline staff in Sarajevo tore off the other part right after agreeing that the picture in my passport is likely enough to be me. The little paper bird tickles my palm before it flies away, a whiff of air against my cheek and all the hairs on my body stand up, an orchestra of sleepwalkers wandering along unfamiliar streets. My feet run to follow it, the sound of an abandoned ball tapping against the stairwell runs alongside me, someone else's shoes hop down the apart-ment building stairs after the shot. Oh no, the little bird is disappearing. I can no longer see. I try to run faster, but my body feels as heavy as the mountain of suitcases no one will pick up. I feel hot. There is sweat on my skin and I feel like something suffocating is surrounding me. The sound of a flutter moves my feet, the blanket is tangling itself between my feet. My eyelids are pulsating. The strange wallpaper appears again. An ugly flower pattern swirls to a doorknob I do not recognize before it gets dark again. I am in a tunnel. The sound of the bird's wings is filling the dark space around me until the voices of the airline staff rushing me to board the plane are fully covered. The flapping of the bird's wings sounds like fire; it is getting quieter and quieter, the airplane doors are closing, the tunnel is moving. Where am I? It is as dark here as inside my grandparents' fireplace. What happened? Someone has to add more coal or they will get cold. What is this warmth in my ear? I can feel a peck on my earlobe, a light pain, the bird's beak. This makes no sense. What is the bird suddenly doing inside the hotel and why is it scratch-ing my ear? I feel like I am everywhere all at once. Maybe I won't feel that way anymore once I am fully awake. My hand lightly brushes past my ear as I rub one of my eyes. The hotel room emerges again. I think I hurt myself on the edge of the nightstand beside my bed. It is just too sharp. Maybe someone should tell them that nothing that harsh should be near a place of waking up. I rub my eyes again. Now, like a prisoner, I can see my suitcase through my eyelashes. Only a few seconds later do I realize that it is the other way around. The suitcase stands guard beside the bed, making sure I do not escape. How long has this alarm clock been beeping? My ear is ringing and I want to go back to the bird instead of waking up in this cold hotel room.

Where was it again that I needed to go? I can't remember why the alarm clock is going off. Someone else is calling me. The squeaking sound of the boy's feet trying to balance on the bicycle pedals convinces the alarm clock to stop. He stops, too. Both his feet are fully aligned now, his legs perfectly still. One of his hands holds the handle, the other reaches up towards the sky. Look, I am taller now, he says. I can be highest with the pedals reaching the same level, just like this: side by side. I wonder if he is tall enough now to touch the branch arching above his head. Before I can find out, I feel my bed covers inside my palm. No. I want to say something to the boy, but I can no longer speak; the outside air is not reaching me. Both my eyes are turning into marbles with which we used to play almost every day. His favourite was the one with the blue-green river inside until it one day became brown, just like the rivers in our city. I guess nobody needed to ask why. Still, he would hold the marble tightly in his hand, hoping next time he opens it, it will look more like he remembers, more like before when the flowers by the river were not yet trying to escape. What is this shattering sound? The marble is broken. There is water in my mouth, my hair is soaked and I have forgotten how to swim. Petals on my tongue are piling up telling me stories of what they witnessed. Countless photographs of missing people are spiralling around me. Some are smiling. Others look serious, as though they could tell what was coming. On one, a grandmother is knitting an orange sweater with her grandchild sitting beside her. The river is carrying them all away. No, this cannot be, who will remember them then? This one photograph is not enough. I do not know anything about them. I need to know more. I need to know what happened. Why do I feel a pillow behind my head? No, I do not want to wake up. I need to collect all these faces. Each one of them can tell me more than anyone still alive. Why can't I move my arms? Where is all this water going? Why am I dry? My ear is bleeding and the flowers by the river have turned into wallpaper. This looks nothing like them. They no longer resemble themselves. I am not sure I like the way they circle around me. Petals whirl around the room and disappear as the alarm tells them it is time to go. I guess I should have learned by now that this is something the everyday life in my new country tells me to forget. The flowers on the wall here look happy. The colour of their petals is lush and vibrant. They know nothing about a river 6,000 kilometres away or what it carries. They do not wonder why after more than twenty years since the end of the war, the river is still brown. The blood on my ear feels a lot like the dew that became thicker and thicker the more the grownups continued to fight. The cold air is becoming trapped. It is getting harder and harder to escape. Each taken life, a droplet that cannot evaporate. I do not want to wash the blood on my ear away. Maybe the heat will tell me where I need to go, since I do not quite remember what I came here for. Maybe then it will be easier to get out of bed. I do not know what is going on. Usually, I can hardly wait to get up from a bed that is not mine, from a bed I slept in only once. Maybe if I sleep here one more night, getting up will be easier next time. One more night. One more night. What time is it?

The alarm clock is no longer where I left it before going to sleep. All I see is an empty nightstand. I am afraid the river flowing around my dark pupil is disappearing and I will no longer know where I came from. I fear that nothing will be left, but a dry riverbed with the remains of a life long passed, resting at the edge of the growing dark abyss inside my eyes. During the war, my pupil has learned to expand. That was the only way to try to survive. Everybody knows that the war makes you simultaneously less than yourself and more than yourself. Everybody knows that during the war you can hear steps from kilometres away, but nobody told me that they will stay with me years later or what to do with all these people living inside my eyes. They are plunging along the black waters inside my pupil, my iris is pulsating in waves. Everybody knows that during the war, the air is different. Everybody knows you can tell by the fog and the moisture on your window that someone has died. The air bears no secrets. Even the flowers no longer smell the same. But no one told me how to stop fogging up every room I enter with my own breath that still carries the same scent. I cannot see anything at all through this hotel window. My hand draws a circle on the fogged-up glass. The room is looking at me now with an iris showing me a glimpse of the outside. My lips move towards the window. I want to see closer the snowflakes falling outside. But it is clear I am just a stranger to this new place, because the room is closing its eye, my breath has coated the window and I am trapped inside. Maybe everybody knows that, too, that some things can only be communicated in the dark. The war teaches you how to do that with wide-open eyes. But it did not teach me about the growing abyss that would remain in my eye after spending years by candlelight and a small nightstand lamp. It did not tell me that one day, when the war is over, a normal light will seem too bright and burn my eye, that the abyss is too big to contract, and there is nowhere else to put all that has happened. I did not know then that years later I would be in a hotel room, making sure not to turn on most of the lights. I did not know then that my pupil, growing out of fear and instinct for survival, would become a home for everything I ever witnessed, a home that I know neither how to close, nor how to live in.

I still do not remember what I came here for, but there is a dust speck in my eye. A branch brushes my cheek. I must still be waking up. The words "one more night" linger in my mind. I do not want to stay in the hotel another day, but these words will not go away. I don't know why. I don't know where all this dust is coming from, but more of it is falling into my eye. Some looks like broken asphalt. My eye is getting itchy and tells me it is time to leave this room. As I close the curtain, a light bulb falls off the window ledge. I notice the floor lamp is unplugged. Did I do that? It is one of those old-fashioned lamps, whose shade looks like someone's dress. Fine little strings surround it. I touch them with my finger as I walk by to leave and watch them move, little grass blades moving in the river I know back at home or my grandmother's headscarf. This makes me smile. This is the first time I smiled since I came to Canada, I think to myself as I take the hotel room key and close the door.

I can still hear a quiet beep in my head, soon interrupted by the sound of tiny wheels of a suitcase. Other guests are arriving. They have unfolded the city map over the check-in counter; little stars mark all the places worthy of seeing. I feel dizzy and the chandelier is starting to spin. Click. Click. Click. The candy dispenser of a little child waiting in line reminds me of a clock hand unsure of which way to go. My own arm reaches into my pocket as I feel a piece of paper leaning against my thigh. Château Versailles Hotel. My arrival date is listed underneath. The date indicates I arrived yesterday, but I feel like I have been away from home for centuries. The words "one more night" still follow me. Maybe something is wrong with the time. The seconds have turned into days, minutes into months, hours into years. They have turned into the kind of time that still hasn't passed. I try to read the address of this hotel. I can read the numbers, 1659, but the letters begin to blur. An "S" swirls like a man after a night alone at the bar; an "H" tries to balance out his state of mind with order and symmetry; the rest quiver at his sight. The paper between my fingertips is bending; the letters are falling off, gliding down into the lobby carpet like dead skin. My eyelashes feel the need to embrace. Black sparkling little dots fill the air, like those one sees during a heavy migraine. They are turning into letters, rearranging on the business card: 1659 Subproject Street West. It looks like this is the address of my hotel.

Something is pushing against the paper from the other side, the sail of a boat turning over. The edge leaves a mark on my finger as I flip the paper around. I must be tired still, because it has been a while since I had a paper cut. Maybe in this new country everything just feels different from what I am used to. Seeing my own handwriting on the other side surprises me as I do not recall having written anything at all: 68 Subproject Street West, 4 p.m., February 29. I am guessing I must have a meeting there with someone. I wonder who it is and what it is for. It is today and, as it looks, on the same street as my hotel. A sense of relief weaves through me at the thought that I only have to walk straight for a change. Thank goodness, because my head feels heavy as though it is filled with thousands of tiny pebbles. My hair smells like river moss with a hint of vanilla shampoo. I hope whoever it is I am meeting won't mind the scent, or the drops of Sarajevo rain in my hair that simply won't go away. During the war, the clouds turn into giant pillows that don't fit inside a washing machine. At night, when it was time to sleep and everything seemed quiet again, when the time came to lie down and rest my head, for a moment I may believe that outside everything is okay. But in my sleep my lips move without a sound, the unsayable soaks into my pillowcase that flies out my window, floats into the sky, becomes cloud and moves restlessly through the city. Like a water sprinkler for a tiny plant, a drop from someone's mouth on my cheek while they speak, quietly the words fall into my hair in the shape of little drops, noticeable years later when everyone thinks that the war is now over.

Two

A breeze of fresh winter air against my cheek as a man with a cane opens the front door for me reminds me it is time to go. My legs won't bend; my knees are frozen. They no longer feel like they are part of my own body. The man at the door moves slowly, but gracefully, as if he is recalling dance moves from his youth, now long forgotten. No one really knows those dances anymore. He holds the door handle the way he would hold a child's hand. The lines below his eyes have multiplied. They look like traces of eyelashes that fell on his cheek during a time when there was too much wind. Now, only the imprints remain, his hat just wide enough to cast enough shade to protect them from being seen by the passersby.

I wonder which eyelashes were his. The closer I look, the more I see all the lines left behind by the eyelashes are too small to belong to him. I am not surprised, because the grownups have forgotten how easy it is to make a wish. They no longer believe in things like that. I remember the boy picking up my eyelash from beneath my eye with his thumb. Just blow it away and everything will be okay, he said. Warm air leaves my mouth, the eyelash floats up. A gust of wind turns the man's coat into wings. Its inner lining is revealed. A paper rose pinned to the inner pocket seems to have entered into a deep sleep. Sometimes I wish I could fold myself in and live inside someone's pocket instead of trying to figure out why moving my legs is so difficult. The wind has disappeared and the man's coat has landed on my left arm. Now I remember the man in Sarajevo, who put his coat around me on that cold winter night when I was sitting on the bench in front of our apartment feeding the sparrows. All this happened without a single light. The street lanterns look like abandoned homes in a ghost town nobody visits anymore. The electricity is out and there is a draft. I could see the man approaching me from a distance, swaying left and right, like a pendulum measuring someone's sorrow. When he got closer, I did what a child would do and asked him what happened to his legs. He told me that he is now half real-man and half wax-man, not to worry, he is not hurt. He said I should always remember there is not a single good thing that happens in a war, but the good thing is that he was able to walk like this across the entire city without anyone suspecting he is hiding two giant candles, one in each trouser leg. I should remember stealing is not good, he said, but he borrowed these from the Catholic church around the corner. Each of them must be around half a metre. He said he never used to pray before and won't start now, but if there is a God anywhere, he doesn't trust him to get me home safely. After I told him I live in the building behind us, he decided to give me both of his wax-legs. He doesn't need them, he said. He is old and his apartment is already so cold, it is too late. There is nobody waiting for him there anymore, he said, and he is not sure he can get used to warmth again. He placed one candle on each side of me and walked away. A sparrow followed him. The others looked at me and at his coat he left around my back. They stopped eating the breadcrumbs as I watched him, still limping. He is only cold, he is only cold, I tell myself.

Where is this snowflake on my cheek coming from? The man with all the lines beneath his eyes looks at me and I remember again where I am. All the eyelashes have left his cheek again, because the wishes the children made did not work out the first time around. Maybe they will now. I am a bit worried that there are so many eyelashes floating in the air, because I have never seen so many of them fall out at the same time. They are only wishes. They are only wishes.

Inside his eyes, breadcrumbs are floating slowly and gently like snow inside a snow globe. A child's glove floats with them. Maybe it belongs to the lost glove I saw on the Sarajevo street. The falling glove looks like it is trying to collect some breadcrumbs. I think the sparrow that followed the man, who gave me his candle legs and his coat, could use some more of them. Maybe the sparrow is hungry. Maybe they had to walk far to arrive at his home. I think I have to keep walking, too. A coat slides along my arm as I limp down the stairs of the hotel. I am not even sure which coat I felt; that of the man standing at the hotel or the coat the candle man draped around me long ago. These stairs look nothing like the entrance to my apartment, I think as I wonder what happened to him and if he is still alive.

His suspenders hanging on to his trousers look like my hands holding on to the frozen railing. Why is there ice beneath my feet and where did the candles he gave me go? My fingertips are turning blue. Drops are falling from underneath my nails, like those from hand-washed sweaters hanging upside down during the war. Their empty arms stretching out towards the ground are looking for their owners. The puddle is growing larger. A child is running underneath the clothesline with its arms up towards the grey sky. For a moment there is a touch. The sleeves move like an empty swing. They are waving now, but nobody is there anymore. A splash in the puddle before the child is gone. The sound of shoes against the gravel could be thunder. There will be more rain, they say. Another drop falls from the sleeve. A stray dog drinks from the water, sticks out his tongue to catch another falling drop. The stray dogs are always thirsty these days, they say, and nobody knows why. Nobody knows why there is still water dripping down their clothes regardless of how often they twist the wet sleeves. All I know is that my sleeves are full of wrinkles, my socks are wet. I can feel a paw scratching my knee.

But what is this snow on my shin? A snowball against my knee has replaced the scratches and I am confused. A little girl waves at me from the street. Her gloves are covered in white. The street looks like someone has poured tonnes of flour on it just to cover all the rubble underneath. I feel like collecting it all. I may need it one day to survive: ten bags of flour for a car. And that was considered one of the better deals then. An "On Sale" sign peeks between the falling snowflakes: two for the price of one. This is not much different from the war: two lives gone for every one you take. What are they trying to sell me now? There is nothing they can offer me to make up for the missing eggs I needed then to build a snowman out of flour that would not fall apart. Maybe some people would say that is not much of a snowman then when he is not made of snow. But I think he can be anything he wants to be; he can be anything at all, especially when he knows the water he is made of comes from the fresh spring well outside. All the snowflakes go there and end up in canisters people carry with them when there is no more water. He looks out the window from the basement as my hands mould him and wonders why he is not allowed to go outside. I used coffee beans for his eyes, but did not know how to tell him we cannot afford eggs and the water alone is not strong enough. I try to give him hands, but the flour dissipates. Maybe he does not need them, I tell myself. Maybe if I secretly open the window every night, he will not just disappear, and will decide to stay. Maybe no one will notice my quiet slippers as I sneak out of bed to check up on him. I have learned by now to fall asleep in the draft. The wind is blowing. There is a snowflake on my eyelash. One eyelash falls out, floats up on the wavy air, like an escalating swing. Another snowflake passes by in front of my eye. I am reminded again that I am nowhere near my old bed. Besides, there is a scarf around my neck and I never used to sleep that way. It glides on the Montréal air like a wave before it folds up and covers my mouth. There is wool in my mouth and gravel beneath my feet. How did the stairs leading down into the basement get to the front of the hotel? As I walk down, a taxi driver asks if there is any place I need to go. His car is full of coal and potatoes. He looks at me not knowing that at the moment I cannot say anything at all. My warm breath behind the scarf returns back to me in the shape of the log in the fireplace too damp to catch fire. Snowflakes are collecting in my hair. The scarf bends around my ear, points to the left. It is high time I start walking to the place that may reveal to me the reason I came.

I don't know if I am walking in the right direction, but this way more snowflakes are landing on my face. One lands on my nose. Its six arms cover every direction in perfect symmetry. What is this cosmic order that makes the water flower and the flowers bend down towards the soil? What is it that the cosmic order does not want us to know about? It is hiding something underneath the earth. What is this horror hiding beyond the beauty of the dying flower? It bows so gracefully like a conductor after a beautiful symphony. Her death looks beautiful, yet her death, and death altogether is forgotten at the sight of her long, elegant neck. I see a lot of flowers right in front of me. They are lining the street all the way into the distance, farther than I am able to see. Crystals adorn the edges of their petals. They are frozen in the position of their last moment of life in flowerpots that line the street. Like an audience that gave a standing ovation, but never sat down again, they lean tiredly. The symphony seemed to be over, but it continues. It is embarrassing to sit back down, so everyone keeps standing, pretending they knew all along it was not yet the end. But something did end, just not what everyone thought. Or maybe they thought it was finally time for the *scherzo,* because life is moving slower than the memory of it and they need to catch up, they need to move faster. But it is too late for that now. Another *adagio.* Another slow movement around the flowers. If only I knew how to move straight, maybe I could get there faster. But I can't. Instead, I swerve from left to right, surrounding the flowers. My arms hover over them every time I pass another one. This is the only way to walk and be safe. I think I have to continue to swerve even though this may make me lightheaded. The snipers will be too confused that way. If I change directions all the time, they will never be able to tell where I am. One night, after hearing a shot, I taught myself how to walk. They can't get me like this, I tell myself. I walked the way I imagine people would walk if they lived on the moon. But I knew even then the man on the moon is asleep. He is no longer watching me. His blinds are long closed. He no longer opens the window when he drinks his morning coffee. Something brushes lightly against my wrist. It feels like the corner of a newspaper, but that can't be, because he has stopped his subscription and refuses to read anything at all. It is only a cold blade of grass from one of the flowerpots

I must have walked far, because I can no longer see the hotel. A snowman is standing right in front of me. He is larger than I am and is stretching out his arm. I think he wants to shake my hand. He can see

I don't trust him and tells me it's okay, he wanted me to know I am standing on the street that accounted for most of Canada's wealth at the end of the 19th century. Most of the mansions that used to be here are gone now, he says, but the past never truly goes away. I am not sure why he is telling me this or why I can see a talking snowman. His eyes are made of old stamps. His nose is a rolled-up letter. There is a pipe in his mouth, which he is loading with pages of a history book. The smoke is hurting my eyes. My eyelids close over the abyss. The boy flicks a marble. The closer it rolls towards the marbles inside the chalk circle, the closer it gets to the edge of my pupil. Oh no. My pupil is expanding again. Too late. The marble falls into the black water inside my eyes. It sinks deeper while the street trembles for a moment and the flowers remain the same.

A large flower stands right in front of the Montreal Museum of Fine Arts and keeps company with the man made of bronze leaning his head towards me. Hands are reaching from behind him, covering his nonexistent face, as if to tell me what awaits. He has no eyes, no nose, no mouth, yet I can feel him looking at me, trying to tell me which way to go. My mother's hands are on my cheek. It is dark again, but I can see through the crack between her fingers like through a broken blind. No, I do not see anything, it is completely dark, I answer her. It is just a game we play, she tells me, and I pretend to believe it. We are walking home, but this looks nothing like our usual way. I see an arm resting on the ground, a hand facing upwards like a flower about to open as though looking for answers in the sky. His sleeve is buttoned way too tightly. He needs more air. He needs more air. This must be the reason he cannot breathe. What was it you said, my mother asks. I did not even realize I was speaking out loud. Someone has to unbutton his sleeve. Someone needs to help him breathe. My mother moves her fingers slightly. Now I can see a woman's hand covering the left pocket of his button-up shirt. She is pressing down on his chest. One. Two. Three. My ears fill with a sound I knew even then I could never forget. It turns the little air particles into black stars. They howl quietly beneath the blanket covering a body, dead skin lands on a petal, the button falls off his shirt and rolls along the street. Her hand pushes down again. One. Two. Her hair covers his neck. Three. A scarf made of human pain protects the best. My mother's hand trembles. Her fingers squeeze together, hoping I won't see anything. The blinds before my eyes close fully for a moment. Darkness comes like an unwanted pacifier at first, a closing drawer I want to get out of. Then it becomes just the inside of what is there, like a coat left on the chair inside out. Nothing can keep out the motion of his little finger or her head on his chest. My mother's palm over my eyes becomes a galaxy. Swallowed by a black hole, I open my eyes. The bronze man at the end of the flower-lined street is in front of me again. There is a giant hole in his chest. Two hands are reaching through it from the other side, resting on the edge, almost in forgiveness, resigned with a sense of grace. A ray of sunlight flows through the hole all the way to my hair. I am a little afraid of that, because I don't want any of the snowflakes in my hair to melt away. A drop of water slides down my forehead, sweat that smells like her sweater which she had placed softly over his head. She only wanted to hide him. She only wanted to hide him. If he can't see, no one will be able to see him either. One of the sweater sleeves covers his one eye, the second sleeve covers the other. The sleeves fold in towards each other like the wings of the bronze man without a face. Something is attacking his wings. Mud slides through the feathers, never-ending rain mixed with the dirt from soldiers' boots and unfinished sandcastles at the playground. There was never so much mud in the city streets before the war, but now my fingernails are black. My arm reaches up, trying to roll up the sleeve. There is too much dirt around me. The winged man's hand touches mine. As he moves his arm from underneath his wing, I can see the flesh around his arm is missing. Maybe he, too, knows what it is like to walk home without a single streetlight on. A sparrow lands on one of the hands replacing his face and I wonder if he knows the man who gave me the tall candles, long ago. Maybe he will be able to tell me if he ever made it home. I know we are in a different city on a different continent, but he has wings and the mud on them looks the same as the one I was playing with on that bench. Maybe when I stood up and went home, he swept over the bench with one of his wings and covered the man with the other. After all, someone needed to keep him warm, since he gave me his coat and he was cold. I remember a street-light flickered beside him for a second when he was already far away. A sparrow fluttered. A light breeze combed through my hair as my shoe stepped on one of the breadcrumbs I threw.

Maybe the winged man was also inside the church with him, because his legs look like they are melting away. The fingers around the winged man's head form a braid, the kind I used to make for myself before the boy and I would go out and play. I did not yet know how to properly braid then, but he likes it that way, he said. It reminds him of the winding paths he takes to get from his home to mine. The wheel of his bicycle rotates in my eye, divides, spins up into the sky. It passes by the Wheel of Fire upon which Ixion is bound. He has been spinning through the sky for centuries now. Maybe this is punishment enough. I know he did something bad, but maybe he has changed. I know he was the first to be accused of killing family, at least by the Greeks, but I think a lot of grownups have done something like that now and they are still on the ground. Maybe they can talk to him. Maybe they can talk to history. Maybe he knows the future now after spinning in the universe for so long. Maybe the grownups could figure things out like that. Or they could talk to the boy instead and find out what went wrong.

I think the fire on Ixion's wheel must be long out. I don't think anyone has checked, but it has been raining for days and the matches are all wet. Still, there is a sound coming from the sky. Maybe it's the boy's bicycle wheel swerving through the clouds. The bars on his wheel are slicing through the future determined by the grownups. Maybe we can have a different one now.

Another slice. The tear in the universe expands. The bicycle wheel keeps rotating. I can hear marbles spinning inside a plastic bag, the one he carried with him at all times. The faster he pedals, the more they spin. The plastic bag has wrapped itself around the handle of the bike. He is holding it down with his palm, making sure it does not fall off. His other arm lifts up again. The hole in the sky tears some more. A hand reaches through it, touches my eyelid with a wet fingertip.

Another snowflake. My eyelids lift for a moment and I see the winged man again, but he flickers before me like a dying light bulb. Why am I feeling so warm when outside it is at least ten below zero? My head feels like a helium balloon about to rise up into the sky and float away. The street in front of me is getting fuzzy. The bricks of the museum are

moving in and out like piano keys. Who is playing them? What is the
boy's marble doing in the winged man's hand? I jump up to reach for
it, but I can't. Maybe if I wasn't so out of breath, I could simply blow it
away. I jump again, but I am not good at that anymore. In school we
learned that if we step on a landmine, it is best to throw oneself sideways
onto the ground, the same way a kite would fall after the wind decides
it has had enough of playing. The lower the jump, the better. The more
horizontally one falls, the less chance of dying. The marble is too high.
I am not supposed to jump up like that. I need to jump like I am going
to sleep, lying down. It is starting to snow more. I am happy to see that,
because I do not want to be here anymore. I want to go back to that
bench, where I used to sit waiting for the boy to arrive. Maybe then
I could take one of the large candles and lean it on the winged man's
thigh. Then I could climb up like on a slide, push the marble out of his
hand with my fingertips, watch it fall together with the snowflakes, like
a planet tumbling through the universe. We lost the marble not too long
before we were supposed to run away. I think it may be my fault he got
lost, too. Maybe if he still had his favourite marble in his hand, he would
have somehow found his way to the bench. I know I always felt safe
when he placed it in my palm, folded my fingers around it and said: The
river inside it has turned brown, but the moment you close it in, it turns
blue-green, just the way it was before the war. The rivers in our city can
one day turn back, too. I don't know if that's true. Through the blinds my
mother placed over my eyes, I could hear someone cry: Oh no! There is
another one in the river. Oh no! Please. Why? The hand is not moving.
A drop of river mixed with red lands on my cheek. The wind must have
carried it. Turn around! Turn around! You can't breathe with your face
in the water like that! My mother covers one of my ears with her other
hand, but I can still hear. Another brown drop lands near my eye.

Snowflakes are whirling around me. I am, once again, on the snowy
street far away. No! I need to go back! I need to see who else is in the
river, who doesn't know how to swim. I need to help! The more I try to
go back, the higher my scarf billows up in the wind. It brushes against
the marble, nudges it out of the statue's hand. I can hear it falling to the
ground. I cannot see anything. Like a giant white bedsheet, the sky has
covered the street as if telling it to go to sleep. The sound of the marble

against the street is hurting my head, but all I can do is follow it. What is going on? The sound it makes is the same as rolling over cobblestone. This cannot be, because the street is full of snow. The sound repeats. Why am I running after it? I want to stop, but my legs keep running. Where am I? I cannot hear my own feet. The snow has silenced the present and placed it inside a drawer in one of its six arms according to the so-called cosmic order. I don't understand anything at all and, most of all, I don't understand why I am so out of breath and why there is wax dripping from the corner of my eye.

The wax is hardening on my skin, turning into a seal. Lines branch underneath it, like the roots of trees pushing up against shelled asphalt. I feel the street beneath me stretch, form little cracks. The marble is rolling towards the edge. I can see it now, but I cannot hear. Snow is falling around me, yet nothing sticks to the ground. I look left and right, but there is nothing there, except thousands of snowflakes. Between them I recognize petals. Each one of them disappears as soon as it hits the ground. The marble rolls without a sound. I try to run faster, but I am too late. It falls off into the empty space. A wave in my eye swallows it, one extra spin in the washing machine. Some days I stayed outside on the bench for so long that my clothes were spinning for days, but nothing would get out the stains. With each cycle, the flushed water flows into my iris. My eyes are brown, because of all the days he never came. My clothes just kept soaking in the Sarajevo rain along with the rubble collecting on the bench every time someone passed me by all dressed in black while I waited for him. Another cycle. The washing machine is just not strong enough. Another wave of water flows into my iris. Little shredded pieces of paper float inside. A letter he wrote to me and secretly placed in my pocket now resides inside my eye. Maybe if my clothes hadn't been so dirty, the washing machine would not have destroyed his letter. Maybe it is my fault, because I stayed out too long. Maybe I thought he is only late.

I am swimming inside my own eyes. There is too much water in my hands. All I want is to know what he wanted to say, but the paper slides between my fingers and I cannot catch a single one. The water is flowing inside my ear; sound returns to me in the same way as after a shot. First follows a barely perceivable silence, yet one that never leaves, one whose echoes fold around everything that comes next. Oh no, the water is being sucked away, the ground shakes, the washing machine grunts at me like someone clearing his throat after too much brandy. My hands move to no avail, a child pointing at a moving cloud in the sky. Only snowflakes are in my palm, nothing else. They almost look the same as the letter remains left by the washing machine. I look up at the sky and stick out my tongue, hoping to taste something familiar. Instead, a sign looks at me, "Crescent Street"; the streetlight beside it turns on as if to say hello.

It is still the same day as this morning when I woke up in the hotel, but I feel like I am just waking up one more time. Everything starts all over, to be experienced again. Maybe the first time was not enough. I keep missing something on the way. It feels like I never got out of that bed, where every morning I would have to remind myself of what it is like outside. A sparrow would knock on my window to tell me that nothing has changed. Every day the war began all over again as though for the first time. There was one second of peace that managed to sneak in between sleep and waking up, a second of neither forgetting nor remembering. In this second there is nothing there except the weight of my body against the bedsheet that rolls around me like warm water in a bubble bath. The water particles can invade my skin without permission. The soap can grow on my fingertips, turn into leaves, my fingers morphing into trees. The bubbles smell like lavender I used as a bookmark in my Mickey Mouse comics. That was before all the lavender fields became dangerous. Mines started growing there instead of grass. The water flows into my ear and muffles the walk of limping shoes from outside. Its waves rustle like the shredding of identity documents nobody needs anymore. The warmth on my skin for a moment makes me forget that outside it is cold and there is not enough wool left anymore to knit all the sweaters everybody would need. They would not help anyway because there is nothing that can protect from this kind of wind. All the umbrellas are turning inside out and collecting water inside. A draft from an open door tips the flowers in the vase. The water in my mouth tastes like flower food. My eyebrows are closed umbrellas, too wet to protect my eyes. My wet hair covers them. It is dark again. Drops are sliding down my eyelids. The sparrow is trying to drink from the water sliding down the window. The tapping sound against the window turns into the soles of my shoes against the snow. My second of peace is over. It resides somewhere in the cracks on my shoe's tongue, pressed down by the shoelaces pulled too tightly.

How did I get onto this street? What happened to the other street where I have my meeting? Someone's shoulder brushes against my elbow. The torn sleeve makes me feel comfortable enough to ask the person wearing it where I can find Subproject Street. An elderly lady turns towards my voice. Her arm bends as if to follow its echo. Now her arm moves through the air like a butterfly circling a flower, deciding whether to land. Her hand goes nowhere. Her eyes look at me. I cannot find her pupil. Instead, there is a blue sea. The bracelet around her wrist is made of different buttons. It slides down her arm and falls in. Sighing deeply as though from the glass bottom of a finished drink, she tells me the street does not exist. It must be kind of fun in there, because she also goes on to point at a giant building and say maybe the man up there with the suave hat can help. He died not too long ago, but he knows his way around here. A man towering across around twenty-five floors looks at me. Maybe this is how things work in this city. Once you die, you are turned into a mural. The lady tells me she knew him. His appearance evoked mixed feelings in her. A strange fella, used to refer to himself as a lazy bastard living in a suit. Met him in Parc du Portugal decades ago feeding the sparrows in front of his house at four in the morning. Folks liked him. A poet of some sort, but she does not know much more about that. All she knows is sometimes he sat there, hunched, like a bridge about to fall apart. But he told her he's all right, that's just his way. And, besides, there are more interesting things to see down below. He would write things down on a napkin, crumble some bread on it, and hold it in his palm. The sparrows ate right out of his hand. He would always sit on the same bench, between his fingers a cigarette. At night it looked like a shivering star falling through the sky. A little moody, but overall a good kid.

For a moment I imagine the light moving in the sky must be God moving his hand, in his hand a lit cigarette. God strikes me as someone who wouldn't mind the taste. It might help him forget all the things that went wrong. After one or two he may confess there has been a mistake in the grand design and now things are out of his hands. I never used to smoke before, but I would like to light one now. Maybe God would trust me then and tell me what he became. Maybe he would tell me there are no reasons for how broken he is. All his reasons turned into ash, fell on the table that is swept every night. There was no ashtray to help him collect all the ruins that remained. Now he is what he is, a regular at all the bars, staying way past closing time. He always sits alone, because even his clothes have started smelling like alcohol. His hair looks dirty and messy. I know it is wrong, but this looks endearing to me. His nails are black and no one wants to be in indecent company, at least not openly. If I ever saw him, I think I would want to sit with him at the table and try to be his friend again. Maybe if I confess all of my mistakes, he would confess all of his. Maybe then something would change. We may both remember that everything was different once, before darkness became somewhat enjoyable, before pain became as black as the hollow space inside an empty cigarette box. I may not understand any more than I do now, but maybe a kind gesture, the pulling out of my chair, a gentle tap on my shoulder, blowing the smoke in the other direction, would make life clearer again. I know this may be wrong, too, but maybe I do not want any of that. Sometimes I feel I am not any different. Sometimes I feel I would pour God another glass of whiskey, offer him another smoke, and agree that I like this bar, why don't we stay, it is too late for anything else anyway. With a cigarette between my lips, a lighter in his left pocket, I lean in. His right finger touches my lips as if to tell me not to speak and I cannot help, but like the smell of his hand.

I can feel his dry skin sinking into my lips, not unlike a paper cut after licking an envelope in complete darkness, because the last candle has reached its end. The edge of his thumb, hardened from centuries and centuries of turning the wheel on the lighter, rests underneath my chin, moves towards my neck without leaving a trace. That's how gentle the touch of a broken God could maybe be. Touching my Adam's apple, he could do anything he wants to now and I would not move away. Water is rising up in my throat. His head is facing down. If I swallow now, maybe the burning in my throat will disappear. Maybe the Wheel of Fire on which Ixion is bound will fully dry out. I wish I could see God's eyes, but I guess he is not ready yet to find out whether he could possibly be forgiven. For now, his finger on my neck is soothing me, underneath a fingerprint: roads curving nowhere, the path of someone who has given up on reaching any end. I don't know how to tell him I like his touch, without pardoning that he allowed all the lavender fields to go away. I also don't know how to tell him I feel I am equally to blame. I want to tell him I am not angry anymore, but my pockets are filled with burnt-out candles that I don't know what to do with. All the used-up wicks are winding around my left arm, pulling tight. It could be much too late. If I wanted them to stay away, I could not manage to do that anyway. I have no right to ask. After all these years, I am too tired of trying to find out whose fault it is that my arm is turning blue. All I want to do is fold my hand into a cup and catch the ash falling from God's cigarette. He may let me smear it between my fingertips before I run over his lips with what remains. Nothing ever truly goes away, especially not lipstick made of what once used to be. I know I am just a fool. I know all my attempts may amount to nothing more than a drunken night that will surrender to the morning when we will be nothing but strangers again. But for now, his hand is still on my neck. It may be a confession or it may be something else. It may be remorse or it may be he just wanted to feel my skin. He knows I won't convict him. He knows I feel too guilty for that. He knows I still like the smell of his hand. I want to move my left arm to catch the ash, but I can't. My right one is holding my head and I feel too buzzed to change anything about that. I guess I'll stay. I guess for leaving there is just too much to say. The ash from the cigarette hovers around us like we are in a snow globe. My hair floats up in waves, reaching for the grey flakes. There are too many in my eyes. It hurts. I feel like thousands of candles are burning inside. My eyelids are fluttering and the bar I am in is flickering. He glances at his watch tied around the same wrist as the hand resting on my neck before he slides it up and covers my eyes. No, I want to stay, but it is too late. Only darkness surrounds me now and his voice telling me it is 4 p.m. and I have to go.

Just like that, God is gone. At least for now. I should feel a sense of relief, I guess, considering our history. Besides, he does not smell too good anyway and he never was of the reliable kind. I am not sure why he wanted me to go, but I was just starting to like him again, despite all of that. Out here, the sky looks as wrinkled as his forehead going through all of the many regrets. Year by year, another line appears just as he makes the call for another glass. I wish he would have allowed me to stay long enough to see what happens to him at closing time and if there is anywhere else for him to go.

Sometimes I hear steps late at night. Maybe some of them are his. Or maybe most of them are my own from when I still used to walk in my sleep. One. Two. Three. Steps back, so I can see more than just brown brick reveal to me the number 68. I seem to be at the right address, but all I want to do is go back to the bar and light another cigarette with God.

The two light bulbs hanging above our table were both broken. Only the candle beside the ashtray was on. Maybe he knew this is how I liked it. Maybe he is not so bad after all.

I am running late. The winter night is slowly catching up to the day. This is just the time for me to stay outside, but the paper in my pocket reminding me I have to meet someone now is rustling again. It flies out of my pocket, folds itself into an airplane. The crackling sound it makes lights the fire in my grandparents' fireplace. They are warm again. They don't even need their house shoes anymore and can walk only in socks, like they used to do before the war.

The airplane flies around my head a few times. My grandfather turns the dial up on the fireplace with every round the plane makes. I still don't know why during the war, I never got used to the cold, but I got used to the darkness. I remember wrapping myself up in a blanket hoping that one day, when the war is over, the streetlights would still look like black pupils watching me. They know about everything that happens. They know what goes on when outside it gets darker.

The airplane flies in a spiral, farther and farther away. What happened to its wing? One wing is missing, but it seems to be all right. I wish it would tell me how it manages to fly in every direction and change its way. My eyes follow it as it gets closer and closer to the brown building I have to walk into. The building towers into the sky stacking floors higher and higher as though there is something on the ground to run away from. It is the tallest one around and wears a jacket made of glass. From where I am standing it looks very proud, like a kid who feels he owns the street. This one has style and even made sure there are flowers up front, the perfectly coloured napkin to accent the elegant suit.

My hand reaches for the paper plane flying away from me. I feel cold glass beneath my shriveled fingertips, before I realize the plane now only exists inside the jacket of the building. Its one wing reflects in the glass and opens the door for me. The one it opens is the door farthest to the right and the only one with a sign on it. With a slight squint, I can read that it says to use this door when leaving after hours. All the other ones lock, because they don't want to know about anything that goes on after 10 p.m. I never liked skyscrapers, but I guess if I have to walk into a building this giant, there is no better way to do so than through a door like this. I can feel the snowflakes on my back as I walk in and, for a moment, I am at least glad to be warm. A fire crackles beneath my palm. My grandfather throws in another piece of coal. The airplane circles another round. God takes another puff and I think to myself, what a lucky bastard, he is at least sitting down. I have no memory of how far I walked, but I feel tired and the muscles in my legs are killing me.

Three

My scarf is still fluttering. My jacket clings to my skin as though I am still outside. Maybe I did not close the door behind me or maybe it is only the air conditioning, but it does not feel that way. I think it is a breeze from the airplane's wing telling me which way to go. All the hairs on my skin stand up like a child lifting his head at the sound of a light switch. I loved those moments when one of the grownups would turn the light off and leave my room thinking I am asleep. My grandmother would always close the window right before that. Even in this strange building with the air blowing at my back, I can hear my grandmother's voice in my head telling me to get away from the draft. People die from that, you know, she used to say. Maybe I should have listened, but every time she left, I would open the window again by a tiny crack. The walls seemed to start talking when I did that. Little popping sounds would lull me into sleep and if my grandmother knew what soothing companions I found them to be, I do not think she would be mad at me.

I think she would have much more to say about this place. Where is my paper airplane? It must be somewhere nearby, because the hairs on my skin are still reaching up, waving to the passengers, who were somewhere else only yesterday. That day sinks into the light brown walls surrounding me. I do not usually mind beige, but these walls are ugly. The closer I look at them, the more they start to look like pieces of sand. A coughing engine muffles from underneath the grains. Someone turned the hourglass too soon. Someone did not know anything about grace, or at least to have the patience to let the passengers leave the plane before turning everything on its head. As I look at these walls accusing them of stealing my plane, I think about God again. I think about how I should not have been so friendly to him. He probably chose this boring looking paint for the walls himself and laid the industrial looking few rows of grey tiles at the bottom. I imagine a bathroom in a prison would have something similar to that. I guess in his drunken state he lost all sense of taste. Or maybe he lost much more than that. A growling sound fills the entire space, the sound of a struggling plane. God's stomach turning. The dryer kicking in. My hands collecting the boy's marbles as fast as I can, because we heard the sound of thunder and this time it sounded nothing like before. It also did not smell the same. God is tapping on the table with his dirty nails. His stomach growls again, before I realize all these sounds I am hearing again are coming from the escalator in front of me.

Its never-ending stairs going up multiply like my silver teeth after the war, fillings trying to stop the decay. But it was already way too late then to put on armour. The holes were too big, the war lasted too long and my teeth were not used to the food in the packages dropping from the sky. I can see God's hand hanging from the edge of the table, the cigarette ash is falling, the little parachutes look so pretty, just like the dim fire as he breathes in.

These stairs make me feel like I am at the airport, but I must have forgotten my suitcase. Or maybe God decided to be a gentleman today and take care of that, so I can travel light for a change. But I am not sure he is awake enough for that. At the moment, this is probably for the best, because something about this building is making me feel strange. A current flows through my finger as my hand rests on the black rubber belt. One of the light bulbs above God's table buzzes, flickers, and for a split second I can see the white of his eyes. Red veins branch from his dark pupil not looking at anything in particular.

I try to look closer to see what is inside, but there is nothing there to see, except my own face reflecting back at me. For a moment, I am angry again and wonder why he is doing this. How is it fair that he knows everything about me and I know nothing at all about him? One moment I think this is just the nature of the game and the next I feel the mafia is running this game, with God as their head. Whose side is he on anyway? I often feel like he doesn't know himself anymore or if he does, he does not want to tell me. Maybe this is a strategy to get me more attached to him, because he knows my character flaws, one of them being that I often tend to think that maybe someone is not being deliberately secretive, maybe it is just a sign of sorrow or of intelligence. Besides, he knows that my eyes have long switched to preferring darkness.

The light bulb he removed rolls underneath my old bed, spins around itself. He knows this way my pupil can expand and for a brief moment, there will be more space inside, everything will hurt a little less. Maybe seeing the red veins in his eyes makes me feel close to him, because I feel he understands, a child's glove floats on top of them. I try to catch it, but God takes another drink and it drifts away.

With every wave of my hand, a red bird flies out of his veins. Why did he have to lift his glass now? Why couldn't he wait?

I am not sure if it's from the sip he took, but suddenly my fingers are wet, cold liquid is burning my skin. A current of electricity flows through my hand, static from the belt I am holding onto snows into my body – just enough to short circuit the light bulbs swinging as he continues to drink. It is dark again and I can't see his eyes anymore at all. Only his arm sways from the edge of the table, a rusty swing, the red bird's wing. Three of these birds now hang above my head, mummified on a giant scroll hanging down from the ceiling above the escalator.

The birds look so unfriendly, I think to myself. I wonder what happened to them and if they always looked this way. Their wings are sharp and fully erected towards the sky. If they were needles, they may just pierce the universe like a giant balloon about to burst. Everything that ever happened, past, present, future, could spill into a giant puddle, disappear into a black hole, never to be seen again. Like a finished cigarette pressed into the ashtray, nothing else remains but the trace of someone's mouth covered in silence.

Sometimes I wonder where all these lives that were ever lived go. Sometimes I like to think of them as foam inside a cappuccino cup slowly melting into the liquid. Little air bubbles signal a special kind of emptiness, nothing like the holes I see where the birds' eyes are supposed to be. They look like they never had any eyes to begin with. My own are beginning to see everything a little blurry, but I am pretty sure the shape of the birds' heads reveals they are wearing helmets of a kind unfamiliar to me. They could be right out of a science fiction film, one of those where they take away your memory, or pick it apart and piece it together differently. Maybe that is what these birds are trained to do, I think to myself, as the stairs bring me closer and closer to them. The nearer I get, the more they are starting to look like little soldiers lined up behind each other about to perform their unknown duty. They are lined up sideways, facing the right, like the priest turning towards the altar on his right side after bestowing his priestly blessing upon the community. I learned that the right side is supposed to represent kindness and the left side discipline. I also learned that kindness is always supposed to be placed above discipline. I guess these birds have got the proper order, but for some reason they do not seem genuine. It feels like they have other motives. It feels like their wings are about to fold around me and I will again be trapped in that tunnel between the boarding gate and the airplane.

Something else is strange about these red birds. A crown hovers over each of the two birds on the outside edges. An open book floats above the middle bird. It takes me a moment to decipher the letters. I am not sure if it is because I am slightly dizzy from these long stairs or if this is how the letters really are, but the words are written in fragments and they are written upside down. Maybe they are this way because God wrote them while sitting drunk in a bar, hoping someone will still want to be his friend.

IN   CON
DOM   FI
INO   DO

In domino confido: In God I trust. Come to think of it, I am fairly certain I remember seeing God scribble down something on the other side of the receipt while resting his hand on my neck. What a strange thing for him to write. I guess the words are broken up, because the paper was too narrow, like all the receipts, and they did not fit. I guess he was too sad to write some of the letters properly. This is probably too innocent of a thought. He may also have been angry or he may have done it deliberately. Maybe I need to stop thinking of him as a grownup, who is still just a child learning how to write, but sometimes I feel this is who God is. Some of my notebooks from the first grade look exactly like this. He is still learning, he is still learning, I tell myself as the moving stairs take me far enough that all of that is now behind me.

A drop is sliding down my neck to my back. It must be snow melting from my hair. My back is itchy. I am approaching the top, but the sliding drop inside my coat makes me feel sad. The last time a drop was sliding down like that, I was leaning on the wet bench. My mother told me so often not to slouch, that it is not good for my back. I know she is right, but I am not sure I can sit straight anymore. I started out that way when I first arrived on the bench. After all, I wanted the boy to know I am well prepared to run away. But I am tired now. The longer I waited for him, the further I slid down. I leaned the back of my head on the edge of the backrest. I guess the edge was too close, because a drop slid down into my collar and down my back. Another one fell, I think from the branch above my head.

A red feather falls from the ceiling, rocks from left to right like a cradle lulling an infant into sleep. It looks so soothing and sweet, I could almost forget that it comes from one of the birds that flew out of God's eye after telling me it is time for me to leave, after the twitch of his hand as he lets the glove just float away.

I wish I could understand why I still follow the feather knowing all that. It looks even more eerie up here. Empty chairs are arranged in a half circle facing the escalator. I feel like I am at the airport. I just walked through to the arrival gate, but nobody came to pick me up. Maybe I should not be here, because it is empty, maybe I took the wrong plane. Maybe God confused me with somebody else. It could be that he barely took a look at me at all and even if he did, what does he know about who I am and where I need to go?

The feather lands on an open newspaper left on one of the chairs. Maybe someone was here after all. I can barely make it over to look at it because something inside me feels like it is disintegrating. My bones feel like they are made of wax and the lighter is in someone else's hand. If only I knew how those old breadcrumbs ended up on my tongue again. If only I knew why the feather fell onto a black and white photograph of a sleeping man. Giant tube-like structures are covering his arms and hands, extending further in length. The end of the tube is a black pupil of a tunnel staring at me, telling me I have no access to its darkness. Little does it know I have seen such eyes before. I have crawled into them while sitting under Sarajevo bridges listening to the tips of umbrellas against the cobblestone above my head. More and more often, they are used as a replacement for a cane, more and more often people are walking out of step. It has not stopped raining, yet more umbrellas are closing, because they are needed for something else. People are getting wet, but they have to lean on something. I just don't know if the umbrellas are able to handle all the heaviness. I just don't know if anything can.

I imagine the arm of the sleeping man in the photograph and wonder if his palm is facing upwards just like the man's hand I saw on the street while my mother was covering my eyes. It was raining then. A drop fell into his palm, his fingers opened towards the sky like a flower in an empty vase. I guess this is the same God, who forgot to put more water in, who forgot he said he would be there, but who never came.

There are too many closed umbrellas now being leaned on. I am afraid one of the umbrellas will be too tired to see. I am afraid its tip will land in the middle of his palm. I know he is no longer moving. I know his fingers will never button up his shirt again, but I am still afraid someone will hurt his hand. I wish I could pick one of the *Akšamčići* flowers from my grandparents' garden and place it in his palm. When the night falls, they would open, and he would no longer be alone.

It is dark inside the tunnels covering the sleeping man's hands. I am out of breath. Smoke is coming out of my mouth, petals are flying from my tongue into his tunnel arms. Why is there tape around them? Why are his eyes also covered? Large pillow-looking shapes are pressed tightly against both his ears.

Why does he need two pillows? Doesn't he want to hear what is going on outside? The odd looking tape surrounds the pillows, too. I wish I could pull on it, like on the string of a falling kite that has had an irreconcilable squabble with the sky. Something here doesn't feel right. He must be hurting. There is too much pressure on his head. Why is he sleeping in an elegant button-up shirt and a tie? Where are his pyjamas and why didn't he put them on before bedtime? Someone must have told him there is no more time.

Or maybe he was so sleepy he just couldn't wait, just like the man I saw through my mother's fingers. I didn't have the heart to tell her then that I am old enough to know no one sleeps that way, with the tips of their fingers reaching for the grey cloud, a dirty pillowcase. I saw his nail dig into its fabric, and the tip of a feather emerge, a drop hanging on its edge, still unsure of the final verdict, before it fell.

My fingers feel sticky as I reach for the newspaper. With a closer look, I can see a tiny wire coming out of his ear and disappearing into his shirt. I used to do this when I was little and couldn't fall asleep. Maybe he is just doing the same and listening to music, I tell myself, as all the letters in the article below his picture begin to separate from the page. They are tugging at my shoulder, attaching to my jacket, rearranging themselves into all the unused drying clips left on the clothesline in front of my grandparents' house. My toes are hurting as I try to reach for the one spinning in the wind, but I can't, I am not grownup enough yet. The stray dog licks my ankle as I flick the clip that spins on along with the washing machine hopelessly attempting to wash the pants I wore while sitting on that bench, waiting.

The puddle beneath my feet disappears, the drying clips on my jacket are lifting me up into the air. The stray dog lifts his head and looks at me like I am a sweater billowing in the cold wind. His black pupil expands and inside the sleeping man continues to sleep. Maybe the dog's eyelid could close over him like a warm, comforting blanket, freshly dried. I know this is probably only in my mind, but I am glad he has left the newspaper for a while, because the stray dog knows better about what goes on in the streets. Maybe he can protect him. Maybe he can tell him which back-alleys to avoid and where not to walk. There are some memories he is just not yet ready for.

The clothesline is stuck between my toes. I wish I could float up higher, but I can't. Maybe from up there I could find out where I am. Instead I feel like a plastic bag caught in a tree. If I have to be a plastic bag at all, I would like to be the boy's, the one he always had with him to carry all the marbles. Once he tied it into a bow and placed it on his neck. He asked if I would run away with him now that he is all fancy, grownup and well-dressed. People may assume he is an adult, he said. He also said there must be a different world somewhere out there and if we try hard enough, we will find it. I believed him. But what did we know? We were only children then. We devised the entire plan. Both of us would sneak out at midnight and meet at our favourite bench under our favourite street lamp half way between his home and mine. Once there, we would wait for the stray dog that used to come by the same spot every day. He was dark brown with black ears and black paws that looked like boots. They looked like boots a cool rebel would wear, someone who wouldn't believe you can solve anything by filling up the city with more and more sleeping people, who did not even get the time granted to put on their pyjamas. He would know how to tell between the good guys and the bad guys. We could simply follow him and wherever he goes at night must be a better kind of place. At least that is what we thought back then. Besides, we no longer trusted the grownups to tell us about the world or what it is like.

I remember my feet dangling back and forth in the air while sitting on the bench. Each movement cut through the black air, invisible cracks swallowed every step I thought was his. I didn't know that with each hopeful movement, I was dividing my life in two and that one day the crack between them would be too wide for me to step over.

I have no idea how suddenly I am in an elevator, in this unfamiliar building, no longer a child, yet still the rustling of him taking out the marbles flows through my ears, the paper airplane flies by in front of my eyes and disappears into one of the buttons in the elevator. The number four is already lit up, but I do not recall pressing it.

What is going on with the mirrors in this elevator? Each one of them is reflecting back to me a different face, a face I am not sure I know how to recognize. In one of the mirrors two giant Ferris wheels are spinning inside of my eyes. This seems innocent enough, but when I look closer I can see a little girl in each wagon and in each wagon the same one. Her back is turned towards me and the windows of the wagon are fogged up. I wish she would turn around, because her hair looks just like mine. Besides, she is sitting there in the same way as I used to sit underneath the blinking street lamp, my fingertips holding onto the little world I am about to flick over the ground into the circle with the other marbles inside. When the war started, the boy and I changed the rules and we began playing the marble game in a different way. The goal was no longer to flick as many marbles outside of the circle, but to get as many as possible inside. The boy told me the game makes more sense this way, because there is plenty of room for all of the marbles inside. He also said that the game is much harder this way, because it takes a better person to get the marble as close to the others as possible without disturbing them than to just kick them out. Any bozo can do that, and he does not want to be one of them. Maybe the grownups will also play by these rules if they see us play that way, he told me and put on his hat. Maybe one day they will stop ordering more chalk for thicker borders and smaller circles. For now the sounds outside are making the ground tremble and the flowers along the border bury their heads.

The elevator skips a step and shakes. The Ferris wheel has stopped turning, all the wagons are swinging, but none of them in the same way. The squeaking sound is giving me goosebumps, the rust is eating away at the motions of the universe. Its melody is all off, this can't be right. Yet, God continues to chew on the squeaky end of his pen. Nothing will be written. Nothing is coming next. At least not for quite a while, because he is dizzy from what happened and needs rest.

But nothing in life waits, not even for God. What was he thinking? I want the little girl inside the foggy wagon to turn around and tell me why she is still sitting there. For a brief moment her hand moves her hair behind her ear and I remember the boy telling me he loves it when I do that, that every time my hand reaches for my hair and moves it to the side, a curtain is lifted from the windows in the bar where God is drinking. Only my hair never stays. There is too much of it. Only the curtain never remains open, because the bar is old, everything there is broken.

Maybe what he sees is similar to what is happening to me. In the other mirror, a light that does not know whether to stay or go is covering my face like a blanket constantly pulled away, the last second of a candle before it falls into another yesterday. Suddenly I feel very cold and I wonder who it is that keeps uncovering me, there is no one in my bed. My winter jacket is heavy and wet, another cold drop is sliding down my back. I slide further down on the bench as another person passes by. I just don't know why he never came. My back is getting very wet. A drop of beer glides down the glass and onto God's thumb. Grey clouds are floating out of my mouth, little pillows thrown onto the mirrors around me in a futile pillow fight. Nothing will make me who I once used to be. It is too late for that.

I feel like an open umbrella is spinning inside of my lungs. I want to lie down inside, because I am tired of fighting and trying to see straight. I want to see everything turn and not have a problem with that. Nothing makes sense anyway. All these fragments inside me can whirl inside the umbrella like invisible dead skin in the air. They can put themselves together any way they wish as long as they let me sleep only for a moment, as long as they tell me why I no longer see any reflection in the mirrors anymore at all.

If only I could take a nap inside the umbrella, I would hold on to its handle like to the arm of a stranger, who was just passing me by, but lightly brushed my shoulder by accident. We would walk across the shelled bridge as it falls. I could tell him everything about me, yet he would still not know who I am, and I would prefer it that way. I could slip in some falling rubble into the pocket of his coat as he puts his hand on my lower back. Maybe I would pull at the edge of his pocket playfully while he tries to lead me to the next step without stumbling. But the bridge is trembling and his hand is pressing tighter against me. The lines on his palm are seeping through to my skin, but I do not wish to tell him that. If I do, he may start thinking we will be able to cross the bridge, that we are going somewhere. The bridge shakes one more time. He pulls me into his chest until my mouth is touching the collar of his coat. My teeth bite into the fabric only to stop myself from telling him what is about to happen.

I do not know if he is able to sense something or if it is just his natural male protective instinct, but his hand moves up my back, sneaks into my hair, nestles my head. I wish strands of my hair would not wind around his fingers with every rotation the abandoned umbrella makes. It must have flown out of somebody's hand, because it is still open and has landed upside down on the street. It was just the wind. It was just the wind. Another round. The umbrella spins around itself on the cobble stone. Its wooden handle curves softly as if to reach out for something. I want to hang the open umbrella on my grandparents' clothesline for no other reason except to feel it react to the wind or to the movements of the stray dog standing underneath. The dog's hair would stand up in the same way as the tiny little hairs on this strange man's back. They look like the dried-out stems of flowers long dead, whose petals I tried to save. I want to tell him not to be afraid to show me, that I prefer it that way, that the smell of fresh flowers makes me sad. I almost want to tell him if he ever plans to give me any flowers to only give me those that are no longer alive, but then I remember we only exist in the black pupil of the stray dog whose eyelids are closing; a drop of grey rain caught in his eyelash captures the present.

I can feel the man's hand on my head getting heavier and heavier, his sweat soaking into my hair. It smells just the way I like it, like the earth after the rain, after all the flowers tucked in their heads, because they are tired of what is going on around them. His coat smells the same way, without a trace of cologne. I am glad, because if I smelled any, I may like him just a little bit less. I don't know if he is pulling on my hair or if the winding is getting tighter, but the pain is making me feel closer to him and like he understands. With every pull, one more stone in the bridge is turning into dirty freckles falling onto my cheek, star systems he can wipe away with just one touch or rearrange. For a moment he reminds me my life could have turned out differently. For one second I even started believing we can make it to the other side, but my shoe-laces are open, the button on his sleeve is touching my ear. I can no longer hear anything except the crackling fire inside my grandparents' fireplace. His hand moves over my other ear as the crackling starts getting louder. The stones are each moving in their own direction. The bridge is falling apart. Grey petals made of ash swirl all around us. Two land on my eyelids and I think to myself, how can something so horrible feel this soft?

Maybe it is morbid of me to feel a sense of relief at the thought of complete darkness surrounding me now when I should make sure I witness what is happening. Yet, this stranger seems to know exactly what I want. His fingertips are gently pressing down the petals on my eyelids, a black sheet calms all the people in my eyes, waking up, trying to swim. With his fingertips on my eyelids and his coat's collar still between my lips, I can be somebody other than who I am, or I can be nobody at all.

My stomach turns as we fall through the air together with the rubble and the petals that look like the tongues of angels, prophecies gone wrong. A jolt shakes the ground. God's cough from too much smoke. A beeping sound lifts my eyelids. I am in the elevator again and the door is opening.

The paper airplane flies out of the lit-up button that turns black the moment the plane is gone. As soon as my eyes adjust, I realize the button looks like the one from someone's sleeve. The number is no longer there and thread is coming out of the holes in the button as it spins. I recognize it now, but what is it doing here? The button belongs to the sleeve of the man whose hands I saw through my mother's fingers long ago. He needs it back, because he will get cold. I know he won't get up anymore, I know the signal of his palm, but winter is still here, grey petals are falling instead of snow and I am afraid.

Suddenly seeing all the other numbered buttons disturbs me. They may only be counting floors, but with each one I see, my eyelid blinks. In between darkness and light, I see each floor. On each one is rubble and stepping out doesn't look safe. Besides, it doesn't look like anyone is there. Where did all these people go?

I don't want to stay in this elevator anymore. My breaths are becoming shallow. The umbrella inside my lungs is closing and pressing against my throat. Besides, I think I may already be late. The dust particles from the paper plane's trail fall into my eyes, ash from God's cigarette.

I have to follow it before it disappears, before all the lives I ever had fall through into the crack between the elevator and the floor.

The moment I step out, more rubble falls around me. I am a bit dizzy, so I try to hold on to the staircase railing right beside me, but it disappears. My hand floats through the empty air. A memory comes back to me: The boy slides down the staircase railing inside his building and jumps. Maybe he is here. Maybe he is here.

My eyes are burning as I walk through the hallway. Everything here feels just a little strange. I am trying to find the stairs to the boy's apartment door, but they aren't there. With every step I make, another drop from the bench slides down my back. I hear someone else's steps, while I try to straighten myself back out again. I push my palms down on the bench, my knees try to help. But what is this underneath my hand? A wall is pressing against my palm as I lean.

I must have been dizzy while walking down the hallway trying to find him. Everything around me is blurry. The walls are too white and the lights are too bright. Maybe I am locked up inside my old bedroom, the taxi's headlights are beaming into my eyes telling me it is time to go, the suitcase's wheels are rolling across the hardwood floor. If only my pupil still knew how to contract, maybe then I would be able to see where I am going. We can't leave now. I have to go back to the bench. I know he will come. I hold on to the wall inside this unfamiliar place and try not to fall. I just know. I need to hold on.

I remember holding the leather handle on the taxi door. It was peeling like a life long defeated, but a life not yet ready to go. I never knew once I closed that door, the morning dew would chew through the window and swallow the street, that I would never be able to go back. The taxi door closes. It must have been the wind. It couldn't have been me. I am not yet ready to go. I am not yet ready to leave. I try to push open the door and get out of the car, but I can't. The hallway wall is back again beneath my hand. My head is getting heavy, I need to rest. I notice a ray of light on the floor the moment my head bends down. It comes all the way from the end of the hallway. The tiny crack underneath the door makes the light travel all the way to my shoes. Maybe he is here. Maybe he is here.

The light on the floor is flickering. Someone is walking on the other side of the door. Maybe the steps are his. My head is hurting. Where is the railing? Why is all this rubble here again? I keep forgetting where I am. My forehead is burning.

The light ray nudges my feet again. This time, I see my mother's and my father's houseshoes passing by underneath my bedroom door as they make sure one last time that we packed everything we need. I did not want to pack anything at all except for the little night lamp my grandfather gave me. He told me that whenever I feel sad or whenever I cannot sleep, all I need to do is flip on the switch and all my fears will go away. The light bulb in it is missing. My bedsheet is covering me, maybe my parents won't find me here and I will be allowed to stay. I need to sneak out and go back to the bench.

Underneath my covers, the crumpled pieces of his letter to me are still in my hand. The darkness rolls around them promising to decipher the washed-out words, but it is too late. My bedroom door opens, the thread in the fabric is too thin. The light from the other room lands in my palm, erases his thoughts, my mother tells me it is time for me to put on my shoes.

The covers slide away from me, the curtain beside God's table brushes against his cheek, falls, flutters again as he pours himself another drink. The sound of his glass against the table blends with the sound of an opening door. Maybe the boy will come out now. Maybe he will make it to the bench on time and wait underneath the flickering light. Sometimes the street lamp was dark longer than it was light even before the war. Maybe it knew before the others the darkness that was coming and wanted to warn us. The curtain in the bar lifts up again, falls, and with each fall it becomes a little darker than before. One more shadow is born. I liked the shadow of the boy's arm appearing when the street lamp came back on. I knew exactly where to sit, so when the boy's shadow appeared, it would look like it was hugging me. For a moment, my shoulder would no longer be cold.

The light flickers again. A shadow moves across the light strip on the floor of the hallway. The door opens a little bit more. A shadow in the form of a hand touches my knee. I am glad because my knee still hurts from sitting on the bench for so long. The shadow hand is enclosing my entire knee, trying to protect it from something. The boy's shadow moves away from my shoulder as he leaves. The last time I saw him, a cloud was sheltering the moon. It stayed there longer than the other clouds and didn't move. The shadow hand on my knee stays longer, too. This is something the boy would do. This is my first memory of you.

Ten Months

The shadow hand slides down my leg, your scarf lands on my shoulder, its tassels swing behind me through the smoky trail left by the taxi exhaust. Maybe you can help me tell the driver to turn back. Maybe you can help me reach into my past that follows me. Already now I see the tassels from your scarf sweeping away the dirty clouds coming from the car. Maybe it is leaving. Maybe it is leaving. Maybe we can stay. The more you whirl your scarf around your neck, the more the smoke is going away. Maybe the driver has at least turned off the engine now. I hope he is no longer waiting for me to find my shoes. Maybe you can help me hide them even more.

I want to tell you the tassels on your scarf look just like the ones on the pull-string switch inside the lamp my grandfather gave me. I want to ask you to pull on the one that turns off the taxi's headlights and makes it drive away. Or maybe you could pull on the one that makes the light sneaking through at the bottom of my bedroom door disappear. My parents would stop packing then and just go to sleep. They would turn off the lights and it would be completely dark. The last twenty years will never have happened. We would have never left then, I know, because the grownups can't see so well anymore. The car's headlights are glaring at the window. Turn them off. Turn them off. I try again to ask you if you can help, but I cannot say anything at all because the tip of the umbrella is still scratching my throat.

It turns out I do not need to say anything at all. From the corner of my eye I can see your elbow float in the air, your arm bend towards me like the wet tree branch scratching the stray dog's back. I think his back is itchy from all the dirty rain. The boy's plastic bag rustles as you move your arm. I don't know how that can be, but I am happy to hear the sound with you here. I think I see the plastic bag around your wrist, but I am not sure, because I am still looking down and your arm is gliding in and out of my sight. It glides out again now. I think you are touching the wet branches above my head from the night I walked back home with the boy walking the opposite way. Drops fall from each branch. Some land on my lips. Others disappear in the air. For once they do not taste like Sarajevo rain, but like your coat. I do not know yet what I can taste, but my tongue rolls towards my upper lip, scoops up a drop of cologne, but it tastes a little grainy. The little particles crackle between my teeth. I think they taste like rubble from the street where the boy and I used to play. The rubble could be coming from inside the plastic bag. The marbles pick up the tiniest parts of the broken street as they roll along. Later, when the marbles in the bag rearranged themselves as the boy moved, the rubble fell, collected at the bottom of the bag. I need to pour this into my pocket now, the boy said. I need to collect the broken parts to one day remind me of the life no longer there. His elbow lifts in the air.

Your elbow lifts again, too. Your scarf gently slides through your fingers. Another piece of rubble lands on my tongue. This is it, the boy says. The broken world is in my pocket now. He lets his fingers fold into his palm.

You curve your fingers in as you walk closer towards me. I can't hear your steps at all, but your smell is getting stronger. The boy's steps walking home have gone silent, too. He just stopped walking for a moment. Maybe he stopped just to turn around and watch me walk through the night before our big escape, I don't know. You smell the way he did then: flowers wrapped into a cigarette. The tongue of the stray dog licks the dead man's hand, the cigarette paper folds itself in, wraps the flower, tucks it in, prepares it for a deep sleep. A second before, a drop from the dog's saliva falls onto the flower's head. Its petals open, a moment before death. I cannot help but want more of your coat's taste.

I do not know what your life was like or where on this planet you tapped the stray dog on his head, but I recognize his smell coming from your hand. He was there, too, that night when the boy and I parted. I think he heard everything. Both, the boy and I, touched him on his head. See you tomorrow, we said to him. I think I heard him breathe heavily. You are so close now, I can feel your breath on my cheek. The boy moves a strand of my hair away right after the stray dog's deep breath. I remember how it tickled my skin. The closer you move towards me, the more I feel the way I did then. I could not tell you why, but I can tell by the goosebumps on my arm.

The boy moves his arm again. One more time. The strand is still covering your eye, he says. Your hand moves again, too. The plastic bag with the marbles rustles again. I don't know if the sound is coming from the boy or from you. My hair is still covering my eyes, but I think I can see the handle of the plastic bag curve around your wrist. I may be just imagining this, but for now I can see it clearly. Its handle looks like a wrinkled cloud full of lines drawn by broken doorknobs, the beginning of new lives before old ones end.

The boy moves another strand of my hair away. I can see your hand now. The lines on your fingers curve just like his. I know he was only a boy then and you would think he would have barely any lines at all, but the air is bad. The air is bad. It is not that, the boy tried to tell me. I started drinking coffee, hoping I would understand the grownups better that way. Ever since then my skin has been strange.

Your hand smells strange, too. Maybe it smells something like marshmallows above a fire deep in some forest away from everything else that has happened or like piano keys that keep falling out of your piano and that you keep putting back every night. They may also smell like an Espresso you dipped your finger into one night at midnight when you decided this was the only time you may have a chance at understanding your life, at figuring out why your tablecloth moves sometimes while you sit in your kitchen and read, like there is a breeze, yet your window is closed.

Your fingers are the first thing I notice as you move your hand closer to my shoulder. They bend in a way I imagine you hold a spoon when you stir your morning coffee, still thinking about what you saw behind your closed eyelids when life was still calm. Your coffee is just as black as the moments you are turning into foam in your cup. Tomorrow, when we meet, this dark night we are in now will feel much lighter, the boy said. It won't be as black anymore. The black will rise up and turn into foam. Some of the black is sliding away from your shoulder even now, he added with his eyelids shut. Your hand brushes my shoulder as you reach for your scarf still covering my neck. The hardened wax on your sleeve makes me stand still instead of move away.

My eyes are still almost fully hidden underneath my childhood bed-covers as they slide even further down your sleeve. I will stay. I will stay here in my bed. The two of you can leave, I remember saying to my parents back then. I won't even open my eyes, I told my mother. With you here, at least for a second, I feel like we stayed. My eyelashes are almost touching my cheek, the moist fire log inside my pupil is beginning to crackle and suddenly I feel so warm I wish I could take off my socks. Little flakes of ash float up in the air. I used to try and catch the ones coming out of my grandparents' fireplace and put them on my tongue. At first I started doing that because I was afraid if my grandparents breathe in too many, they won't live too much longer. I am young, I thought to myself then, and I can handle it much easier. Then I began wanting more and more once I realized that this way I could still taste something that was long gone.

Only I did not know that all this ash would float inside my dark pupil without going away like the ice forming inside your coffee because in your apartment it is too cold. You haven't told me anything about yourself, but I can see from the hardened skin on the side of your fingers that you have been turning the knob on your heater for too long. Or maybe you were turning the dial on your watch backwards because you feel you could have done something differently, something that would not have left so many empty clothes hangers in your closet lining up beside your coat. Maybe then it would not smell this way. Or for all I know, you were trying to turn the watch forward because the present swirls around the same axis without going anywhere like the scarf spinning around your neck.

Something is happening to my eyes. More and more ash is coming out of them the closer you move in. The clothesline between them is becoming dirty, underneath an abyss of memories lifting their arms at me asking me to pick them up. Your hand moves your scarf away from my neck, brushes over the wire so I can walk across the abyss without falling in. I can still barely see. I don't know what else to do other than blow at the ash right in front of me. Some of it falls into your sleeve, some into your pocket and some hides in your armpit, the dog licks its paw after stepping into someone's palm. I am slightly embarrassed because I know this is too intimate, but you do not seem to mind. Your arm moves closer to me, your scarf glides down my arm. All the tassels on your scarf are now swinging.

Something strange is happening. I can hear them swinging loudly inside me. The sound of a window opening and closing repeats over and over again. Maybe when you enter your apartment, you will wonder why there is all this snow inside your kitchen and why the window is open. The string for your blinds is moving with the tassels, knocking at the glass. The light switch inside the lamp my grandfather gave me is swinging, the light is flickering. Its shade spins and lifts like my dress revealing too much after a gust of air tickles my knee. I think the breeze is coming from the taxi that you just told to drive away without even knowing it. The hallway light inside my bedroom is no longer on and my parents have gone to sleep. You are the only one here. The streetlights in Sarajevo have come back on, at least the ones I can see from my bench where I used to sit waiting for him. Maybe now the man who left me his candle legs will finally be able to find his way home.

The tassels hanging on to your scarf are no longer moving. They are as calm as the sparrow that stopped and decided to no longer follow him.

Maybe now it is calm enough for me to lift up my eyelids and look into your eyes the same way I turned around while sitting on the bench and looked up at my bedroom window only to find the curtain stuck between the window and the outside wall. I guess it is just like me, always trying to go outside when my mother told me it is not safe to go out and I may get hurt. I hope she won't see that I did not close the window properly. I hope she won't see that I am still sitting on that bench with a little dried flower the boy gave me and told me to bring. Right now your scarf glides over my hand and through my fingers, like the curtain that managed to sneak out of the room regardless of the dangers outside.

The curtains in my old bedroom are these old-fashioned ones made of fine white thread weaving itself into intertwining roses. They bend around each other in a way one would hold a dying person. I am not sure when I began to see them this way, but often from my bed, I would look at them hold each other underneath the street lamp below my window. When the war began and even the lamps could no longer keep their eyes open, a black blanket rolled around the curtains and I thought to myself: no one will see them now. People will pass underneath the window not knowing that above their heads the entire next century is being prophesied. Your hair weaves and curves in the same way. There is something about it that makes me feel that if you walked underneath my bedroom window twenty years ago you would have stopped. It would not have been because of me, but because your hair got caught between the thread, because you felt the curtain's breeze on your eyelid, the dying roses admitting to you they no longer want to be saved. You would know this is not the right moment to speak, that there is nothing you can say to change the air that makes them move around each other this way. One of them may hold on to your hair like to the string of a balloon rising up into the dark sky. The clouds are too grey, it would not survive, so she holds on tighter. For some reason the balloon really wants to go up, I don't know why. Maybe it feels the world is no longer as innocent as it used to be, or it wants to find out what the world looks like from up there. But the dying flower holds on to it, pulls at your hair, not knowing that it hurts your head, not knowing it is pulling at your window blinds you may not wish to open yet. But, then again, maybe you do, because your fingers are touching your elegant looking black hat the same way you would spread apart two blinds, lightly lifting the brim, revealing your eyes to me, like a gentleman would do. It has been a while since someone said hello to me this way. Come to think of it, I can only remember the boy doing that.

Your hair curls above your ear as you move your hat. It curves up, turns into feathers from inside my pillow. I accidentally scratched it open with my nails in my sleep the night the boy never came. It was just too loud outside. The raindrops kept knocking on my window and the stray dog continued barking at the plastic bag stuck in the tree. Maybe I should say something to you now, tell you I am sorry if I arrived too late, but my mouth is full of feathers and I can taste your hair. It tastes like a burnt lampshade, the kind of burn that appears after you fall asleep in your bed before you manage to reach over to your nightstand. I know the feeling when the switch right beside your head is just too far away. I wish I could stop all the empty hangers in your closet from swinging, playing you a lullaby that tells you the way life is now is the way life is always going to be.

You haven't said a word to me, yet you must have felt my shallow breaths. I feel like you just removed the lampshade from its stand, placed it over my mouth like an oxygen mask. The bulb stands naked facing your ceiling, the light is escaping onto your wallpaper, revealing the tiny tears along its edges. I can breathe better again. Some of the feathers are flying out of my mouth, but I am worried about your bedroom being too bright now and what will happen to you when you wake up. After they told us how to jump should we step on any mines, they also told us not to stand near the window with the light on. I don't really remember this often, because the light came less and less often anyway. But I am glad I thought of it now, so I can prevent you from getting hurt. You need to stay in the dark. You need to stay in the dark tomorrow when you walk back to our bench. I am sorry. I don't know if I am saying this out loud. I should have said it to the boy then. Maybe he can hear me now from where I am if I say it to you again.

Some people would not mind the extra light, but I can see you are not like that, I can see wallpaper underneath your fingernails. This reminds me of myself standing on my bed, peeling away the strange wallpaper in my hotel room, because it had nothing to do with who I am. I wonder what it is that happened to you that makes you reach behind you in your sleep and start scratching the wall that folds over you like an envelope you can no longer get out of. The moment you turn over to the other side in your bed, your arm spreads out, an airplane's wing trying to glide on an empty bedsheet. The sweat from your pyjama sleeve is speeding up the air. The pressure below the wing is falling. Flakes of wallpaper are falling on top of your arm. Your breath is going in the opposite direction and I am afraid something will happen to you. I do not want to scare you, but I learned in first grade that for a plane to fly, the air on top of the wing has to travel faster than the air at the bottom. I can see your arm move up to the empty pillow beside you, your nails dig in, a tip of a feather is coming out of it. I grab it with my teeth while you still gently press the lampshade against me and leave a circle around my lips.

A giant light circle has appeared on your ceiling and watches you sleep ever since you removed your lampshade to help me breathe. I am not sure what to think of it yet, but instead of pulling your bedcovers over your head, you move your hat up even more, and turn in your bed onto your back. Your eyelids are vibrating, your bedroom curtain floats up, a sparrow flies away and sits on top of a street lamp.

My feet feel warm. I feel like I am walking on the wire inside your light bulb. Maybe if I sit down on the wire and try to swing, I will be able to cast enough shade for you to be safe. The boy is walking too far away. I stand on my toes just to try and make my shadow grow enough to cover him. But I am still limping and my knees are hurting. All I can do is try and blow all the feathers inside of my mouth onto the light bulb to soften it. Maybe some will land on your eyelids and calm them. Maybe then I will be able to speak. One of the feathers from your pillow is still between your fingertips, the same one I pulled out with my teeth. It takes me a while to notice that the touch I feel on my lips is a touch coming from your hand holding mine in a tight grip. It seems like we already went through introductions and some conversation I do not recall, because while I am still watching you adjust your scarf, you say to me that you are glad I found the place all right, you are glad that I am here, that you cannot wait to get out of this building and call it a day.

Thank goodness you said that. Without even knowing where I am, this place makes me want to leave as soon as I can and that is a lot coming from someone like me, someone who has never learned how to properly leave. As soon as I want to ask you if you could tell me your name again, the little girl inside the Ferris wheel shakes her head. Her hair whirls around her the way your scarf moves as you reach for the light switch beside the door. The moment you touch it, the Ferris wheel stops. The light disappears. I can tell she likes it this way. I can feel it is better that for now I do not know your name. Instead, the darkness from the room we were just in can flow into the hallway like a river flowing under a bridge at night. It does not tell you what all is inside, but if you look carefully enough you can tell by the way the light glides on its skin that there is too much ash. The river is too warm, just like the milk you left on your stovetop too long one morning when you were looking out the window, wanting to catch that moment when the street lamp turns itself back off.

The little girl inside the Ferris wheel writes something on the fogged-up window as you close the door. Maybe she is trying to tell you her name, I don't know. But I think you would like her, because I remember her pulling on her shoelaces the same way as you are pulling on yours now. The boy taught me how. Somehow it feels like it was you who tied my shoelace back then. It seems impossible that this was the case, but even the war seemed impossible, and it happened anyway. Somehow the colour of your coat reminds me of the dark blue morning that I remember as the only beautiful part of that day when the taxi came. It was that type of morning when you realize that even some ugly things have their special kind of beauty to them. Even many years later, I often think about the beauty of that dark blue morning, that moment when there is an overlap between something ending and something beginning, and how I imagined it wrapping around me like a blanket. I never saw it look that way before. It must have had that special kind of blue, because of all the extra fog coming out of all the mouths of sleeping people who fell asleep on the street. It looked more beautiful than it ever looked before. I folded this ugly kind of beauty around me like a blanket, because it was the only way I knew how to put on my shoes and leave a whole life behind with my window beating against the wall in protest, telling me not to go.

Something about your slow walk makes me feel like you understand the pain of this beautiful kind of ugliness, that you felt it before, that you understand if you walk any faster my shoelaces will come undone. I think you moved your lips, but the boy's voice comes out. How can that be? I think I heard him say to just hold the loop between my two fingers lightly, there is no need to press hard. Your lips are still moving, but this time there is no sound. I could not press any harder even if I wanted to. It is not that I did not know how to tie them, but on that morning, I had no more strength left in my fingers after carrying my suitcase down the stairs. Although I do not remember the suitcase being very heavy at all, so I am not sure why even pulling on my shoelaces seemed as difficult as getting my parents to go back to bed and forget about what they had planned. I wanted the morning dew to fall onto their eyelids until they are as wet as laundry fresh out of a washing machine. Their eyelashes would touch the way our hands did. The wet curtains would close over their pupils. With every button on your coat you slide through the buttonhole, it is getting darker and darker. My parents are getting sleepier and sleepier. Maybe their heads fell onto their pillows long ago like onto a balloon. Maybe we never left at all.

The plastic bag around your wrist is rustling as you hold open the entrance door for me. Even though you knew that with me you have to walk slowly, somehow the way from your door to the street seems much shorter now with you here than when I was walking alone. I do not even recall seeing any of the things I saw on my way before meeting you. I do not remember walking past ugly walls or taking the elevator, seeing red birds or escalators. Even the awkward photograph I saw of the man in the newspaper is gone. Outside it is still snowing and looks just the same as it did before, but I no longer feel cold. It was so cold when I walked away from the boy, I think I saw one raindrop turn into a snowflake the moment I started walking alone. Your scarf brushes against the back of my neck as the door behind us closes. My mother's fingers lightly touch the same spot as I am about the perfect height for her hand to gently rest on my shoulder. She pulls on our apartment door with her other arm. We need to wait for the boy. We need to wait for the boy. My father waves to the car, while I pull my suitcase. I can still hear my bedroom window, one of the apartment's eyelids. It is pulsating. This must mean it is in deep sleep. I wonder if it is dreaming that we are leaving. I wonder when one of the sparrows I used to feed lands on the window ledge and pecks at the glass from inside, what it will see. The window will open widely, our apartment will open its eyes and wake from its sleep. What will my room see? What will it think of me for not even saying goodbye and will it forgive me?

A little part of me catches myself wondering what you think of me. How did you even know all these little things you did to get me to walk with you without me having told you anything at all. Somehow it feels like you have known me all along. Or maybe I said something to you when I was in the back of the car, when my finger buried itself inside the hole in the torn seat. The stuffing I picked out from inside looked like cotton candy, so I put it inside of my mouth only not to have to answer the driver's question if I have everything. He doesn't know anything at all. If he knew, he would never want me to leave without the boy. Maybe you knew better. Maybe you know not to ask me anything, at least not yet.

I am sitting right behind the driver. My feet are pushing against his seat as I watch his hair curl up above the edge of his collar. While the grownups are talking about which border will have the kindest people checking our fake passports, all I can think about is how the movement of his hair resembles the way the petals I plucked from the flower folded up once I lit up one of the large candles the limping man gave me. The warm air from the flame lands in the middle of the petal like on a cushion, my warm feet jump onto the mattress on my bed before it is time to sleep. I started doing that every time before I lay down, because after the war began it was impossible for me to fall asleep on a bed that was neatly made. I wanted my sheets to be as wrinkled as the petals on my nightstand breathing in the heat of one of the man's wax legs. I continued to jump until my pillowcase looked just like the lines forming on the back of the stray dog's neck after he looks up at my bedroom curtain moving in the wind. The driver looks up at the rear-view mirror. You lift your head towards the snowflakes falling into your hair. Your hair moves up even more after you gently touch my shoulder indicating for me to stop. You probably want to ask me where I want to go, but I don't know how to tell you that I have no say in that. Maybe you can sneak into the car I am still in and drive it instead. Maybe you can change the past from where we are now. For a moment, I see your breath on the car window. I just don't know if it is coming from the inside or the outside. I think it's okay. I think you should come in, too. Maybe the driver would be okay with that, because I think he is very tired. I can see his eyes in the rear-view mirror. The dark circles below his eyes look like the coffee stains on his sleeve. His hand was too shaky that morning and it still trembles while resting on the steering wheel. I think he should really get some rest. Maybe if I continue pushing against his back, this time with my knees, he will get up. Maybe he will listen to me and just go back home to lie down. My mother touches my shoulder the way you did and tells me that I am being rude and to please stop. She may listen to you if you tell her that you see in the way I walk that it is not yet time to go. Regardless of what I say, the grownups won't listen to anything. They do not even see that my mouth is filled with the stuffing from the car seat or that my pupils are turning into marbles every time I hear them speak about trying to figure out the best way to escape.

The boy and I had it already figured out better than them and all I want to do is go back to our bench. His plastic bag is still rustling around your hand, so you must know where to go. Besides, I think they are all so tired, maybe if you get into the car, they won't even notice. Or maybe I can hold my hand over my mother's eyes while you climb in, just like she used to cover mine. But I don't know who would cover all the others.

Meanwhile, all I can do is cover my own eyes while the windshield wipers move left and right inside my palm. Between them I see you standing outside, opening the plastic bag, trying to catch as many snowflakes falling around you as you can. You spread it like a fishnet, glide it through the air. Maybe you also have a snowman inside your room that no longer knows how to go outside and you are hoping you will be able to keep him alive. A few more snowflakes fall onto your scarf. Their hands are holding on tightly to its thread. One shakes in the wind and almost leaves, but then decides to stay. If only the driver's hand was not reaching for the key. If only my mother's hand did not grip at the headrest in front of her so firmly. If only my mother had let me keep pushing against the driver's seat, maybe I would not wonder if one day you will blow at one of the snowflakes on your scarf until it lands on my tongue. I could tell you then that I am glad outside everything is covered in snow, because this way, if only for a moment, I do not have to see my bedroom window getting smaller as the car drives away. Through the fingers covering my eyes all I can see is your dark blue coat. One of your hands is still on my shoulder and I do not know if you are standing so close to me because I have not answered you yet where I want to go or because you are trying to protect me from the wind. Or maybe it is something else entirely, I think to myself, as I notice the last button on your coat is unbuttoned. Only a loose thread hangs in the air like a long abandoned swing still moving. I know how that feels. Sometimes when you lose a button, it is just too late to replace it. And, anyway, none of the new buttons would fit. I think you know that looking for a new one would not help. I remember the grownups telling me back then that everything comes to an end, but that is not really true. Everything at some point goes away, but nothing truly passes, nothing ever ends, at least not for me. The missing button on your coat makes me feel like you would understand. The cold outside air sneaks in through the opening, knocks against your neck, slides down to your chest. There is no more reason to close the window beside my childhood bed. The candle on the table beside it is long spent. All the adults used to tell me then that the draft is dangerous, but they don't know that it is the only thing that kept my snowman alive. I feel you may be like him. I feel you would never tell me that.

The wind is getting heavier. My hair is moving across my eyes. My mother tells me to roll the window back up now, because the car has started moving, but I can't. Your hand is covering mine, spinning the handle in the opposite direction. How fitting that we are driving away in one of those cars where to open the window, you have to keep spinning the handle around and around. The window is opening even more. Through my hair, I am watching all the snowflakes from your scarf float into the car. The snow whirls like God's hand spinning his cigarette around, while he tries to figure out what happened. All the car windows are white, the snowflakes have turned them into my bedsheets. For a split second, I am under my covers again trying to hide from my parents. I think they will all get sleepy now. They will have to stop the car now, because they cannot see anything at all.

Your hair is flapping against your hat. The wind is turning all the wet sleeves around, empty sweaters waiting for their owners. I can feel drops falling onto my cheeks. A drop of dew glides down the window. I hear you say to me that the snowflakes are turning into rain, that we should find a nice, warm place inside as soon as we can. You mention to me that a drink would be refreshing, but a coffee and a cookie may be more suitable for a day like today.

Today. Today looks like yesterday, only a little older. Today has just stumbled out of bed, with one slipper on and the other hiding underneath the bedframe. This is the only way I know how to walk with you through the snow that hides where we are. We are walking alongside today. It takes us by the hand and shows us the way to the café. But today is still walking through the hallway of my old apartment to the kitchen only to find two coffee cups on the dining table from the morning we left. There is still coffee inside. I guess my parents did not have enough time. The car came too early or they were running late, because they could not get me to leave my bed at the hour I promised them I would.

So this is what everything looked like when we left. My mother's coffee spoon leans on the little plate underneath her cup. This time it is lying on its back. My mother never leaves it that way. Somehow I am finding it difficult to tell whether it is lying there in defeat, resignation or acceptance. A flash of the man with his back on the street comes back to me, his hand still facing the sky. I can't see his feet. My shoes are hiding somewhere underneath the driver's seat. My socks are curled up in a ball I threw out the window just because I could. Or maybe I threw it in front of the car hoping that may be enough to stop it from driving away, but nothing worked. If only I had been a little older. If only my sock size had been a bit bigger. Maybe the car's tire would not have been able to just drive over the ball I made out of my socks. Now they are just a flattened Earth covered in dirt. The tire marks still swirl around my ankles like the roots growing underneath my abandoned bed. Sometimes they sneak into my day and spiral around my forehead reminding me our apartment key is still swinging in the lock on the other side of the door. No one came to pick it up.

My headache is making me dizzy. My head is getting heavy. Sometimes I imagine the boy came to see me after we left and found the keys we left in the door. But I know that can't be, because I still hear them rattle against each other in the wind. Maybe one day I will be able to understand what happened. Maybe I will know where the boy went and why he never came that night like he said he would. That is not like him. He would never just leave me like that.

The stray dog's paws rest on my upper legs as I wait for the boy on the bench. I want to touch the top of his head, but my arms won't move. My fingers hold on to one of the coffee cups left on the table when I was still little. How can this be? We left over twenty years ago and the coffee is not stale yet. The brown puddle moves inside the cup, drops are falling in. The ceiling is leaking from too much rain. The dog's brown eyes are watering from too much wind. I can feel something dripping onto my knees. He is trying to tell me something. I know because his pupil is expanding as he looks straight at me. Inside it, the boy's curly hair is weaving through the holes in my shoes where my shoelaces should be. A tight grip is telling me to get up, but I can't move. The dog's eyelids close for a moment as a gust of wind scatters the dirt collecting on the streets.

My eyes are hurting. Suddenly it is very foggy around me. The dog's breath smells like coffee. The steam from the car's exhaust rises into my pupil. A voice breaks through it telling me "*Voila Mademoiselle.*" A hand places a fresh cup of coffee on the table in front of me. Some of it spills over the edge onto my wrist. "*Pardonnez moi,*" a voice glides through the cracked open car window you helped me open. A fresh breeze glides over my cheeks. Briefly, I get the feeling the boy is here. There is no need to apologize for anything, I think to myself, but I don't say anything. If I tell the waitress it was not her, but me, or the stray dog's paw that stepped into the coffee, she may at best think I have a fever and at worst that I am crazy. I get a slight urge to tell her that the cup looks just like the one my mother left on the kitchen table back then when I still believed it is possible to return to places one left. I decide to bite my tongue instead. This does not sound much more sane and is probably better left in my head.

Your arm moves across the table and lands on my wrist. The tip of your sleeve is touching my skin, soaking in the spilled coffee. You brush over it with your deep blue coat as lightly as the deep blue morning sprinkles the car's windows with sweat dripping from God's forehead. My own head leans on the window, only now I can feel the soft fabric of your sleeve underneath my cheek. Thank you for allowing your sleeve to be my pillow for a bit. You are telling me something, but I can't hear you, because all I hear is the car keys jingling as the tires drive over the wounded street. Maybe I could at least tell you that with your coat there between my head and the window it hurts a little bit less when the car drives over a wound especially big. Who would have thought that many years later these wounds would be filled with red resin and turn into flowers? Something broken now resembles flower heads. Who would have thought they would be called Sarajevo Roses? This is what the pain will be eternalized as in history. The holes left by the shells have turned into scattered petals. Some have flown too far from where they are supposed to be. We need to make sure not to lose a single one. The red resin is fading on some. Maybe it is fading, because of all these people's steps walking over them too many times. People are searching for something they can no longer find. We need more rain. The petals become more visible then. The red resin becomes more saturated when the clouds decide to drop water from the sky. Even though it is raining all the time, I pour some water over one of the wounds and watch the Sarajevo Rose bloom. Who would have thought the streets would one day bloom as the result of horror? I need to pour more. I need to pour more. I think you know, because you slide a glass of water across the table all the way to my hand.

There is something black underneath your nails. I guess it would be the logical thing to do to ask you about yourself. After all, I do not remember why we are meant to meet. Yet, I feel if I ask you, you will be just the same person you always are and I will be even more the person I always am. Maybe without mentioning too much, we can be something other than our past. Instead, maybe I am hoping you could pick a petal out of every Sarajevo Rose you find and put it in your coffee. Maybe I am hoping I will not have to ask you anything about your life and I will be able to tell by the way your sleeve leaves a trace on the glass of water you pushed closer to me.

Maybe I just want to take the little chocolate on your coffee plate, unwrap it, put it in my mouth, so for once I do not have to taste the glue underneath the wallpaper I keep peeling away. With its wrapping, I would make a little paper wing and put it in the upper left pocket of your button-up shirt. That way, if anything in your life breaks, you would not have to be afraid.

I would rather not tell you that the older gentleman behind you reminds me of the man with the rifle I saw in the shade of the tree while waiting for the boy. I recognized him by the way he slants onto one side when he has been standing for way too long. This is how he used to lean over in the park when he was somebody else, when all he did was sell helium balloons. A lot of people, who used to sell helium balloons, now needed their hands to hold something else. I looked forward to seeing him every weekend when my father took me for our regular visit to the park near our apartment. The man would always give me one extra balloon, but only if I promised him to release it into the sky. He said if I watched closely enough and followed the way the string swerves, I would be able to read invisible letters in the air. He said if I watch the balloon fly up often enough, I would learn to decipher the secret language of the universe.

I wonder what he would tell me now. Would he be able to trace the line left by your hand as you try to speak to me from the other side of the table? I can see you opening your mouth, but I cannot hear a word you are saying. Maybe you are explaining to me why I came. Is it strange that I do not really want to know that anymore anyway? Somehow all I want to do is sit here with you and not think about anything at all.

I want to watch you unbutton your coat as if you were unbuttoning the dark blue morning sky. Underneath, there would be nothing but a mist, the same as the one forming on the glasses beside the man that was lying on the street with his open hand, reaching towards something in the sky. There would be nothing much left to say as you take your coat off, because everything would be clear anyway. I watch you cloak the chair behind you with your coat, with that morning from the day of departure. Maybe if it wasn't so cold outside, you could leave it there for someone else to find, someone whose pillowcase is full of holes from biting into it during sleep. Or it could just stay there watching people come in like the barely visible moon looking at me in the backseat. I waved at it through the window and for a moment I thought I saw the moon wink at me as though it was telling me everything will be okay one day, but I am not so sure about that. Maybe I imagined it.

I remember one of the days the man gave me a balloon that looked like the moon. Instead of letting it go into the air like I promised him I would, I gave it to the boy. He told me to tie it around his wrist because in one hand he was holding the plastic bag with the marbles and in the other my hand. He used to tell me how one day he will figure out how to build me a switch that connects to the moon. He said whenever something bad is happening around me and I do not want the moon to see it, I could just turn it off, and it would not notice anything at all. That way, one day we can find a way to get there and it won't always remind us of how we kept losing more and more marbles, because the cracks inside the streets were getting too big. They kept splitting open like the ugliness inside that was no longer able to remain contained. That way, the moon won't know anything I do not want it to know. He said this while winding the plastic bag around his finger until it was tight enough for him to let it go and watch it spin, then come to a standstill. Maybe one day the war, too, will come to an end. But I don't know, because the car's wheels have been spinning for so long the sky is no longer blue and the moon is long gone.

The sound of the marbles bumping against each other is in my head. Or maybe it is just your spoon touching your cup as you stir your espresso. I do not know anymore.

A light bulb is swinging above our table. I touch it with my fingertip just to see what would happen. Nothing does. Everything is still the same. I don't know why you lift your finger to touch the light bulb again. Maybe you looked at me and thought my eyes look too sad. Something happens this time. The light flickers. He came. He came. In the brief slice of time when the light is about to go out, I see him moving towards the bench. He is still too far away, but I know it is him. I know it is him. You push the light bulb as if you could tell I want to see his face. But he is just too far away. The light bulb swings across the broken street towards him. Only a little bit more. Only a little bit more and I will see him again. Oh no. The ground shakes. A burning smell grows outwards into the air. Darkness again, before I realize the light bulb above our table seems to be burnt out now. I am sorry, I hear you say.

A dark stain is covering part of the glass. It is still warm, but the light bulb seems broken. There is no light. The stain has the same shape as the flower that grew out of the street where we used to play. Maybe God likes the way these flower heads smell. The light bulb continues to sway. A whiff of burnt air brushes against my nose, God puts another stem in his vase. One of his eyelashes falls in. I wonder if he blew it away from his finger and made a wish. I wonder what that wish would be. Or maybe he did not even notice it at all.

An eyelash is glued to your cheek and it looks like mine. It looks like one of the ones I plucked out myself the night I waited. I do not know if making wishes that way counts, but I have to try. I do not know how one of those eyelashes landed on your cheek, but I am glad to see it there. It curves up like the tip of your collar, because another button is missing there. Maybe that is what you are looking for as you place one of your hands in your coat's pocket, I don't know. But there is nothing in there except grains of what feels like sand, but you know is something else. The boy takes more of the broken street and puts it inside his pocket. The plastic bag rustles again. I think some of the pieces landed in both your pocket and mine. I do not know how. I just know every time I place my hands in my pockets, they appear again, regardless of how many times I try to empty them, so after a while I just stopped.

I hear you ask me if I would like some of them inside of my coffee. Maybe some of the past you have to keep and some of it you have to let go, in order to move on. I am not sure which is which or if I ever had much of a choice, but I nod.

You say this to me as if it is the most usual thing to say, as if you were inquiring with me about my day. Thank goodness you are not asking me anything of that sort, because I am not interested in little chitchat like that. You add that you would recommend some sugar with that, at least for the beginning, that you drink your espresso black, but for me you would suggest something else. With other people I am much more stubborn than to simply say yes so easily, but with you I am different. As I nod again, a strand of hair falls across your forehead as though you were the one who lowered your head. You leave it there while you sprinkle the inside of your pockets into my coffee as though you have done it many times before and it is by now just part of our regular morning routine. The more of it you pour into my coffee, the more familiar around you I feel. Suddenly, I feel like I am still in my pyjamas, my favourite ones. I have not seen them since the morning we left. I left them in the bottom drawer for when we come back. They are my favourite, because on the top part Snoopy sleeps on the roof of his house. I guess he never liked to sleep inside. Or maybe that is just what everyone assumes. Maybe it is not like that at all and maybe something happened, so he can only fall asleep outside. Maybe he cannot fall asleep at all.

The particles fall into my coffee from your hand like dandelion seeds floating in the wind. It is not even spring and too soon for everything, but here they are, and I do not want to stop them now. Maybe God coughed, because he is sitting in the draft. I think he did, because there was a dandelion flower hiding in the vase where he is collecting all the stems of roses, while the Sarajevo streets fill up with their heads. I feel something like close to happy and like we are drinking coffee together on that roof with Snoopy beside us. I know this sounds silly and maybe all this is only happening because God has caught a cold, but right now I do not care about that. For once, I am not inside an apartment from some life long ago. For once, the keychain in my pocket does not have a single key and is nothing but an empty ring. For once, I no longer hear the sound of the keys we left behind in the apartment door. For once, I feel the boy is near. At least it is easier to tell myself that with one of your dandelion seeds caught between my eyelashes.

After all, everything I see is blurred through a white fluffy cloud in front of my eye. It muffles my parents' and the driver's voices trying to get through to me still. Yet, I hear yours perfectly clearly. You tell me that is enough from your pocket and it is time for some sugar now. I have no idea where the "ah sugar, ah honey honey," tune suddenly came from, but it loops through my head as you say that. Another song I do not recognize is playing in the coffee shop, so it must be coming from somewhere else. I do not even like that song much. I think it is cheesy. Regardless, I allow it to remain in my head as I watch you tear at the little sugar pack. One is enough, you preface your act, because you still want me to be able to taste the street from which the roses bloom. If only you knew how many times the boy's steps followed the cracks from which they came, but maybe you do. A little bit of sugar makes it all more bearable, you add. A little bit of sugar adds a rainbow over the grey sky, a colourful bridge replacing the fallen one. Sometimes we need to believe in things that are not there in order to survive. The more sugar you pour, the stronger the colours become. I notice you took your own sugar pack and not mine. Who knows whether you had any reason for that at all, but the moon just peeked through for the moment you did that and blinked for a second. Both the rainbow and the moon are here at the same time. Another reason to think we somehow ended up on that roof. Maybe we could lie down on our backs while the clear sky flows over us like a soft blanket. Maybe we need to do that fast, because the rainbow may not be around for too long. It could start peeling any second like wallpaper that is becoming too old, together with the sky.

I twirl the empty sugar bag in the middle until it starts shaping into a bow. How strange. That is what I did with the plastic bag a long time ago before I gave it to the boy. I haven't done this since, as I would only do something like that for him. Before I am able to give it to you, you softly take the bow out of my hand and place it in my hair, right above my ear. It goes with your playful style, you say to me. Besides, you are like a little mischievous detective, aren't you, you continue. Now it can be your earpiece, so you can hear everything better, and this one suits you well, with a hint of sweet. What a line. You tried to be imaginative, I give you that. And, hey, since we are on the roof with Snoopy around, I guess I am in the mood for a little more silliness, so I forgive the somewhat corny sentiment. I guess you knew that. I have no clue how you appear to know me so well. I have even less of an idea why the moment you push my coffee cup even closer to me, crumpled paper pieces resembling the boy's letter I left in the pocket of my dirty pants start falling all around us.

They look like little snowflakes made out of Styrofoam. Instead of making me sad as they usually do, because I have not yet managed to put them together and find out what the boy tried to say, your presence is making me want to play. Right now may be the first time in my life I am able to at least for a second accept I may never know what exactly was in that letter he hid in my pocket. Maybe now, after all this time, he would want to tell me something else. His thoughts are falling around us in fragments. Some land in your hair. Others are bouncing off your arm. I don't think you can see them, because you are continuing as though nothing is happening. As for me, I scoop a few into my palm and blow them in your direction, rather than trying to collect them. I think I caught you closing your eyes. Maybe one landed on your eyelid, slid down your cheek and fell into your espresso. There is a little brown stain now on your collar where the button used to be. I am surprised that I am throwing these your way mostly just to tease you and because for a change I feel at peace, and not because I need you to know anything. I am even starting to think the little white pieces that have collected in your hair look somewhat endearing. I bet you do not know the reason I am leaning in closer to you is because I like the way my breath is making them move. I almost want to ruffle your hair and make it even messier than it already is, but I am not sure yet how you would interpret my playfulness. Besides, we are not close enough for that yet, even though I am letting you prepare my coffee for me. I almost want to tell you the more coffee I drink, the more you look like the boy, but I don't know what you would think of that. I feel like having another sip. Maybe I will see him if I close my eyes. Your hand is still on my cup. You smirk at me as I lean in further. Your mouth looks like a thin slice of the moon, a thin crack in the fabric of God's pillowcase, maybe the one the button needs to slide through. But I do not really want to think about God right now, either.

He can no longer see anything. His chair is facing the entrance door, but no one is walking through. Only a shadow occasionally passes by on the other side in an unclear shape. I want him to stay there and watch them pass like the black silhouettes of car lights I see through my closed eyelids. The boy is nowhere in sight. Instead, I am back inside the car, my head still leaning on the window, while I pretend to sleep. Another car's headlights pass through my closed eyelids. Every once in a while, a human being sneaks in, someone standing on the side of the street, leaning. Sometimes I would pretend they are just holding balloons, but I know they are holding something else. I watched the balloon strings often enough to know they are not that stiff. Besides, there is no need to hold a balloon with both hands, at least not like that. I have also never seen anyone wear special clothes just to sell balloons, especially not the kind of clothes that would scare away any adult, let alone a child. Green waves flow over poufy fabric. Maybe the clothes turned out this way because they did not know how to wash their clothes properly. That must be it. Why else would someone wear an ugly outfit like that? Just one of them was holding an empty canister in his hand instead. I wondered if he is on his way to my grandparents' house to get water from their garden. Or maybe this one came from the future. Maybe he just poured all the water onto one of the Sarajevo Roses making sure it does not die. Everyone will be able to see it now. If the red is stronger, they will come and help.

I will let God wonder that now. His hand is buried in his hair while he waits. I wonder who he is waiting for or if he is waiting at all.

He is scratching his head. Some dandruff lands in the vase. My eyelid twitches. It feels like someone is pressing against it from the inside with his hand like against a curtain that won't move aside. You lift your hand up to the brim of your hat and slide across it. This makes me grin because it is making me think of a happy memory even though the war was already there. I used to slide like that across the long hallway floor of our apartment in my old slippers early in the morning before anyone got up. I would run from one end towards the window on the other, and then let my feet go pretending I am sliding on the Milky Way. I called it my Moon Slide, because this was how I was going to catapult myself to the moon. I just needed to get a proper head start, run fast enough, let go at the right time and slide out through the window. I tried to practise every day. One day I think I was going too fast or maybe I just did not let go in the right moment. The window on the other end was suddenly so close to my eyes that I grabbed onto the curtain on the side. My hands held onto it like I was some astronaut climbing into my spaceship. The curtain twirled around and spun me around myself. The stars I glued onto the ceiling turned into all the planets I visited right then. Even as I pulled down the curtain and broke the rings that held it, I thought to myself, no one can catch me now. Neither of my parents was mad at me when they came out of their bed and asked me what happened. I just told them that I was launching myself onto the moon and obviously still need more practise. I asked them if they had any tips and apologized for the curtain. I do not think they had any answers for me, but the lines that formed in the corners of their eyes as they smiled told me that they did not mind I broke the curtain rings. I took one and rolled it across the floor. It stopped at my father's foot. He just left it there as we all watched a helium balloon rise up and fly by our naked window. I knew it would come. I know I just need to learn the Moon Slide better. I know I just need to learn when to stop running and just let my magic slippers carry me across the floor to the window. Another helium balloon will appear, just like now, and it will take me up all the way to the moon. I know another one will come, because there are just so many abandoned ones now.

I must have been telling you about this memory all along while we are sitting in the café, because the lines in the corners of your eyes have formed just the same. They are tiny airplane trails. They look pretty, so I will refrain from telling you that when the war started getting longer, one of my magic slippers went missing. I still continued practising my Moon Slide, while the cracks in the hallway floor grew beneath my feet.

The airplane trails are multiplying as you tell me that you like me already, that you would prefer to disappear onto the moon for a while, because you feel the building we came from, and maybe even your entire life, is turning into a giant octopus spreading its arms trying to get you.

I do not know what has got into me, but I am going to tell you my secret about how to deal with situations like that. All you have to do is walk up to the light switch inside the room I picked you up from and keep pushing it on and off as fast as you can. That is the best way to get rid of any monsters that may be around. Even with all their superpowers in some areas, when it comes to this, they are just like us. Sudden change hurts them the most and they just run away. I also think they are weak and do not have the strength to keep adjusting their eyes. I do not really know for sure, but something also tells me that in the moment right after the switch, when the second of complete blindness follows, we may see nothing at all, but we feel everything we have ever done in this life. The monster may survive one such moment, but too many of them in a row will be too much for it to bear. You will see, its giant arms will let go of your shoulder and all you may hear is the scratching sound of its nails against the wall in the building's hallway. It may knock on a few doors along the way asking for help, but nobody will care to come out anyway. Who knows, this may also be one of the steps of getting to the moon and activating the invisible space tunnel connecting it to the Earth.

You smirk as I say this. Another line appears by your eye. Even though I did not see it, this must mean a little airplane flew out of your pupil. One of the birds' red feathers from the building lands on your ear. The bird must have fluttered as the monster ran underneath it trying to find the exit door. I hope the man I saw in the newspaper was also woken up by its sounds. I hope the long tunnels around his arms cracked open the way a Kinder chocolate egg splits down the middle. After a while I stopped wondering about what I will find inside, because it was always the same. All I would see is an empty hand. I wish I could help the man in the photograph. I wish I could wake him up. No one would want to sleep with the collar buttoned up all the way to the top.

I could ask you some details about the kind of institution the building is part of, I guess, but I feel I can sense enough about it, I do not need to know more. I have walked the same hallway before, while the Sarajevo rain was dripping on my head as if a clock hand was counting down the time I have left. Underneath, all the major institutions of the Earth grow roots and connect in a giant knot. Yes, I have been there while in another city, I have been there before. There is no need to disclose more.

Maybe on some other day I would want to try and figure out with you how we can find this knot and untie it, but today I would rather stay on the roof of Snoopy's house and not go underground. We can count all the little dots in the sky that you sprinkled on there from inside your pocket. One has landed on our table. I tap it with my finger to pick it up, blow on it and watch it drift through the air. A breadcrumb falls on my old bedroom's window ledge. A sparrow flies towards it with warm feet. I wonder whether it just came from the street lamp where the boy and I would always meet. Maybe the lamp is working again. Maybe he is there now waiting for me while I am spending my days in this strange city. I have no idea why I just thought that. I know this cannot be, because he always preferred the dark.

Something strange is happening with the light in the café or it may be just my eyes. It keeps shaking like the man's arm on the street. Maybe he can't breathe because his breathing machine is connected to our chimney. Maybe I turned the knob on the fireplace in the wrong direction, because I am not awake enough yet. Or maybe I am too cold walking in the apartment without one of my house shoes. Maybe it is my fault he is shivering. The blinds in front of my eyes are trembling. Passing car lights are brushing against my eyelids again. Ferris wheel wagons are spinning inside of my pupil. I think the little girl is waving at me. I am not sure, because everything is appearing as a silhouette, the light bulb above our table is swinging. God has taken the cocktail umbrella out of his drink and he is spinning it above our heads. I am angry at him for doing this. Why is he reminding me of these things now when

I just want to be left in peace while I watch your eyebrows rise up and down as you talk to me. They are calming me down. Every time you raise them, the man on the street is breathing again. His stomach rises up. His eyelids lift. I wonder what he sees, because two of the boy's marbles are spinning where his pupils are supposed to be. If he saw you, I wonder if he would see what I see.

I do not know exactly what is happening, but my eyes are so tired suddenly. As if you could sense this, you pull down the blinds in my bedroom and place your hat on my head. The sparrow on my window ledge jumps up as the blinds send a whiff of air to its wing and lands on your hat's brim. Its little feet fold the blind shut as it walks along the edge of your hat. Everything is closed and the many lights can no longer get to me. I can't even feel all the cars' wheels passing on top of the brim. I guess the sparrow must be redirecting all the traffic. I like the irregular rhythm of its feet pushing the shadow to expand over my eyes.

I can feel my pupil growing in the darkness. Thank goodness your hat is protecting me, because I am not ready yet for you to see what all is inside. With the lights gone, all the little details around your eyes start appearing to me. I am not sure how I know that the tiny scar on your left eyelid is from when you were a boy and fell down the stairs while running to tell your mother that you can smell smoke and that your curtain is burning. It was only a dream then, but the dream folded itself into tomorrow and grabbed your curtain in the morning. God's cigarette was too close to it. Too much smoke is rising into the chimney. The man on the street can't breathe again. I do not know how I can see this scene from your life. Maybe I am not even sure if the memory is yours or mine. It may also be that you told me this story about being able to sense the future while pouring the sugar into my coffee. Or maybe I know this because I am wearing your hat. Its edge circles around my head like the smoke ring coming out of God's mouth, the eye of prophecy. Maybe if you blow into it, it will take on a different shape and everything can still turn out differently.

I hope you won't mind that your hat is soaking in some of the remains of the Sarajevo rain. I think you will be okay, though, since I can see your own hair now and it looks like you haven't washed it in a while. Don't worry, that is a compliment, coming from me. The longer you go without washing your hair, the more of the world you have in there, the boy says. Sometimes we would try and see which one of us can go longer without washing it. Sometimes we would count the days until we could no longer keep track. An invisible ring left by your hat circles around your hair before you ruffle it with your hand. One of God's smoke rings dissipates. It swirls into the same shape as the strand of hair falling over your eyes. The curtain I am holding onto is swinging again. The café is spinning and I feel like I am in a bumper car circling in the invisible lane surrounding your head. I like it this way even if I keep passing the same spot all the time. At least like this we have no chance at arriving at the border. At least if I just keep spinning around you, you may never ask me for my passport and find a photograph of somebody else there instead. I wonder what you would do then. You may like me too much to just send me back home. But you may not like me enough to wink at me like the moon did, then turn your back to me gently the way he does, and let me go wherever I want to go, as if you never saw anything strange about my passport at all. One thing I would find out about you, though, is whether the spoon in your hand would turn into a balloon or into something else.

Even if I wanted to, I cannot find that out now. The curtain I am holding onto has twisted itself up to the end and is starting to spin the other way. The silly song is continuing to play as you open another packet of sugar. "You are my candy girl ... " whooshes by the moment I pass your ear. I try not to let it stick in my mind that your ear's curve reminds me of one of the hills surrounding Sarajevo, where the people with the ugly clothes used to hide once the war got even worse than it already was. I try to remember that the hills are not the ones to blame and that it's the grownups who started fighting. The driver's voice runs through my head again. He says to my parents that it would be much easier to escape the city if it was not in a valley, with all those people watching us from the hills. I just think to myself, maybe if they had been able to sell more balloons, they would not be up there at all.

I want to ask my parents why we cannot just go up to them and talk. I am sure we would recognize some of them. Maybe at least a few came to get fresh spring water from our garden. If I ask one of them why everyone is so mad at each other, maybe he would tell me. After all, everyone was always kind to me before. But maybe that was because if I recognized someone coming to get water more than once, I would give them one of the *Akšamčići* flowers before they left, and I do not have one now.

If I did maybe everything would be all right again, because this flower talks to the moon all the time. The only time it opens is at night. It is never awake during the day and knows what happens when it is dark. Maybe it could say something that nobody has heard yet, maybe then nobody would be mad at each other anymore.

I hear you say to me that I will have to get one for you then. I am somewhat surprised, since I was not aware I was telling you any of this at all. I just wanted to keep spinning around your head in my bumper car the way the moon travels around the Earth. I do want you to know about me, but I am afraid the more you know, the sooner the clear sky above our heads will go away, and everything between us will end. If you let me move with you like the moon, we can just circle around the present until it becomes more bearable, until it does not make us go anywhere else.

Maybe you would like to have the *Akšamčići* flower I tied to the chalk I threw onto the roof of my grandparents' house. When the war started getting worse, I became worse and worse at the marble game. Regardless of how hard I tried to keep all the marbles inside, more and more of them would escape outside of the line the boy and I drew on the ground.

The circle is too small. It needs to be bigger to hold them in. The boy's arm circles around the asphalt while I try blowing away the old circle we drew. Snowflakes of chalk flow up into the air and land in the propeller underneath his arm stretching out as far as it can. The air underneath the wing is speeding up again. The circles you are making with your spoon inside of my coffee are getting larger. White sugar flakes are on your fingertips. Or maybe you brushed your hand over the chalk on the ground, but I do not know if anything is helping at all, because the other circle the boy is drawing is still too small.

The further he tries to stretch out his arm, the more chalk dust appears on your hand. He is pushing down harder now, his balance is tilting to one side. Your hand is almost entirely white now. You lift your hands as if to dust them off, but instead, you just look at your palm. I almost feel like you are remembering this, too, because another line formed in the corner of your eye. The line doesn't only appear when you smile. Sometimes it comes together with a long-forgotten memory.

The boy keeps stretching. Your line expands some more. I am afraid the circle is not big enough to hold everything. I flick the marble anyway, but it crosses the borderline. It still lands outside, just like the letter piece I flick across the table towards you. It flies against your arm and falls onto the floor beside your shoe. The boy steps on the marble I rolled too far and puts it back inside the circle. Don't worry, he tells me, I won't let any of the marbles get lost. I want to tell him that is not the same. Once the marbles have been on the other side of the line, it is already too late. I want to tell him they do not feel at home anymore and it is all my fault. Maybe I keep missing because I can no longer see properly. Maybe I ruined my eyes when I was standing too close to the candle flame on that night when I felt really cold. That was the night when I heard my father's voice through the wall. He said one of the men standing guard on the hill told him the situation in this country is not going to get any better and that we must leave as soon as we can. I wish I never heard that at all. Maybe then I would still be just as good at the marble game as I always was and we would not have lost a single one of them.

If I had gone to sleep, like my parents told me to do, instead of continuing to look at the flame, maybe my eyes would still be good enough to play. Maybe the boy would have never lost his favourite marble then and none of this would have happened. I would not be in this strange city in a spinning café, because the boy would have been there that night. He would have come to our bench and we would have run away, like we planned.

I notice you are done preparing my coffee for me. Your hands fold around the little candle on our table. I thought we already warmed up as we have been sitting inside for a while, but I guess your hands must have gotten cold again. The outline of the flame is blurring in my eyes. You rub your palms against each other, maybe to warm them up. Chalk dust starts falling from your hands into the flame, the circle the boy drew expands. The flame shivers as if in apology for swallowing all this chalk. It trembles some more. The edge of the puddle trembles, too, as the stray dog steps into it. God blows another smoke ring into my eyes. This is the perfect time to throw the chalk right through it before it lands on the roof of my grandparents' house. I tell the boy that with the chalk gone we no longer need to draw any circles at all and all the borders will go away. Maybe then we will be able to stay. This way no one will be able to tell anymore what is inside and what is outside. None of the marbles will feel like they do not belong and since I cannot do anything wrong anymore with the circle gone, we will get to keep them all.

The roof of my grandparents' house is the best place for the chalk to go, because this is where I put all the things I no longer want to see, but am not yet ready to let go. It is already late and all the windows are dark. My grandparents are asleep and I do not want to wake them, so I decide to tie an *Akšamčići* flower to the chalk before throwing it to soften the fall.

I am glad the chalk lands without making a sound. My throat keeps stretching as I watch the chalk roll down the roof. This is the way I used to lie down in the grass and roll down the hill where I am no longer allowed to play. The umbrella inside of my throat is trying to open. There is too much rain. I think there is just so much of it, it has worn down the tiles on the roof, because one of them is loose. If I promise my parents to take an umbrella with me to the hill and use it to move aside the grass in front of me, they may let me go into the woods. The chalk lands in the roof rain gutter safely without touching the loose tile. The chalk made it and I can, too. It makes me believe I would not step on anything dangerous, either. I know if I still had both of my magic slippers, I could go. I know this because they diffuse any mines immediately. The first time I tried my launch to the moon in them, my Moon Slide, I attached stickers to the soles that would help me with that. The stickers are of Snoopy with a blanket he borrowed from his friend. When I slid across the hallway floor, Snoopy promised to sweep it with the blanket and make the ground more slippery for me, so I would have the speed I need once I stop running and let go. He also told me not to worry about the cracks that came, because of all the loud sounds outside that make the ground shake. He will make all of them go away. I am sure if I asked him, he could also help me with the mines. He could just place the blanket on any mine he sees and it would stop working. The mine would not feel any pressure from my foot. You may not believe me, but trust me, Snoopy could help, I have seen how thick the blanket is. I felt it with my bare feet and I can tell you the blanket feels just like your hat.

I hope you are not too cold without it. You slide my coffee cup closer to me and tell me I should drink it while it is still warm. Now that my eyes are protected by the shade, I notice your eyes look like the boy's favourite marble. The same blue-green river runs through them in a faint wave. At some point I should tell you that I have been looking for it everywhere since I came. The boy threw it onto the roof hoping to get the chalk back. He said all I need to do is wait by the down pipe and open my hands. The marble would push it along the gutter and down the pipe, a planet sliding down a secret time tunnel. I asked him if maybe the marble is too small for that and what if we never see it again. He assured me that is not going to happen. He said he sleeps with it under his pillow every night and every good dream he has charges it with extra powers. Besides, now that we are running away, we need the chalk, so I can draw an invisible circle around you in the air. He told me that now that things are getting worse, we need some borders for protection, and not to be sad, we can figure out how to get rid of them later.

The only circle I see now is the one left on my saucer as I lift the cup to take a sip. Warm coffee slides down my throat. Rain is pouring down the pipe. It is getting heavier and heavier. Little droplets splash against the roof tiles, fall from the oar of Charon. He has to row faster and faster now. I don't know if you know who he is, but I am glad they made the time to introduce him to us in school even though we had to spend so much time practising what to do if we step on any mines. I guess we had to know who he is if something went wrong. They told us that he is the ferryman of the underworld, that when you die, he is there with his boat on the river Acheron. If you have a coin under your tongue, he will take you on his boat to the place you need to go. We learned that some think he is ugly and mean, but I don't really know what to believe.

Some say if you have nothing in your mouth, he will let you wander the shores between the living and the dead for a hundred years. Somehow that does not seem like him. Even though we have never met, I think maybe when he says you need to have something under your tongue, he just means he wants you to have something to say about your life that will make him want to take you anywhere you desire to go. I think in my sleep I heard him weep every time another Sarajevo Rose appeared on the street. I think I saw petals fall all around him. One night I could see him lean over the edge of his boat and lift a few petals out of the water with his palm.

One of the petals is stuck underneath my tongue. I know he would take me on his boat, even though I don't have a coin. I just know. I think the petal would be enough.

I can hear his oar splashing inside the Acheron river, while the rain in the city continues to fall. I am a little worried about him, because I do not think even he is used to this. There is just so much water and the drops are getting stronger and stronger. What if something happens to his boat? Where will all these people go?

The raindrops keep falling. The rain gutter on the roof of my grand-parents' house is filling up with water. I think maybe now the marble will finally come down. I have to prepare. I have to catch it when it rolls down. Both my palms are facing up underneath the pipe opening like wings. Any time now, the marble will land in my hand. It just has to with all this water falling from the sky.

Centuries of sorrow collect in my palm. The river Acheron grows and I can hear Charon breathing faster. Or maybe the breaths are my own as the marble still hasn't landed in my palm. I think I can feel the river from Charon's oar dripping between my fingers. My hands are still empty. I know the marble was up on the roof. Where did it go? Maybe I can ask Charon. Maybe the rain was already heavy enough before and already pushed it down. I want to ask him if he has seen it, if he knows what happened, but for some reason I cannot open my mouth. He may not hear me anyway as he is barely keeping his boat afloat and there are too many people lined up waiting for him to bring them safely across the river to the other side. With every loud tear in the sky, more people appear along his shore. With every tear I can hear, the steps along the street are getting quieter and all I can think of is the boy.

No. None of these people that appeared are him. I try to say something to Charon again. My tongue lifts up with his oar. The flower petal is still there. I can't tell if it is from a rose or from the *Akšamčići* flower I threw on the roof, together with the chalk. I think I can taste some moon dust. In that case, it can only be the *Akšamčići*, since its petals talk to the moon. Chalk dust appears on my tongue. Maybe this means the marble is somewhere nearby, too. It must be. It must be. Then again, I don't know, because so many days have passed and so much sugar is still on my tongue.

You adjust the bow behind my ear made out of the empty sugar pack. The moment your fingers touch it, one of its sides lifts up. The loose tile on the roof of my grandparents' house moves up, too, before it moves back down. Oh no. Rain is leaking from the ceiling into their fireplace. It is getting darker inside. My pupil is dilating again to adjust. Drops are falling in. Circles form. I think some are from the rain and some from Charon's oar. Your pupil expands, too, as you look straight into mine. The black abyss of your pupil is pushing aside the green-blue iris wrapped around it. Its waters move aside in waves.

Maybe I could tell you now how the colour of your eyes reminds me of the wave inside the boy's favourite marble. I just still don't know if it's the right time. Your pupil expands more as you keep looking at me. More and more raindrops keep falling onto my grandparents' fireplace. Maybe your pupil keeps growing, because it is getting darker where they are. I don't want my grandparents to catch a cold, because the fireplace is no longer warm, but part of me thinks the darker it is everywhere, the more chance I have of seeing the boy. I don't know if I am right, but your iris turns into the river inside his marble again.

A little bit of the green-blue river from the marble splashes into Charon's boat and flows into his shoes. I don't know if seeing different colours may give him some hope. I am worried about his boat. If any more water gets in, it may sink and I am not sure he knows how to swim. A wave pushes his boat in the wrong direction. It bumps against the riverbank. I think it hit something that connects to the electrical wiring, because another light bulb in the café we are in turns off. Your pupil grows again. More raindrops fall from my grandparents' ceiling.

One lands inside Charon's boat. The overflowing boat reminds me of all the puddles in Sarajevo collecting inside the broken streets. They keep growing, too. I think maybe the stray dog drinks from the puddles, because he is worried if too much water covers the streets, no one will be able to find their way home. He licks the puddle again. I wish he could help Charon, too, but I don't think he can. I think he knows he needs to stay on the street and make sure he sees what is happening.

The stray dog's paw lands in a puddle. You lick your finger and run it across your eyelid as if you were turning a page in a book. I guess your eye feels dry. Maybe it feels dry because your growing pupil pushed too much of your iris aside. Or maybe the smoke from my grandparents' fireplace trying to survive in the rain came all the way to the café and irritated your eye. I remember one day the boy placed some coal inside the fireplace. Smoke rose up as he rubbed his eyes and blinked. I need some water, he said. I can imagine you doing the same. I think I remember I even gave him some ice for his eyes.

God chews on an ice cube, because he put the cigarette back into his mouth the wrong way. It sounds like he is chewing on a light bulb. Tiny pieces of glass are falling on my head, since he is too tipsy to eat properly. Rain from the ceiling is dripping into my hair. I am not sure if it is coming from inside the café or from somewhere else. I know you already gave me your hat to protect me, but I wonder if you know your widening pupil has a similar effect of making me feel safe. The longer you look at me the way you have been, the more your pupil is turning into a black umbrella above my head. Nothing can happen to me with you here. The boy is the only one who made me feel this way. At least until now.

I am still waiting for his marble to roll down. Instead, the handle of the black umbrella falls into my opened hands. I spin it slowly between my palms and look up. A rotating black circle is above my head. Your dark pupil rotates, too. I am still looking up at the inside of the umbrella at the same time. I can see one of the umbrella's arms is broken. You blink every time the broken umbrella arm rotates past the spot I am looking at. It comes around again. Even though part of the umbrella is broken and you keep blinking, I feel closer to you the longer we sit here and the more often the broken umbrella spins above our heads.

I spin the umbrella faster now. The sparrow flies away from your hat. The faster I spin, the less I can see where the broken umbrella arm is. Another round and it disappears entirely. I know the broken arm is still there, but only for a little while, I want to make you forget and make you feel sheltered. A line in the corner of your eye appears as you look up. I think you smiled. I think if you smile any more, I may start believing you are the boy. The rainbow appears again as I spin.

The boy taught me how to spin something properly when he showed me how to make fire with a stick during the war when we had to save as many matches as we could. He told me all I need to do is spin the stick really firmly and quickly inside the notch. Once there is enough friction, I just need to blow. We used dry petals as tinder.

I feel your breath brush against my eyelid. There was an eyelash on your cheek, you say. Now make a wish. I open my mouth to tell you how sweet that is. The petal from underneath my tongue flies out, rises up to the ceiling. That's okay. I won't need it, I know. I won't need to get into Charon's boat at all now that you are here with me. I don't know from where, but a light breeze comes in. One of the boy's letter pieces slides underneath your shoe.

The curtain in your bedroom moves as I breathe towards the floor. It falls over the exposed light bulb, a cloud moves over the moon, smoke rises into my eye as you glide your finger through the candle flame beside my coffee cup hoping it will dry. I think it is wet from all that rain. Your hand so close to the candle flame is creating a shadow on my cheek. I think I may have missed the letter piece, but you are making me forget about that, because the shadow your finger forms on my cheek is helping me run away. It comes just in time. My palm is making it feel too warm from leaning on the car's armrest for too long. My elbow opens the ashtray as my father's hand nudges me. He is waking me up to tell me we are taking a short break and to put on my shoes. I think my elbow is still asleep. God takes another puff from his cigarette. My fingers keep pushing the lid on the ashtray up and down, up and down. I keep telling my father I can't get out of the car now, to leave me alone, that I want to keep sleeping. I tell him my eyes are hurting, because God keeps playing with his cigarette and blowing the smoke right into my eyes. Please stop playing with the ashtray, you are talking nonsense. Don't be such a child now, even though you are one, my father says gently. And what happened to your socks? God stole them. His circulation is horrible now, since he drinks too much. He is a loser. He can have them. He doesn't have anything else anyway. I hope my socks smell as bad as the air in this car and he passes out and hurts his head on the table. Besides, what kind of weird car is this, with an ashtray where my arm is supposed to lean. My father tells me to please calm down and not to talk that way. I am not sorry I said any of that even though I did not really mean it. I do not really want anyone at all to hurt anymore, not even whoever is at fault. He asks me again to please come out, because we won't be able to stop for a long time after this, the coming stretch is not safe. His hand lands on my elbow again trying to move it away from the door. Your finger touches my wrist. Be careful, your sleeve is too close to the candle. The only way I can respond to you is to tap the flame the way I tapped the old-fashioned lock on the car once my father tried to get me to leave the car by opening the door from the outside.

My finger is approaching the flame. It pushes down the head of the lock and I watch its body disappear in the car's door. My father's face disappears in the glare of the street lamp behind him. Not surprisingly, his hair looks as messy as yours. I guess that must be because I hid away his comb the night before we left. I thought maybe he would not want to leave the house looking that way. I roll down the window just enough for him to hear me when I say that I can't see who he is and my father told me not to open the door for strangers.

My father's jacket flutters in the breeze. Our table shakes. Maybe I kicked it when I stretched out my leg trying to reach my shoe hiding underneath the driver's seat. Oh no, I just pushed it further away. I try to stretch more, but I think I hit your shoe instead. I am sorry. Your smile tells me you do not really mind. More little airplane trails appear in the corner of your eyes as you ask me how much longer I let my father wait for me in the cold.

It could be a while, because I am about to climb over to the front seat. My father thinks I am simply trying to get my shoe. He has always had something very innocent about him and believes everything I say. If only he knew I am actually planning to drive away. This is the perfect moment to escape. I run my finger through the flame on our table the way you did. I can use it as the car key now. My nail will be soft enough to mould itself to fit the cracks on the ignition. Do you maybe know of any places I could go? Do you maybe want to come with me? This is the perfect time for you to come in, with nobody here. We could escape together and go anywhere we want. I can't drive home. My parents would just find me there and make me leave again. I have to drive somewhere else, somewhere far away. I am also not sure I remember the way back anyway. Too many streetlights were broken until there were only trees. It could be that the driver turned the steering wheel when a bird fluttered by the windshield. All I know is my head kept bumping against the window while the tires drove on a path not meant for cars. Every time we drove over a larger bump, I thought of the man who gave me his candle legs, that maybe I should have run after him and given him one back. Now it's too late. The gravel from underneath the tires is stuck between my teeth. It tastes just like the contents from your pocket you gave me. This is why I trust you when you tell me that Montréal may be just the place I need. A lot of apartments there have just the kind of hallway you need, you continue, long and dark leading to a window. You could practise your moon launch there every day. Some of them may have a floor with cracks, but I could help you out with that. It's nothing that a little bit of sand can't fix and I have plenty still left in my pockets. You and I both know it's not sand, but I guess for now you are more comfortable referring to it that way.

My pupil widens at that thought, one of the car lights turns on. The other one remains dark. From the outside it must look like the car is winking, wishing us a good journey. If I say anything to you now, I am afraid I will fall through my own abyss and land in yours. Yours grows in front of me while the stray dog stares into my pupil and tugs at my sleeve some more. I don't want to leave the bench yet. I want to wait longer. The stray dog tugs again. You fold down your collar and tell me you like to feel your scarf on your skin. I pull your hat down over my eyes and fold down the visor in the car. I think you know that I just told you I am ready to open the car door for you, so you can tell me where to go.

Coffee is dripping from the table onto my leg. I think I bumped it when I tried to climb over the gearshift and hit my knee. I thought you were about to whirl your scarf around your neck, but instead you place it on my leg. Actually, there is an apartment for rent in the house beside mine. An oar lifts through the black air inside your pupil and makes a full circle the moment you say this. It spins again through the dark space. A light breeze passes my eyelid. I think the car is moving. You are spinning your scarf around me. The car window on your side keeps rolling down. I am glad you like the draft, just like me. I am glad you decided to come in and drive away with me. I am happy we are leaving.

I think you will like my street, you tell me while putting on your coat. My father's coat flutters again as he watches me sit in the front seat with the wheel between my hands. One of them waves to him through the wet window, motions that it's okay, I will be fine, he can leave. A bird flies behind him and touches the back of his ear. The moment he turns away, I turn the key and press on the gas pedal. Your shoe steps on the little piece of the boy's letter I blew at you. Maybe I can help you figure out what he tried to say. I think the many trees lining my street could recognize his handwriting, you say to me after you pick up the crumpled letter piece. Maybe a broken branch can reach through the air and touch the eyelash on your cheek. I wonder if it is the same one as from before or if it is another one.

Maybe the wind in your street moves the branches underneath the street lamp the way my mother's hands moved underneath the lamp-shade beside my bed. That night the boy never came, she tried to make me less sad by telling me a story about how one day I will make it to the moon despite everything. Her hands fold in near the light bulb. A shadow in the shape of a spaceship appears on the wallpaper beside my pillow. See, I built you a way to get there. All you have to do is scoop the light, fold it into your palm, and leave at least one crack open between your fingers. If you bend your fingers just right, the shadow will appear as a door. It will not be a problem then for you to enter the spaceship any time you wish to get away. My mother says all this to me again while I watch the same spaceship appear on our tabletop.

It could also be that the tassels from your scarf moved in front of the candle flame when you leaned in a bit more to dry my knee. One end is soaking in the coffee I spilled, the other folds around your neck, hangs down, the little strings are touching the edge of my cup.

I move my cup away not because I don't want your scarf to get dirty, but because I want to watch it move in the air. Maybe I could pull on it like on a light switch connected to nothing, yet it may be the perfect kind that can set the mood just right. In this light people may look a tiny bit different, but different enough for everyone to start liking each other again.

I hope you don't mind that I am pulling on your scarf. The light at the border is too bright. If I dim it just a little bit, it won't be able to get all the way to where we are and beam into my eyes. The people at the border think they need all this light to be able to check if the passport photo matches what they see, but I don't understand. Did they forget that everyone has changed? Even if everyone remained the same, no one looks like they usually do in that bright neon light anyway. They are bound to make some kind of mistake.

Inside your pupil Charon's oar takes another spin in the air as your scarf glides over your neck. He knows he is not going to get anywhere that way, but it looks like he doesn't mind for a change. He runs his hand through the water in his boat and taps some onto the back of his neck. He spreads his fingers. A drop slides between them and flows down the back of his collar. I feel something wet slide down my back. The underworld leaves a path on my skin. The little girl slides with her finger across the fogged-up window inside the wagon of the Ferris wheel. No one could save them all. Not even Charon. There were too many that came all at the same time before they were expected. His boat is too small. Maybe he is still trying to figure out what to do with the drying petals inside all these people's mouths. I know they taught us that those who Charon would not accept onto his boat would wander along the shores for one hundred years. I think it will take much longer than that now. There are too many lost house shoes floating on top of the waves that broke Charon's original oar. I think they may wander for centuries now.

He slides his hand into one of them floating in the river like a lost boat. It looks way too small for his hand, but I think he does not want to wait for another one. He lifts his arm. The ceiling is leaking again. Drops are falling onto the windshield. I turn towards the window to ask my father how to activate the windshield wipers, but I can no longer see him. Maybe he tried to get away from the rain, but that would be unlike him. It could be that I pulled on your scarf a little too much, because all the streetlights in the parking lot are off.

I think I turned on the high beams instead. The light spreads out into the fog. A ray of light is widening on the floor of the bar God is in, the door is opening. Someone else must be entering. The light glides underneath his table, like children often enjoy doing, but without running and skipping. I can't tell if God has moved his feet, but his trouser legs are rolled up to his knees. Little droplets are forming on his skin. One rolls down a tiny hair on his leg as I roll down my window entirely hoping to wash away the rain. This will make it easier to drive away. Before

I roll the window back up to see if it worked, my finger brushes over the drops in the side mirror. God hangs on tighter to the glass holding his drink. All I see is the edge of a door, a hand pushing down the handle. More drops roll down God's leg. Maybe he is nervous. Maybe he is afraid of who it is that's coming in. A thread hangs down from the buttonhole on the sleeve. I wonder who it is, too, but everything is blurry and the rain is falling faster than I can brush it away. Whoever it is, even though God seems pretty nervous, maybe at least part of him is glad that he may no longer be alone.

The door is squeaky. The car window is coming back up reluctantly. The draft pulls on the thread hanging down the sleeve of the person coming in, the string of a balloon moves between the branches made visible by the light coming from one of the car's eyes. If I only knew what is inside the other eye. Maybe it is better only one of them is working. Who knows how many more balloons are hiding in the trees. It is better nobody can see them, because I think they ran away from home. Their owners just stopped playing with them, but now they have nowhere else to go anymore. The sky is too dark for them to fly up into it as they usually do. There are too many grey clouds and the rain is hurting them.

Come to think of it, the spaceship my mother told me about also only had one beam. Maybe the car is transforming into it now that you are inside it with me. Maybe on our way up to the moon we can collect as many of the balloons as we can find hiding between the branches. They will help lift us up faster. I think I am going to tell you that the reason I want to take them is because I need a few to hang up the curtain that I tore down and I think it will look sweet. I can use their string instead of the curtain rings I broke. I will let you believe this until I have found the right moment to tell you that the reason they are not at home is because the people they were living with started building new toys, and they needed helium. Ever since the war started, helium became more and more in demand and more and more balloons were opened up again because of that. Their inside was needed for something that can fit into a hand, but spread into the entire universe if you throw it correctly. This is why they are all afraid. I think the grownups call these new toys grenades. The balloons know they never had much time on this planet, but they were prepared for that. They were not prepared for a sudden death that was to come from the same person that gave them life. Lips surround its body. A tongue lifts up. The air is sucked in. There is nothing underneath. The mouth is empty.

One of your hands rests on the naked chair back, the other reaches over towards the steering wheel. The falling drops on the windshield are the sounds of our shoes against the stairs. The boy is running down in front of me quickly. Today the electricity is out, the elevator is not working, and we are using the dark stairwell to practise how quickly we will run if one of the grownups sees us sneaking out on the night we plan to leave this place. The only light around is a small orange emergency light that lights up only when I step on the brake or on a broken step. There is no way the grownups will be able to get us, because they are taking too many naps. Their eyes need too much time to adjust to the dark.

The boy is running faster. The clouds are twisting themselves in the middle. Drops are falling as fast as they can as if to warn me of something. I feel I will never be able to understand even the smallest detail about this life, but the drops keep trying.

A strand of your hair touches my eyelash as you lean in and push another button near the steering wheel hoping the wipers will start moving. Your umbrella opens. The snowflakes have turned into rain. I think you will like this rain we sometimes have here in Montréal, you tell me as you try leaning your umbrella over my head. Sometimes it keeps raining for days.

A gust of wind flips your umbrella upside down, its arms are reaching towards the sky. Your lips form into a thin slice of the moon again, lying on its back. I feel if I touched it lightly in one corner, it would sway back and forth like a cradle, still waiting for a lullaby.

You are right. I like the rain. I think we need more of it. This is all I say to you, but your eye starts rotating the same way as the boy's marble in my palm as if you know why I need more rain. Every time before the marble game, the boy would take my hand and place the marble inside. He told me to stretch out my fingers as much as I can, so that there is a smooth surface. He would spin the marble and watch all its colours mix into one. He told me if I want to get to the moon, I have to learn how to keep it spinning in my hand. What exactly the method is, he couldn't really tell me. One day I will just know how. There is a way to never make it stop, he said, but for now I will bring you a balloon for every second you manage to keep it moving. The lines on my palm were not as deep then.

I think we need more rain. You raise your umbrella up like a giant chalice. It almost looks like you are making a toast before we drink the dark blessing recited by the clouds. The umbrella is filling up. God's glass is getting emptier. A drop from the flickering street lamp falls on top of the wax man's head. Your umbrella must be leaking. The fabric along one of your umbrella arms is coming undone. The thread touches the side of my neck.

If you tell me your old address, I can tilt my umbrella above the roof of your house, you say to me with your pupil widening. Maybe if I pour out all the rain onto it, the marble will finally land in your hand. I guess I must have told you about the marble and that I feel it is my fault it got lost. You tilt your umbrella some more. I think I hear water running down the pipes. I stretch open my hand. My pupil widens, more details appear on the lines in the corner of your eyes. I can't help but think again how much you look like the boy. I just don't know how much I can trust myself to see well enough with so many pieces of the broken street caught between my eyelashes. Another one flies out of your pocket and lands.

The bird from my bedroom window ledge flies into your umbrella. Maybe the street lamp beside our bench is working again after all and the bird's feet are warm. Maybe it is just trying to cool them off. Its wings are splashing inside. Your eyelid is getting dry again. Nothing is spinning anymore. I can see my own messy hair inside your eye. Even Charon is gone for a moment. Maybe he lay down in his boat to rest.

I would really like to see you again, you say to me while the bird in the giant chalice you are holding above us is taking a bath. Maybe you can tell me more about your life and I can help you decipher what the boy tried to say. Another fragment of his letter is in my hair. You take it and place it into your pocket. Maybe you can send me more. It has been a while since I received a real letter, you continue, and you seem like the kind of person who knows how to write one. It has been even longer since I told anyone about my life, you disclose to me. I am not so good at that anymore, but I can tell you I would love to jump into my umbrella, just like the little bird you told me is swimming there now, and take a bath, if I remembered how. The Romans knew how to live properly. At least in that regard, I mean when it comes to baths. I am sorry, you look at me and blink. Maybe this was an inappropriate comment. I told you I am not so good at all this.

You lower your umbrella for a moment, dip your finger in the rain and run it across my eyelid. I guess you must have noticed that my eye got dry. I don't know how you knew that I just saw the boy place another piece of coal inside my grandparents' fireplace. The button on his sleeve is undone, the fabric curves up. When the war started, he began wearing his shirt that way. Now that the air outside is becoming so bad, every-one's circulation is getting worse and worse, he said. We need to open up our sleeves, so everything can flow the way it is supposed to. It is not safe anymore to keep them buttoned, not anymore. Sometimes when you can't breathe, it's not only your mouth that becomes dry, but also your eyes. You run your wet finger over my eyelid again. You say you are not so good at this, but it looks to me like you are, because the winter is gone. I don't know how long we were in the café for. Only ice cubes are left in God's glass, but over here it is getting warm. A dandelion seed lands on your eyelash. A few more land in your hair while the little girl walking past us blows at the flower in her hand and throws away the stem. It lands on your shoe. I don't know what happened to all the snow-flakes, but I hope they are okay. How strange that spring already came.

It must be May. I always leave the city at the height of spring and come back in late August, you lean in slightly as you tell me this. I would pre-fer to come back even later, but it takes me time to prepare to watch the leaves fall. Hopefully you do not think this is a bit gruesome, but there is just too much life here for me in the spring. Your eyelid twitches the moment you say this to me. Your bedroom window squeaks. A snowflake floats in and lands on your pillow. I hope you can tell I do not think there is anything strange about how you feel. I like it when it is quiet around me, too, so you don't have to worry. There are just too many sounds. There are just too many sounds leaking through the sky. Sometimes snowflakes help with that and muffle the echo before it can get to my ear. But it is spring now. I am worried about the one snowflake that found its way to your bedroom. I am worried it will not survive, because your lampshade is gone. I think maybe you took it off, because you could hear my breaths becoming too shallow. There is too much smoke in the air. Even though it is a little odd to use a lampshade as an oxygen mask, this is just what I need. Sometimes it helps to pretend. Sometimes pretending becomes more real than anything else around me. The light circle on your ceiling is widening. My lips are widening, too, as you ask me if I want to return to the city once you are back in August and I say yes.

I can breathe just a little bit better now that you asked me that. I guess you must have some kind of magic lampshade. Or maybe when I am around you, for short fragments of time, I manage to forget that anything bad ever happened to me. As I remember the rain that turned more and more grey, I watch one of the drops slide down the broken umbrella arm and fall onto the ground.

A thread is hanging loose from its tip. I pull on it just because I am curious what will happen then. The thread escapes through the holes, flows out of each dark vortex in a wave, the sky is getting loose, a star or two or more fall through the evening sky. The main stitch of the universe is unraveling. Maybe now I will be able to find out what all is there behind the sky. You smirk as I tell you this and ask me again if I am going to come. I can't stop myself from pulling more on the thread, so I tell you I will answer if you give me your hand. Don't worry, it's not like I want to hold it, there is just too much thread coming out of the universe.

I roll the thread falling inside your hand into a spiral. The spiral is widening. More and more of the thread is coming out of your umbrella. The seam along God's hand is disentangling. He is too tired to notice anything.

The curtain in my old bedroom is coming undone. Oh no, I can't sleep if there is too much light. Maybe you can hang your coat on my curtain rings, because I keep pulling. It will be dark enough then and I can watch the sleeves move in the draft.

I think the apartment for rent right beside mine may have a bedroom that will be dark enough, if it is anything like mine, you say to me as you spin your umbrella. I guess you know by the thread in your hand that I said yes. I could even go with you when I come back, if you like, or at the very least give you the phone number and address. Of course I would like that, because the universe is folding in. It seems to roll around my bedroom like the paper I used to make cigarettes for my parents. Maybe one day everything will turn into ash, even my bed. I don't know, but I can no longer even see where my bed is. Everything inside my old room is as black as your umbrella. It is too dark and the sky keeps rolling over it. Maybe God will lick the edge and close it shut the way I closed the cigarette. Everything will go back to dark. From far away the window looks like a pupil long friends with the night. The stray dog barks at me. One of his claws digs into my leg.

The umbrella slips out of your hand as you are reaching into your pocket. The tip of one of its arms scratches my upper thigh before it lands on the ground. The stray dog slides his paw over my leg. I think he wants me to get up from the bench. I think he doesn't think it is a good idea for me to continue to wait. The umbrella lands on its back. The stray dog barks again. With every motion of his paw, the umbrella spins around itself. It almost looks like he is spinning it, because he keeps tapping his paw against my knee. I don't want to upset him, but I am not sure I can get up just yet. He looks at me with worry in his eyes, while I watch the umbrella limp away in the wind. How strange that it moves just the same as the sleepy people before they fell asleep on the street.

I like that you are not trying to catch it. Maybe you are wondering where it will end up or you are enjoying the larger puddle beneath our shoes. The chalice has done its job and blessed our encounter, you say in a cheeky way as you take out a stamp. In the meantime, before we see each other again, you can write to me. I am sorry about the umbrella and getting you wet, you say as you hand me the stamp. Maybe I can make up for it by showing you the city and helping you with the apartment search, you smirk and bend down to roll up your pants. Besides, I want to know more about the bird that flew all the way from your home into my umbrella just to take a swim. I know I am far from being like the little bird, but I do like to feel the rain around my ankles, you remark as the puddle folds around your feet.

You dip your finger in the puddle and tap it on my palm. I would not want the stamp to fly away. This way it will stay. You open my fingers and place the stamp in my hand. A black and white portrait of a man is now covering some of the lines flowing through my skin. This is my friend, Paul Antschel, maybe he will be able to help you even better than I can. As though someone threw a pebble in, circles expand in one of your eyes as you say this. At the very least, he will keep you company in the car as your finger digs deeper into the seat, its stuffing turning into clouds in your mouth. He knows when not to talk, he knows sometimes you can't. He has many broken nails. Some of them collect in my pockets. I don't know where he lives now, but he was born in 1920 in Czernowitz, then the Kingdom of Romania, and survived the Holocaust. He visits me sometimes in the building, where you and I met. Sometimes he just stays there. Often he just falls asleep. I mostly see him leaning on the armrest in my room, closest to the lamp. His head nestles inside his palm, his eyelids pulsate every time my window flutters. Sometimes he rubs his forehead, maybe because of the dust falling from the bookshelf, maybe because of something else.

I don't know how this is possible, but his forehead looks the same as the man's who gave me his candle legs, high, with wrinkles going up in the shape of broken steps. The cracks in the stairwell make it harder to run. The empty staircase raises its forehead as soon as we run out and the boy closes the door. The echo of his shoes slides through the gap.

A snowflake is hiding there, too. Time meets in its middle. Each of the snowflake's arms fulfills the part it is given, it does not get to choose which fraction of time it becomes. All of time's parts, past, present, future, run to get to the middle first. None of them arrives sooner than the other. They are all here at the same time, so they go on and continue their way, as though there never was any other kind of plan. Each of the six arms has somewhere else to go. Maybe if I slide down the right one, I will land in the dimension where none of this happened. Even if I did, I am not sure anymore I would know what to do there. I am sliding down too far. My wet hand holds on to the climbing bar in the playground in front of my school. This way I do not have to touch the ground at all. I think I am pulling at Charon's oar, because his boat is tilting. One of the snowflake's arms is bending.

The stamp in my hand is bending towards the rain. My grandmother gave me one, too, on the day we left, but I don't know where it went. I think it slid down the hole in my pocket and fell into my shoe. It had enough space, because my shoes were a size too big. You are growing fast, my mother says to me. Just pull on the shoelaces a little bit tighter, and you will be all right. I guess no one knew then there would be so much rain. My socks are getting wet, but with you here, I like it. The water from the puddle is winding around your ankle. Your umbrella rolls farther and farther away down the street we are standing on. I can barely see it now as it recedes farther into the distance. As though it fell off from the edge of the street, it lands on top of the car's windshield. I must have been turning my head strangely, because you ask me if I know where I am and if I will be able to find my way back okay. The little bird is still here, so I say yes, even though I have no idea where I am. I don't think you quite believe me, either. Why else would you have asked me to open the door to the car you know is not going anywhere fun. Part of your coat covers me as you move closer. Your arm stretches out, turns into an airplane wing again. This time it leans in, slants at the angle needed for circling. Something at the airport is not ready yet. All the lights are off. There is nowhere to land. You touch my back the way a wing slices through a cloud.

We are back in the car the moment it slices all the way through. Someone kicks my seat behind me, but there is no one there. The windshield wipers start moving. You lean back into your seat. The road in front of us appears a little clearer through the small slice created by the wipers.

The arc looks like the arc of a rainbow. I wish rainbows could appear at night. You never know, you tell me, as you point at something in front of us. Just look at the balloon aligning with the moon. It looks like the lunar eclipse without making the moon red. Maybe now it will no longer be called the Blood Moon.

I am not so sure about that, but you turn the radio on and the same song as when you were preparing coffee for me is playing again. God lifts his head and lights another cigarette. Another red moon appears at its end. One of the coal pieces the boy threw into my grandparents' fireplace is getting more red along the edge. They will be warmer now. They will be warmer now. God leans back.

The smoke from my grandparents' chimney floats down his throat. The exhaust of the car coughs out clouds made out of words I saw in my dreams with my head resting against the driver's seat. That was before the grownups stopped to take a break. Maybe they stopped to see if something is wrong with the car. Maybe they were worried about the scratching sound it makes every time I snore or the twitching of my eyelids made them think they are driving too fast. But I don't think that can be, because my eyes are facing the floor. They cannot see. Even if they could see my moving eyelids, I don't think they would notice how carefully the boy throws each piece of coal in or the way his collar briefly touches his cheek in the draft. I know they haven't noticed anything, because I can hear my mother's voice through the dense air telling me not to lean forward that way, that it is not healthy, all my blood is seeping into my brain. She tells me to lean back and sleep like that if I am tired or to rest my head in her lap.

You lean your head back and tell me to do the same. Drops of rain are falling into the car. You take off your coat and place it over my head as we are standing on the street by the café. Write to me what kind of apartment you may be looking for, you say, as I notice the worn-out fabric of your collar falling over my eyes. I don't know if you washed it too many times or if you were too cold to take it off. Between the thinning thread, I can still see your eyes. A stray dog's paws are running inside. Drops roll down the windshield. On the other side, the fabric of the sky is tearing apart. I don't know what looks more worn out, the collar of your coat or what I see when I lift up my eyes towards the clouds. What if the sky is sad? What happens then? I don't know, but it looks like it is coming undone: glowing red, yellow, orange, purple, lines are appearing where its fabric is thinning. I am not sure that the sky opening like this is a good thing, but maybe if I am able to see what is behind it, I will be able to understand at least a little bit what is happening, why everyone is fighting. The lines are getting bigger and the openings wider and wider. I think another world is peeking through. I am almost sure. One of the openings widens as God pulls apart the buttonhole on his sleeve. He widens it some more and I watch the orange line in the sky grow. He slides his button through the hole, but the sky is still open. I wonder if he is buttoning his sleeve, because he is getting cold or because he doesn't want anyone to see him this way, so he is trying to close the sky. I don't know why they speak of the end times as though they are something scary. The sky looks mesmerizing while it is falling apart, you quietly whisper. I am not sure you meant to say that to me. Or maybe I misheard.

I watch the balloon string move in the car's headlight. A strand of God's hair falls across his forehead. The light ray coming from the door is making him warm. I don't think I have ever seen God sweat as much as he is sweating now. I guess that means the reason he buttoned his sleeve probably wasn't, because he was cold. Maybe he just did that because he wanted to look good for whoever it is that is opening the door. Maybe he thinks he looks too messy. I don't know if this is such a good idea, because the sleeve looks like it is wrapping too tightly around his wrist. I think it is hurting him, but it looks like it is important to him to try to look somewhat decent for the person arriving. I think this is pretty sweet. The longer I look at him, the more sorry for him I feel, even though I am also still unsure of who God is. Drops of sweat are forming on his hand now. The ice in his glass he is holding has melted from all the heat coming from his palm. A drop from his forehead falls in and turns the water into an unusual shade between pink and red. Wait a minute, it looks just like the colours inside the petals of the Sarajevo Roses, depending on how wet they are, depending on how much it rains. A stripe of all the possible shades appears in the sky. God tightens his sleeve. The stamp you gave me with the sad looking man on it falls into God's glass, sinks to the bottom, yet here it is also in my hand.

The more the sky is opening, the more it rains. Sometimes when I think of where the boy could be this very second, I am so afraid for him that I can't breathe. It starts raining even more than it already is and it feels like each drop is falling into my lungs. I want to tell someone what is going on, but my lips are moving out of synch. They are moving somewhat unpredictably, shivering in harmony with the balloon string moving in the wind on the other side of the windshield. You ask me again if I will write to you, as if you noticed I can barely speak. Even though I feel there is barely any air in my lungs, somehow I manage to tell you, yes I will. My mouth feels dry. God sucks on the filter. The moon is getting big. Time is getting small. Ember from the cigarette is falling through the cracks in the sky, through all the glowing lines. I like the purple one, because it doesn't remind me of anything. God taps on his cigarette. More ember falls through the sky. The light particles are travelling faster than I can rub my eyes. Ash is falling into the stair- well cracks, where the boy and I practised how to run. All the cracks are expanding from the heat and I am afraid of falling in. I remember learning in school about a myth that time does not exist once you reach the inside of the Earth. I don't remember much about it, because I was thinking about Snoopy and how he will want to walk around and look for all the mines, so that he can make them stop working. I keep thinking about how this is way too much for him to handle and I can't let him do that. I know he will say it is not and that's okay. I know he is way too kind. Sometimes I wish I could hide away from time. I try to remember how large the biggest hole on Earth is, but I can't. Besides, I wouldn't want to hide there, anyway. I think maybe the grownups do, because it looks like they are trying to force open the Earth, but its outer shell is too thick. I think every time they try, another Sarajevo Rose blooms on the street. The clouds are trying to water them, but it is too late now. None of them have stems. God is collecting them all and connecting some into a chain and placing some into his vase. I am not sure why he is doing that. Maybe he is making a chain to measure how deep the biggest hole on Earth is, and if it penetrates the entire crust, so that he can hide inside.

He is inhaling again. Another fiery rift appears in the sky. I think the person walking into the bar definitely wants to see him, because I notice God adjust his sleeve. He attempts to straighten his back. My own back is a little bent as I hold on to the steering wheel. It takes me a few seconds to realize I am now in the car driving to see you in Montréal.

Outside, the night looks just like the one when the boy and I said bye, see you tomorrow, without knowing what would happen in between tomorrow and today. Many days have passed since I have seen you. I think it comes to about half a year when I count them all in my head. The passing streetlights outside remind me a little bit of the empty bench and a little bit of all the space between now and when you held the umbrella above my head.

THREE ★ WEEKS

One

I am thinking about your last letter to me as I watch the moon. It is almost touching the highway. It would be easy to believe that the more I think of you, the closer I am getting to the moon. For a brief moment, I imagine that now that I am older, maybe I can slide along the highway with my car and then lift up. But, then again, I don't think the Moon Slide would work without my magic slippers. I don't think I can do it without Snoopy's blanket beneath my soles. Besides, I feel I need to get you first.

The moon is so low right now that it looks like any moment now it will land on the street and roll towards me like a giant marble. Maybe something is off with gravity, because the underworld is getting too full. Charon is asking for a bigger boat, but God is not paying attention. I think he is too nervous right now to think about anything else but the person entering. Right now I am thinking about you. I am thinking about how I hope the moon will stay up for as long as it can, not because I am afraid it will roll over me, but because you wrote to me that sometimes you wish you could build a house on the moon. You would build it over on the other side that never faces the Earth, so no one can see you. The boy and I planned that, too. Maybe from up there you could see why the *Akšamčići* flower I sent you only opens for the moon. Maybe, with you, it could even come back to life again. Even

though I told you I long prefer flowers that are dry, with the *Akšamčići*
it is different. If the one I sent you opens again, maybe it would tell you
what it saw on the roof of my grandparents' house. Maybe it saw where
the boy's marble went. I am sure it could help me find it again. Maybe
the river inside would be blue-green again, because the boy filled it
up with all his superpowers. Maybe everyone would be reminded that
the rivers in our city were not always brown, that there used to be a
time when everyone was on each other's side. Maybe the marble may
remind the grownups that they could stop fighting and play together
instead. I think the *Akšamčići* flower knows where it went. I just don't
know if it saw too much to be able to revive, because it was up there
for a long time. You write you will try, that you will place it beside your
favourite plant, one from the Tradescantia family. The two of them can
speak. I remember reading in your letter that Tradescantia is the only
known plant that can visibly measure radioactivity. I think this could
work then, because they could tell everyone that all this fighting is
making the sky too thin. The stray dog is still barking at the thinning
sky. A helium balloon has tangled itself around one of his paws.

No home should be without it, you wrote, and that you will get one for
me as soon as I find a suitable apartment, in exchange for the keychain
I sent you with the moon attached to it. In a little more shaky handwriting, you also wrote that the Tradescantia plant will let me know
whenever the air is bad, so I no longer have to be afraid. I hope you
like the moon keychain I sent you just as much as I like the thought of
you looking out for me. I decided to pick the New Moon for you, not
because it is supposed to mark the ending to the old and a gateway to
an unfamiliar beginning, but because I like the dim lighting, and I think
you will, too. I think you could even take a walk around to the side facing the Earth without anyone noticing you. Maybe if you walk slowly
enough with the moon, your feet would spin it in the other direction.
Eventually we may see something other than the usual almost winking
moon. I think that is the side the boy mentioned that we should move to.

They say the other side is filled with craters. I think they are wrong.
I think the circles they see from above are where the marbles God
played with once used to be. He stopped, because he wanted something

more exciting than that. The pattern of the circles looks the same as the one formed by our marbles I am watching from the top of the stairs leading to my grandparents' front door. A light ray slides underneath my shoes. The door is opening, because outside it is getting too dark and God is smoking again. My grandmother is at the door and tells me to come in, that is it getting late and it is almost time for sleep. I don't want to go in just yet, because the moon is turning blue and the boy is picking up the marbles we played with faster than usually. I know it is getting too dark now to play and the boy always picks up the marbles around this time, but I see by the lines on his face and the way he looks at the moon that he is concerned. The moon is more blue than the previous nights, the boy says. I guess this must mean God is blowing the smoke in our direction. The man at the border flashes a blue light at me and asks for my name. How did he get there all of the sudden? The last I remember is being in the car with a balloon in front of me. Maybe I fell asleep. He asks me for my name again as he flips a page in my passport. I tell him I do not remember my name, but if he wants to give me one, he can choose the one written on the page he is looking at. Or if he prefers, he can make one up, the way a cloud chooses its path, a petal its time to unfold. I tell him the person he is looking at in the picture is not me, he can check the eyes if he wants to and it will be clear. I am squinting as I say this. The many airplane tracks appearing in the corners of my eyes must be confusing him. After all, I am just a kid. I can't really say that my mother is angry, but she does send me a disapproving glance before telling the man at the border to please not take me seriously, that I am just being moody.

I may be moody, but I meant what I said. I see myself skipping on one leg into the rings I am not allowed to miss. If I step outside, something bad may happen. But the man at the border keeps shifting his eyes, the circles are moving with every glance he empties only to move on to another one. It seems impossible to follow the rules when the rules make no sense, when they keep changing faster than the pupil of a tired man.

The circles won't stand still. Some are disappearing. Your black umbrella closes, a dark pupil watching the sky has gone to sleep, its eyelid folds in. I thought it flew away from your hand, but your finger gets caught between its metal lashes. The squeeze on your skin clenches as lightly as the stray dog's teeth occasionally touching my wrist as he pulls on my sleeve. I guess he is still trying to convince me to leave.

Somehow he manages to pull me off the bench, my feet touch the ground after swinging through the air many times. One of the circles beside the car moves beneath my feet. I think my shoe is touching the line. Maybe I wasn't prepared to jump off the bench. The stray dog moves in closer as if to comfort me, but he can't tell me if everything is going to be okay. I know he can't, because every time I wonder that, he turns his head.

He rubs his head against my leg. I think he is at least a little bit worried about me. The tip of his head pushes against my thigh. What did I do? He looks up at me. His pupils are widening, even though the street lamp flickered for a moment as soon as I stepped on the circle's edge. Inside his eyes, the soldier's boot at the border is touching the car's tire. Every time he asks another question, his iris shrinks, pushed aside by the expanding dark inside his pupil. A crater grows in the gravel in front of the car. I wonder if this is the kind one would find on the moon. I don't know what is happening. Maybe my imagination is trying to help me escape and pretend I am already on the moon, but it is not working. The crater here at the border is starting to look very unfriendly the longer I look at it. The soldier's foot moves closer to mine and I am afraid.

Where are you going, he asks me or my mother, I do not know, but the stray dog answers. He just looks at him without moving his eyelids. The crater is getting larger. The dog blinks as a drop from the street lamp closes his eyelid. I am still finding it hard to move. The circles beneath my feet are turning into soap bubbles floating up into the sky. One of them lands on his eyelid. A drop falls into his black pupil turning into that night I waited. After a long time, I see the limping man again, who gave me his candle legs. He is walking inside the dog's eyes like he has always been there and nowhere else. A trail appears in the air behind his back. He reaches up to touch a branch above his head and for a moment I feel he could be a plane. But his arm falls to the side of his body, swings aimlessly. If he had his coat, maybe he would find a pocket. I am happy to see the candle man again, even if it is only inside the stray dog's eyes. The stray dog is looking at the soldier standing beside our car at the border. Somehow, neither of them wants to look away. I hope the soldier manages to see everything that is inside his eyes, before he blinks again. Peace hides somewhere inside it in the shape of a distant myth now shattered into little pieces that no one remembers how to put together anymore.

The soldier's hand glides through the air now, too, as if to trace the candle man's steps. Charon's arm dangles off his boat's edge. His finger forms a path in the water, a trace of his past. The man walking off in the park without his candle legs is trying to grab onto its end, but he can't. The path is disappearing faster than he can walk.

His shoes step on someone's shoelace. It comes undone and unwinds like God's plan he did not plan so well. Wait a minute. I recognize the handwriting on them. My own words appear before me, the stray dog sticks out his tongue as he still stares at the man, who will decide what happens to us.

The same address, time and place are written on the shoelace as on the piece of paper hiding inside my pocket after waking up in the strange hotel. This is the place and the time we met. I don't think I fully understand what is happening, but the more I look into the stray dog's eyes, the more my memory is coming back to me. I know now. I made that time and place up once the boy and I started our plan to run away. I became very afraid that we would lose each other somewhere along the way of implementing our plan. I knew that if we did, we needed to have a time and place where we would meet. In case something goes wrong, this is where you will find me, I told him, and took out a pen. Even though I made it all up and didn't even know if the place I was writing down really exists, I took it all very seriously. Wherever it is we would meet, needed to be far away from where we are now, I remember thinking. Best somewhere across the ocean, because who knows when this war is going to end. The grownups all said it won't last very long, but it looks like they were wrong. I think we learned about Canada in school, at least a little bit. It sounded okay enough to me.

All I really cared about is that it is far. I remember very well the gravel underneath my palm as I knelt down and pulled slightly on the edge of his shoelace with my other hand. I took out the pen my mother left on my nightstand after she used it to create the shadow of a spaceship on the wall beside my bed. I started writing on the shoelace: Canada. As for the details of time and place, I wrote down whatever appeared first in my head. This place really exists. This place really exists, I know it, I thought to myself as I moved the pen. If my mother used it to create a spaceship for me, I can use it to create a place for us to meet and I know it will be real. The only thought that went through my mind as I was writing is that I will meet the boy there and we will go to the moon. I am confused, because this is where I met you. How is this possible? I don't know, but it makes me want to see you even more. It makes me wonder what else I have buried inside me that is determining all my steps without my knowing it. It makes me wonder whether I am living my entire present only through my memory.

I remember the tip of the pen again on the boy's shoelace. I remember my mother. I think ever since I told her I want to get to the moon, she has not been able to fall asleep properly. Through the wall, I could hear her talking to my father in the other room. They must be trying to think of another way to build a proper engine for the spaceship, because nothing is working so far.

I wonder more about how I could know of a place I have never been to before. I close my eyes, fall deeper down into the memory. The boy's shoelace is in my hand. Ink flows out, an eternal river branding its path. My hand moves as if on its own, yet determined and knowing. I don't think I knew then what I wrote, but the soil beneath me seemed to confirm the writing. Underneath my other hand the Earth pulsed. An invisible stethoscope wire runs into my ear, an almost imperceptible pulse resounds all the way to now. What does it mean that you were there? How did you know to come? I don't know if it is because I am scared or nervous or excited, but my eyelids are fluttering. The boy appears and disappears accordingly, the movements are too quick. He is flickering before me, just like the streetlight beside our bench. I want him to stay longer.

He ruffles my hair and tells me doing something like writing on his shoelace is so like me. The wind from his moving hand shakes the stems in God's vase. God tries to catch them, but nudges the vase instead. I think he still can't concentrate. God's hair moves, too, the more the boy moves his hand. More stems are rolling onto God's table and falling to the ground.

A branch falls onto the road in front of me. Somehow I am not as worried about it as maybe I should be. Or maybe the tear in the sky looks too pretty for me to slow down. Besides, now that I remember we met at the same time and place I told the boy to come if anything happens, I want to get to you as soon as I can. I don't know what exactly to believe, but all the things about you that remind me of him are making my eyelids flutter even faster. Open. Closed. Open. Closed. The boy is here and then he's not. Open. Closed. Open. Closed. If my eyelids move any faster, the boy will always just be here, the boy will stay. I still feel your worn-out collar descending over my eyes.

Through it everything on the other side looks nothing like before. My foot is pressing against the gas. The moon is pulling on my car. The tires climb over the branch. God reaches for the tipping vase, but the car trembles and red petals from the Sarajevo Roses are floating inside. A stem lands beside God's foot. He picks it up and I wonder if he can smell the scent of my car's tire. I think I should have slowed down. I think something is covering my eyes, because the clock in the car is showing it is July 22, 1993, though we arranged to meet tomorrow.

The year is off. Besides, it is only July and you said you would not be back in the city until early August. Maybe the little bird that escaped from your umbrella convinced you to come back early. Then again, even if it did, I don't know if I can make it on time, because grenades are falling all around me. The sky has opened its mouth and inside it the remains of helium balloons appear between its teeth. Behind them, a gaping black hole reaches down into the warped human soul. Every twenty seconds it warps some more. Every twenty seconds its tongue rolls up to the roof of the mouth to leave room for another grenade to fall. 3,777 of them fell in Sarajevo on that day. There aren't enough heads of roses on the streets. What happened to them? Maybe some take more years to bloom, maybe there wasn't enough space. One is blooming inside my eye. A breeze from the open door unfolds God's coat. The lining is coming undone. Thread is hanging down, all the way to the floor. Petals are floating up from inside. More of them end up in my car. What are the petals doing in his coat? Maybe he is too cold after all and he is warmer this way. Or maybe he is hiding them. I hope he is trying to put them back together instead. Even if I asked, I don't think God is the one who has the answer.

The red petals slide in through the tiny crack left by my window. They look like little tongues trying to speak. Spot by spot, they are filling up my windshield. I want even more of them to come in. I can barely see the street outside, but my foot is still pressing on the gas.

The candle man's shoe is still pressing down on the boy's shoelace. Oh no. I think he should move his foot, but I don't know how to tell him. I am worried, because he no longer has the candle legs and maybe he is not used to walking without them anymore. His candle legs he left for me are long spent. They are now the pillars of the gate at the end of the Acheron River.

I guess neither the boy nor the candle man noticed anything; the shoelace is unraveling. One loop disappears into itself, the other one follows, stretches out onto the path as the boy moves his leg. The shoelace is getting longer and I am afraid someone may step on it. I don't want the boy to hurt himself and fall. The shoelace is growing, together with the road that stretches out all the way to the moon. For a moment I believe this is really where it leads. Maybe I am starting to believe this, because part of me thinks it is my fault the man with the candle legs has stepped on the boy's shoelace. Maybe if I hadn't accepted the man's candle legs, he would have walked in a different way. I think the man's knees are wounded. I think he doesn't know how to walk without the candles helping him stand straight. Maybe he simply used them to walk instead of to keep warm, like I thought. I should have left him at least one. I shouldn't have let him walk away like that, regardless of what he said. Usually I would not be this worried about an untied shoelace, but something about the way the stray dog is telling me this is filling up my windshield with red rose petals.

The man steps away from the shoelace just in time to avoid the tension, just in time to avoid a fall. Nothing happened. Nothing happened. The shoelace drags through the black waters inside the stray dog's pupil. The waves are too big. I want to know where the boy is going, but the dog's eyelids are closing. He keeps blinking and the streetlights along the highway are flickering.

His teeth are still holding on to my sleeve even as the highway is quivering. One by one the lights are going out as another one falls. One by one. I don't know what to do, because there are too many red petals to fit them all into my car. One sticks to my side mirror. It covers the stray dog running behind my car, but I can hear the sound of his paws. It sounds nothing like what is falling from the sky. The sky has closed its mouth over us. Inside, the remnants of our grinding teeth are falling in the shape of fatal seeds spreading out violently as soon as they touch the ground. One by one by one by one by one by one. 3,777. Even eternity is exhausted by the endlessness.

Through the fireworks of death falling one by one, the dog's paws are pounding against the street. Two by two. Two by two. Maybe one petal is stuck underneath the boy's shoe. But it is too dark and I don't know. I just don't know.

At the beginning of the war, everyone ran, especially through the streets everyone knew were exposed to the most snipers. Later, everyone walked, even there. It was not because the will to live lessened, but because it grew. Even as a child, I could figure out that much. Sometimes in the early day I could hear my mother thinking: No one will take away my morning stroll with the blue dew forming underneath my hair. I don't know who is watching me and if they will decide to pull. The world is watching, too, but not for long. I can see the world's eyes peeking through the window before they shut close the curtains. I guess they don't like the view.

God rubs his eyes, because there is too much light flowing into the dark bar. I think the door must be fully open now, because the light ray flowing across the floor has gotten as big as the car's headlights reaching across the border. The person walking in lets go of the door, starts moving towards God. I think God is trying to see properly, but little stars are sparkling underneath his eyelids and above his pupils. Someone should have told him not to rub his eyes so much, that it could ruin his sight. A copy of the universe stands between the finished cigarette in his hand and the person walking from the door towards his table. God squints. Headlights are beaming into my eyes through the rose petals. Their worn-out edges are fracturing the light. A crack forms in God's glass. I think he is getting even more nervous now that this visitor is getting closer, he is pressing on his glass too hard. The stray dog pulls harder at my sleeve. My feet give in and follow him. There are so many cracks. So many more than there used to be. I try to jump over them, but it is not working. Besides, every time I stop, the dog barks. I think he is telling me to hurry.

As we are running, I stretch out my arm. All the branches are way too high for me to reach, but I can at least touch all the streetlights we pass. They are all dark, but maybe if I tap them, they will wake up. Maybe they are only pretending to be asleep, just like I did when my parents came into my room not too long ago to check up on me. I could see their silhouettes through my thinning eyelids. My mother's hair rustled like the leaves on the branches surrounding me. Something in the way she lightly touched my shoulder gave away she knew I was awake but allowed me to pretend. In secret the leaves tell me, like her gentle tap, where I am going, but I do not understand. Some day I may comprehend the shallow breaths coming from the stray dog and why they sound like my own when I am in deep sleep.

All the lights continue sleeping. I wonder what they are dreaming and if they can hear us running past them. I hope at least one of them can, because I no longer recognize where I am. We must have made a turn I didn't notice, because I don't think I have ever been on this street. The shape of the leaves looks nothing like what I could see from the bench where the boy is supposed to find me. Here, the darkness rolls around my eyes like a blindfold. The trees' branches pull tightly on it as they cover the moon.

God's Adam's apple gets bigger while the sound of the stray dog's paws recedes. No, where is he going now? I can't keep up with his pace. He is moving farther and farther away and I can barely hear anything at all. He is there still, but I don't know where. All I see is a leafy tree and behind it a hill I don't recognize. What is this hill peeking behind the dishevelled leaves? That is not the hill where I used to play. A cross lights up on top of it and now I remember you telling me about a big cross you can see from your balcony after I told you how one winter day my mother told me we can't have a Christmas tree this year, because they are forbidden now. The same day my father told me that some people think the prayers from the mosques are getting loud and they should stop. I didn't understand why. I loved swirling the lights around the Christmas tree while the Adhan prayer wound itself around the early morning clouds. Only every third light on our set worked and I thought maybe one day if I circle the way I am supposed to, the rest of them will light up, too. Once, when I moved around the Christmas tree at 5 a.m. while the prayers dripped down the window with the rain, I thought I saw one of the dark lights flicker for a moment. Another one came on and off quickly as I hung up the crescent moon I found inside my Christmas present I opened too soon.

I think the grownups misunderstood something. I don't particularly know God very well and I do think he could use some help, but I don't think he minds either the Christmas tree or the prayers from the mosques. Once he walked by me with his hands folded in praying along with the singing minaret. Once I saw him dragging a Christmas tree in the deep snow without wearing a jacket. Twice he asked me when Santa Claus is coming. During all these times he looked like he was lost and had nowhere to go. I know, because he kept turning around. Now he is spinning his empty glass around itself, the shadow of the person approaching him covers his eyes. Maybe he will feel a little bit calmer now, in the dark. He turns his empty glass around itself, the shadow of the figure walking closer to him covers his eyes.

The street becomes even darker after I turn off my car's headlights. I think I have arrived. God is still playing with his glass. One of the ice cubes falls out and lands on my windshield. I like the houses on your street, I think to myself, while I watch the water trail form on the glass as the ice cube slides down. I like that there is no space between most of the buildings. They are all leaning on each other, so there are less windows for all the snipers. I am also glad to see that there are less alleyways than on a lot of other streets here. Sometimes, when the moon seems especially far, I can't help but still think that they are dangerous, even with all the streetlights here.

I think I just saw a sparrow land on top of the street lamp between your apartment and the one I am here to see. I am not sure, because the light bulb is off and the stray dog is no longer here to guide me. I wish I could still hear his steps. The only feet I hear now are the sparrow's. It looks up at your window with its feet pushing backwards. Maybe it thinks this will somehow turn the light on. Instead, I think it rolled up my old street into a ball not knowing I am still trapped inside its hollow. You wrote to me to let you know as soon as I arrive, but I think it is too late now. The drive took much longer than I thought it would. I should have known it would take a while, because there are too many kilometres between your address and where I came from.

I think I hear you opening your window. It sounds a bit like the trunk of our car opening at the border. Maybe the man who looked at our passports wanted to make sure I didn't forget anything. The sparrow looks at me as though it has been waiting for me all this time. I don't know if it is asking me what took so long or if it wonders why I am here at all. It might not approve of my plan to look at the apartment right beside you. It may want me to come back home. It tucks its head into its body the way I slide down in my seat because of the draft coming from the open trunk. I am cold. The wind blowing at my neck moves your curtains aside. Even though I look forward to seeing you tomorrow, I hope you do not notice me now, because I prefer looking at this apartment alone.

Maybe the reason you are opening your window now is to let me know that it is safe here, that I don't have to be afraid. I don't know, but the rusty gate I just walked through reminds me of the crack spreading in the rain pipe barely holding on to my grandparents' house. No. It has to hold on. It has to. I have to recover the marble hiding inside. A rose is growing there too as fast as the dog's ears are flapping over his eyes as he runs. If I could see what he sees maybe I would know why there is an ice cube between God's teeth, why my grandfather sticks his head out the window as soon as I open the car's door. He is 6,000 kilometres away and whispers something to the moon. From his window, he touches the pipe moving in the wind to stabilize it. It might be fluttering in the same beat as my shirt moves against my body the moment I leave my car. My grandfather blows at a leaf on his window ledge. It lands in my hair. Just the right moment, because it is a little too dark here, even for my eyes.

Thank goodness I brought the night lamp my grandfather gave me. Sometimes its switch works without it being connected to any kind of electricity. A long time ago, before everything, it closed a pact with the moon. The moon sprinkles down some lunar energy into its body every time the thin wire inside the bulb starts shaking from all the grenades still falling around me.

The man at the border puts our passports in his pocket before pulling on the cord stuck underneath my suitcase. I think he is trying to pull out the lamp. I don't know if he is done checking our passports or if he just needs two hands. His movements make the lampshade fall off. A star falls from the sky. You pull aside your curtain and watch me open the gate leading to the apartment you suggested. Something is stopping me from looking up now, but I just know you are at the window, the same way I could tell the man at the border only looked through our trunk because he needed some more time to decide what to do with us. I am pretty sure he realized that at least one of us is trying to cross the border without the other grownups allowing it. Even I could tell that my father's brown eyes had very little to do with the blue eyes in his passport picture. Maybe the man pulled out the lamp hoping under its light the eyes would look the same. This way he could nod to his comrade to open the gate without being afraid he will be accused of sending through someone he is supposed to capture. Maybe not all the grownups are so bad. The soldier holding my lamp looks over at the other one. They are both dressed in fairly ugly fashion, but the one farther away has even more badges and there is a belt falling across his shoulder. That is never a good sign. The people shooting have those, too. I definitely don't like his clothes, but I also don't like the way he is looking at the soldier with our passports in his pocket.

While the soldier with our passports is trying to figure out how to turn on the lamp, my father takes my hand and places one of the curtain rings into my palm. Remember, regardless of where I tell the man we are going, you can still go to the moon. Maybe this ring will help. I always knew my father was sweet, but I can't believe he decided to save the ring that rolled to his feet and really isn't mad at me.

I place the curtain ring over my eye the way Sherlock Holmes would examine through the magnifying glass. Instead of seeing everything more clearly, a misty darkness spreads over the outlines. My father's face disappears and so do the others. Their heads look like balloons blowing in the wind tied to an abandoned balcony. Darker clouds are pulling in as the door of the bar God is in closes. The last ray of light cuts through one of the balloon's strings. My father, my mother, the driver, the man at the border, all recede into the darkness resting its hands on their shoulders until there is nothing left, but what I see now – the future came to me already then before its time, as though in a hurry to prepare me. I am not sure I listened well, because now the past is coming to me well before its time.

I am not even interested anymore in seeing what the apartment is like. All I want is to get away from the outside. Out here, the tree branches are pulling at my hair, too many leaves are collecting in my sleeves, the street lamps are too bright. I am so tired. So tired that all I hear when I open the door of the apartment for rent is the sound of an empty canister sliding against the floor.

They are all piling up behind the door. The stray dog swerves through a number of them lying scattered on the street. We are running farther and farther away from the bench. His paw gets caught in one of the handles as he turns around to see if I am still following him.

The hardwood floor beneath my shoes squeaks while he shakes his paw. Only someone like him would recognize the depth of the canister's hollowness escaping with every tap on the uneven asphalt. I hear it echo in each one of my steps moving away from the door. My hand still holds on to the handle. If I let the door close maybe the stray dog won't see me anymore. Sometimes I feel this is exactly what I need, to see him lift his nose in disapproval, grunt at my carelessness, and twitch his ear because I am throwing a paper ball at him.

I could watch him turn his back towards me, his tail wagging as though he is sweeping the air clean of having witnessed me. Sooner or later he will see, he thought too much of me. Not that I think I am such a horrible person (though I have met better ones), but he seems to have a secret mission for me that I am supposed to fulfill. I can barely follow him, let alone manage to overcome the abyss between his black pupil and mine. I ended up here in this apartment instead. I might as well just stay and sit down on the cool floor. Somehow I feel really warm, my hair is getting sticky, a log in the fireplace tumbles over, the dog sneezes. I have no idea where he is. All I see are thousands of branches from the park waving goodbye. I could wave, too.

What am I saying. My own thoughts make no sense. I don't want the stray dog to leave. I want him to stay. More than that, I want him to lick my eyes like an envelope, seal the eyelids shut for the night, before I have time to realize who left all the empty canisters there and why. The water was just too far away, it is just too far away, I repeat and repeat again.

As I drift into sleep, I see all the people with canisters in their hands. They are crossing the Miljacka River, holding on tightly to the railing, because there is no more bridge left. A naked framework was built as its replacement. One day we will collect all the lost rocks, one day, I tell myself the moment my nails dig into the exposed brick that you told me is very Montréal style. It is no use to look at this place. I am somewhere else. Most of them have at least two canisters in their hand. Some have tied even more of them to each other with shoelaces. I guess the more canisters they take now, the less times they will have to perform the balancing act. Each of them lifts their legs so elegantly like they have been doing this all their lives.

One of them is wearing your coat. How can this be? The belt is hanging loosely on the side. I can testify that your coat smells nice, but I don't think this looks safe. It hangs along the edge like your curtain string caught between the wall and the closed window, a strand of God's hair dipped into his drink. In addition, your coat is way too big for the person wearing it. Both his hands are in his pockets. I guess he has enough water at home or he is only going for an unusual walk. I want to tell him to hold on to the railing, to be careful, that he may fall. I know it would be futile, however. Not because this appears to be a dream, but because there is something so determinate in his walk, even the hole-filled sky could not stop him. Lined up amongst all the others, he looks the most out of place, but to say he does not belong would be inaccurate. Quite the contrary. He seems to have seen the ugly side of fate and the equally ugly side of chance. Neither can be said to have much courage. He was adamant on walking defiantly to both, with grace and lightness.

If ever you start thinking I have no courage, the boy told me, the grownups will have won, and I never want to be even remotely like them. A cloud moved over the moon in that instant. It moved as softly, as unnoticeably as I realize the person walking inside my dream looks just like the boy, only twenty years older.

He seems so far away, because I feel twenty years younger than I am. His coat opens as I pull aside the curtain to see if I can see your balcony from the window, like you said I could. That is not what I see at all. A building wall full of little painted-on stars looks straight at me. Each one of them covers a bullet hole. The boy painted a star over the scar inside my palm when the marble cracked a little inside my hand the day the ground shook a bit more than usual. He painted it for me the day my grandmother asked me to go to bed, but I walked back down the stairs instead. I am glad I did even though I hurt my hand, because I got to spend more time with the boy and now I have a star from him in my palm. Now, with the star there, your wound will heal faster and all your pain will go away, the boy said. He was right, because when I took a look at the scar again, all the red had gone away. I carry it with me all the time. The stars I see on the building wall look exactly the same. Some of the holes are turning into large craters despite the attempt to stop the wounds from expanding. I still think the stars will work better than a Band-Aid. I know I will find him now. I know, because who else would have painted these stars twenty years after the war? I recognize the chalk. It must be him. He must be alive. He must be alive.

The stray dog turns again to see if I am coming. I try to wave from the window to tell him to wait for me. I am tired, I can't walk that fast and I don't know where I am. I am looking for the boy and looking at your window at the same time. I point at the stars to show the stray dog what I discovered. My hand hovers in the air with my finger directed at history engraved over apartments where somebody's lives used to be. The stray dog looks up. I think he is happy, even though he is not wagging his tail. He looks up even higher. The person who came to see God is even closer now, his shadow has moved away from God's eyes.

The two windshield wipers turn back on. I guess that means we are allowed to go. I don't know what God sees now, but I see even less than before. My mother is putting our passport back in her purse. We only have one for the both of us. I am inside of her passport right beside her, because the grownups think I am too little to leave on my own. They are wrong. Even if they weren't, they should have remembered that long ago, long ago before they decided it is better not to be together. They are wrong about a lot of things, because they are wrong about that, too.

But something about this grownup, who was looking at our passports seems more like a child. He hands me back all our passports through the car's window. I don't know why he picked me to give them back to, but he smiles. If one day I see a light flicker on the moon, I know it will be you, he says. You are free to go, he motions to the driver with his hand.

I don't know if he saw me, but I waved, too. I think he missed it, because he was looking at the soldier, who was in charge of opening the gate. I hope I am wrong, because even though I didn't like him at first, I like him now, and I am almost sorry I was a little rude. I think I should say thank you, but it is too late. The car is moving now and the gate is opening. From the corner of my eye, I can see the soldier, who opened the gate for us. I can't be sure, but I don't think he smiled. I don't think I saw a single line in the corner of his eyes.

I am happy we have passed him now. A tree branch bends against the window as the car squeezes by the little booth he is sitting in. More branches are knocking against the window as if to tell me something bad is about to happen. I think I need to turn around. My head turns towards the back window, while the car continues to drive slowly over the rubble. Oh no. The soldier is leaving the booth now. He just needs some fresh air. He just needs some fresh air. He is walking towards the soldier, who let us go. He lays a hand on his shoulder softly. Maybe he is trying to comfort him. Another tree branch beats against the car window. Wait. Where is he taking him? Why is he leading him into the woods? It must be too bright for him in the neon lights. Maybe he is trying to tell him to take a break, to just go to sleep for a while. More tiny tree branches knock on the other side of the car. My mother snaps her purse shut. A loud sound penetrates through the forest. A little bird flies out from where the sound came. It looks afraid. I do not think to even ask my mother what that sound was. There is no need to ask, because even I know helium balloons do not pop that loudly.

Only one of the men comes out of the forest, but we are too far away now. Too far away to see who it is that came out. Too far away to recognize whoever it is that came out, both of them are gone. The little bird circles around the car one more time before it flies away.

My finger touches the fogged-up back window of the car. The drainpipe cracks as my grandfather closes his window trying to get away from the shot he heard coming from the border we just crossed. The stray dog is tugging at my sleeve again. Inside his eyes the marble is rolling down the pipe. It falls through the crack before it reaches the end. I hear it splash into a giant puddle. The shot from the border must have been too loud. It is pouring now. It is pouring and I should have waved. There is still no marble in my hand. There are just too many puddles and the waves are too big. This apartment is too big for me, too, and another star is appearing on the wall beside the window.

I do not see a single star in the sky as we drive farther and farther away from the border. Maybe they fell out because the ground trembled too much. Maybe God took them temporarily to remind himself of his greater plan. I don't remember. I don't remember. I hear him repeat through the smoky air in the bar.

The person beside him is not saying anything at all. God motions towards the empty seat with his hand. I guess he still knows how to be polite even after several drinks. I wonder if he knows who came.

The tips of the person's fingers are touching the table as softly as my mother moves away a strand of my hair falling over my eyes after I lean over the back seat of the car. I wish she hadn't because I wanted it there. I think I have seen enough. I think the scratching sounds I hear are the stray dog's paws sliding against the brick wall.

He continues even though he is not getting anywhere. He reminds me of me. I want to go downstairs and place my hand on his head, tell him it is okay, he can leave me right here where I am. But I can't. Here from the window his eyes are even smaller than the drop of sweat rolling down God's forehead.

The stray dog sticks his tongue out. God opens his mouth and for a moment it seems he is going to say something else. Maybe his memory came back. His lips form into an "O", his tongue rolls up like he is trying to blow into a balloon. He takes a deep breath in instead. He doesn't say anything.

No one says anything. The road has turned the car in another direction and the border is now out of sight. The silence descends on me as light as my bedsheet I tried to hide under before we left, without success. I can't say I did not find the silence comforting. I can't say I did not find it burdening. Maybe it was a mistake to see it as a friend, although I know it was not the enemy. At least not then. I don't know. I don't know, because years later it still wraps around me so lightly, I am afraid I no longer notice it is there. The helium spreads inside my mouth. The balloon string gets caught in our tire and I wonder. I wonder if the string wraps around the same spot too often, if the car will break down before we can escape. I wonder if that will be my fault, too.

I hear the skin of the balloon dragging against the street as soon as the stray dog stops pedaling his paws against the wall. He must be getting tired, too. His quick and shallow breaths travel up all the way to the open window. I might have been able to catch them if both of my hands weren't gripping on to the windowsill. My fingers wrap tightly around the bars holding up the driver's headrest. We are nowhere close to safe yet, I think I heard him say. We are now between the borders, in a space that belongs to nobody and in times like these you never know who is here.

I prefer it here. I want to stay. I want him to stop driving. I can see the moon much more clearly, because there are no lights here. Besides, right now I prefer to be in a place that belongs to no one. Maybe this is why I hold on so tightly to a windowsill in an apartment I do not even know. I wish I could remember what it is like to feel at home. Down below the stray dog is looking at me with droopy eyes telling me it is time for me to go. I think he does not want me to rent this apartment, because his eyes are turning black. One of his legs lifts up, bends, in a gentle, almost helpless-looking plea. He limps forward like the man who gave me his candle legs. I hope he can tell through the way my hair moves across my eyes in the draft that I know I am in the wrong place. I know, yet I am not sure it was possible to end up anywhere other than where I am.

Many little feet splash in the dog's pupil. All these children plunging inside the dog's eyes are still looking for their home, too. 1,621 children killed during the war. Maybe more. I hear them moving inside his eyes. I don't want to forget. I need to go back to the monument in Sarajevo reminding me of all of them. Little footprints are scattered everywhere along its wide circular base made of melted bombshell cartridges. In the middle, two glass structures are reaching towards the sky, one taller than the other, representing the mother, and the smaller one representing the child. She is reaching over to protect it from harm, but I don't know if it is working. I don't know if the gap between them is too large. Water is flowing through the space into all the little footprints. We need more water. We need more. The imprints are less and less visible the further away they are from the mother, the closer they are to the edge. We need more water to fall. Everyone will be able to see them then.

Little foot-shaped markings are appearing over the dust in the hallway of this faraway place. I don't know where all of them are going, but somehow they ended up here with me. More of them are appearing, but I don't recognize any of them. They are all overlapping each other, because there is very little space in this hallway. I am afraid they won't get anywhere this way. Where are they going? Some are even appearing on the wall and I am worried. My hand slides across the wall. Another tree branch pushes against our car window as I remember the shot. One more set of footprints is crossing the floor. The hallway floor squeaks.

One of the seven columns next to the monument is turning. I don't think anyone has been turning it in a while, because it squeaks, too. Each cylinder holds 74 or 75 names of children, who never made it home. 521 names altogether. I try to reach the rest of the cylinders and rotate them all, but I can't move. My arm is too short to reach and only gets to the window. The window pushes open as I stretch. Maybe the draft will get to the cylinders and they will spin some more.

The window squeaks, too. I think I saw you pass through the room inside the building on the other side. My fingers are cold. They hover out the window still trying to reach at least one of the other cylinders. Maybe I am also trying to wave at you and let you know that I am here.

My arm stretches through the black outside air. Even if I manage to turn them all, I still won't know what all the other 1,100 names are. 1,621 children. Your silhouette passes by the window again. You stretch out your arm towards the wall and reach for the light switch. The light inside your room dims. 1,621 children. Maybe more.

The window squeaks again as I lean. I guess no one has lived here for a while, because everything is rusty, I think to myself while the cylinders filled with names keep spinning in my head. They are a lot more rusty than anything inside this apartment. I don't know why there is any rust at all. I think everyone should keep turning them. Maybe some people are afraid of being sad. Maybe some people don't want to know all the names.

No. None of them can be him, I think to myself again as I watch the stars on the building change colour in the moonlight. I hope you are not going to sleep yet, I think to myself as I lean on the window ledge and accidentally touch the wand for the blinds. It stumbles against the wall and the window and then comes to a standstill. I push it with my finger only to hear the sound again. Maybe one day the cylinders will also tinkle softly like that.

I don't think I can hear anything, the driver answers me after I tell him maybe he should stop the car, because there is a strange sound coming out of it. Something must be wrong with him, because the sound repeats. Another tinkle falls inside the torn car seat as my grandfather closes his blinds. I hope he will be okay without his lamp, I think to myself while the window keeps moving.

My fingertips are wet. It is raining outside and I am glad, because the footprints will be more visible now. No one can say then they just didn't see them. I wonder when I see you if you will remember that in one of my letters to you I wrote that I am not afraid of much, but that sometimes I am afraid of umbrellas.

I prefer hats like the one you placed on my head. The boy tilts mine down across my eyes just to tease me. What happened to the lights in this apartment? It is dark here across the border. The blackness expands back into my past and forward into my future. It turns the light bulb until it becomes loose and rolls it across the floor. On the moon the sky is always black. Maybe this is where I am. Maybe the grownups did not know their way after we crossed the border or they listened to me after all and took me where I wanted to go the moment I fell asleep in the backseat.

I can barely see anything outside of the car. The fog is falling from the sky like God's curtain he rolls down to keep out the light. He used to like waking up to the sun, but his eyes are no longer the same. Someone's face is appearing before him in flashes. For a moment God's own face relaxes into an older version of himself, but it doesn't last very long.

I remember while you and I were still sitting in the café, you ran your finger through the candle flame and said that you think you could have easily been somebody else. I smelled my finger then and all I could smell is the candle's flame. I wanted to tell you that usually I feel I am all people at once, sometimes I feel I am nobody at all, but in this moment I am only the girl dangling her feet on the too high bench, waiting for the boy still. Even your hair is starting to resemble his. I can't tell you that so all I say is, how strange, my finger smells as though I am the one who ran it through the candle flame. Possibly, this means I knew you in a previous life, you smirk, and I smirk, too, because at least for a few seconds you made me forget about this one.

Two

In this life the emergency lights on our car are flickering through God's bedroom drapery and my eyes are hurting. The light in your window keeps turning on and off. It reflects towards my eyes, like all the cars' headlights going the other way amidst all the painted-on stars in the sky. At least this is what they seemed like when we crossed the border, because once we left, it became difficult to tell which part of my life was lived and which part was mostly in my mind. I remember leaning my head against the car window again, the echo of the shot still expanding through the air. I wished I was in one of the other cars, going back into the direction from which we came. The light from your window reminds me of that. It is on now, then it goes away, before it comes back. Then I remember I told you this is how you will scare away any monsters. It will go away, it will go away now. I see you approach the window and point towards the moon. There is nothing there anymore except a slice as thin as my eyelash on your cheek. Soon it won't be there at all.

Soon we won't be here anymore. Soon we will be even farther away from home. This is what goes through my mind as the driver says that in this weather it is hard to tell how much longer until the second checkpoint. I don't want to be rude, I say, but I think I have a better idea. Why don't we just stop and collect all the helium balloons hiding in the forest. If we tie them all to the car, it will float up to the sky.

Maybe three of them started wrapping around each one of your wrists the day you were reading my letter at the passport office. Maybe you were also preparing to run away. Maybe somewhere in one of my letters to you, I mentioned the helium balloons and escaping to the moon. I am not sure. Maybe you started at least considering going, too. It is true you never mentioned the balloons explicitly, but you wrote that, usually, getting your passport taken is something you would rather avoid, but after reading my letters, you couldn't help but go. How unnatural to not be allowed to smile, you added. You shifted in your seat after that. Maybe one of the helium balloons was in my letters after all and began to lift.

I keep shifting, too, because it is not very comfortable on the floor of this apartment. Regardless of that, I want to stay. God is not comfortable where he is either. He keeps moving in his seat. The figure can feel God's eyelashes brushing quickly against his palm.

I can feel the veins beside my left eye pulsating as I rest my head on my hand. I think I am tired now, and I wish you were here to wrap your scarf around my forehead. Maybe then this migraine would go away, at least for the day. You could pull tightly on both sides until the only pressure I feel is the one coming from your hands. Don't worry, you could pull as hard as you can. Imagine I am a balloon. I have enough air now. All you still need to do is pull on the end and tie a knot. It would make me look like a Ninja Turtle then and the people at the border would be afraid of me, they would all just run away.

It's hard to keep my eyes open even though I know I can't fall asleep now. I don't even mind sleeping on the hardwood floor. It's not that. It's just that every time I rub my forehead with my fingers to make the headache go away, another tree branch knocks against the window. My eyelids are closing and the boy is emerging again from the black. My head is throbbing. The ground beneath his feet is shaking more now. I am worried the railing he is walking over won't be able to take it. Besides, one of his shoes is undone and he is still not holding on to anything. I recognize this sound bouncing off the metal railing. It's that of an anti-aircraft rocket, but it must be my fault everything is shaking. It must be me, because my migraine is making everything around me shake. It must be me. If it is me, I must be able to stop it, but I can't figure out how to make this migraine go away. A drop of sweat is rolling down the side of my left eye.

The sound of the anti-aircraft rocket is getting closer and closer. The water trail on my cheek is getting longer and longer. It is about to touch the ground any time now. I can tell by the approaching smell. I can tell I need to lie down before it's too late. It's getting even closer now that you are pulling down your blinds. Their rattle travels to the front of my brain.

Each blind grinds against the other, louder than the previous one. I need to lie on the ground, as fast as I can, my stomach down. That's what they told us in school to do when the grinding sound chews through the soft fluffy clouds. Don't be fooled by their warm fresh laundry look, they said. Place your hands folded into each other at the back of your head. Everything will be okay. Everything will be okay, they said. I don't know for sure why we had to place our hands that way. I think it's so that all the previous happy memories won't sneak out from the brain and escape. Everything will be okay.

Everything will be okay, I keep repeating to myself. Once you buy new blinds that do not make that sound, everything will go away. I just need to find a way to tell you that and then I know everything will be okay after that.

I hear another sound. Something is rolling with metal clinking on the sides. Maybe it is just the last blind falling down. Maybe it is over now. But the sound continues and your window looks like it has been completely dark for quite a while.

It is darker everywhere now. The dark blue belt of the coat slides along the edge of the fake metal bridge. I guess they had to build something fast. All the water canisters are jingling in hollow panic. I am worried he will trip. The coat is too big. My head is still throbbing in beat with the shaking bridge. His feet are speeding up. I recognize the shoelace. What is the boy doing there? Why is he crossing to the other side of the river away from our bench? He is going the wrong way. Besides, he doesn't even have any canisters in his hands. ·

He keeps twisting his right foot off to the side and into the narrow canal running along the edge of the metal framework. Every time he does that, the rolling sound gets louder. Oh no. It must be the marble I hear. How did it get stuck in there? I am worried, because the boy keeps trying to wedge his shoe into the opening on the side. I know he is trying to get the marble out, but his shoe is just too thick. Oh no. He needs to stop. What if he falls? Sometimes as he runs, he skips once or twice, the way I told him to do when all the surrounding sounds get too loud. You can even imagine you are skipping over an invisible mine and that way when a real one shows up, you will be better prepared.

But he has added on an extra move that isn't mine. I wish he would stop, because it's too dangerous, and doesn't he see his shoelace is undone. The sight of this makes my headache worse. My veins are pushing heavily against the skin beside my eye. Your window is flapping against the wall quickly. I fear if I don't make it stop somehow, the skeleton he is walking on will shake even more.

I push both my hands against my head trying to ease my headache, but the veins flow into the white of my eyes. Maybe they won't burst. Maybe they won't burst and they will simply remain little red lines. A red tear appears in the black sky. A red feather falls into the boy's hair. It looks like it came from one of those unfriendly looking red birds residing inside the building where we met. I wish the feather would go away.

My eyes are starting to burn. I think it is getting warmer where he is, because drops of sweat are sliding down his ankles. He is running faster.

The red lines spread out more inside my eyes as he stretches out his leg, attempts yet another time to stop the marble from rolling on. The bulb in your bedroom is overheating even though you turned the light off. Don't burst now. Don't burst now. A dark round stain appears on top of it. A grey cloud in the same shape slowly slides in front of the moon. It is getting darker now.

It is almost fully dark inside of the stray dog's eyes. I see him clearly right in front of me despite a delirious heat wrapped in cold descending over my forehead. I am not sure how he got into the apartment, but I see the entrance door flapping. He is getting closer now until I can feel his breath mixing with my cold sweat. Inside his pupil, I see the marble rolling, like through a magnifying glass. The blue-green river inside is still mixing with the brown. The cold steel frame surrounds it similar to the material they used at the border to decide what belongs to whom and who belongs where. I guess the chalk wasn't strong enough anymore for that. I wonder if the skeleton of the bridge is strong enough to withstand all these memories trying to escape. The marble rolling on the replacement bridge is making it sound like pebbles are falling outside instead of rain. Maybe it is you throwing little stones against the window to see if I am okay. Another one hits the glass. The marble bumps against the side of the steel.

The marble bumps again. The moon can't get through. Invisible ice has formed in its path. The boy's shoelace enters into frame through the edge of the stray dog's pupil, then disappears as quickly as it came.

There is nothing standing in the marble's way. The shoelace enters again, this time in a different loop. It falls into the thin tunnel, but the marble rolls over it without stopping. Maybe if I had used a thicker pen, the shoelace would be bulky enough to stop it. Or maybe there is something wrong with the time and place I wrote onto the shoelace. Maybe it wasn't part of any kind of greater plan. Or maybe God stopped taking any more requests. I wonder if life would be different had I written down something else.

The stray dog lifts his paw as if to help. His ear twitches every time the marble rolls over the shoelace. I am pressing harder on the side of my eyes, because the draft is getting stronger. The marble is rolling faster. The hairs on the dog's paw are standing up. I think he is getting cold, too.

God bites into another ice cube. A crack forms on the side of the skeleton bridge. I think I can see a tiny scar peeking underneath the hair on his paw. More and more of them are standing up.

More and more of his steps splash into my head. The red veins inside my eyes are growing. Maybe if I close and open my eyelids fast enough, I can stop the veins from blooming. But the streets bloomed, too, and no one could stop them, either. On second thought, I want my eyes to bloom. I want to let the quiet, pulsating, red rivers unfold inside the white of my eye until the pattern speaks, because sometimes my mouth turns itself into a bow. The one around the boy's neck or the one holding the balloon closed. I don't know.

If I look at the moon with red eyes like that, maybe it will come a little closer then. I try to get closer to the stray dog, because he looks so sweet and there is something comforting about him. My elbows are pushing against the hardwood floor as I crawl closer to him. My stomach is too close to the ground. I have to be careful not to sweep any of the footprints away, but I am not allowed to get up. My head has to still remain below the window line, because it is too dangerous outside. If I breathe in as deeply as I can, maybe there will be enough space. I just don't want to inhale the way God did before he exhaled and created the universe, because something went wrong then.

I have to hold my breath. Just a little bit longer. Just a little bit longer until everything has matured enough to be let back out, until all the steps are safely behind me and I can no longer harm them. Little stars are sparkling right in front of my eyes that look nothing like the stars on the building and I don't know what to think about that. A drop of dew on the boy's strand of hair sparkled just like that the last time I saw him. The strand falls over his eye like the tree branch slicing through the flickering streetlight.

The stray dog lifts his paw even higher. Maybe he wants to sweep the boy's hair away from his eye. Maybe he wants to help him see better where he is walking.

My elbow tips up a loose tile from the hardwood floor. The ashtray in the car's door flips up again. If I don't breathe now, maybe nothing will get into my eyes. I remember crawling on the floor like this before. I had to embark on an adventure to get to my magic house shoes that had hidden themselves all the way under my bed, somewhere mid-way. Perfect opportunity to practise some kind of potential maneuvers I will have to know how to do once I am on the moon. For now all the dust is collecting on the sleeve of my pyjama. It's okay, because this is our last night here and my parents won't get the chance to see that I crawled back into bed with dirty pyjamas like that. Last time I did that, they did not like it so much and asked me how I can fall asleep like that with all the dust around me. They wouldn't say that if they knew what all is there. But that's okay. They are just grownups. They don't know. They don't know that the night before we left, I visited the entire universe right under my bed.

The more dust I collect, the better. All the particles are tiny little galaxies I am rescuing from the long forgotten black holes nobody can see. I will know all the secrets now, I think to myself, as dust pillows collect under my arms. I tuck in my head as soon as the bottom of my bed forms a roof over me determining the border between the world of grownups and the world I am entering. I don't even mind the dusty smell. It reminds me of all the moments I ever lived in this room wrapped up into one cell that will float around in the universe for eternity. All I have to do is manage to hold back a sneeze. I don't want to wake up my parents, because they would not understand what I am doing down here. If they open my door, the light from the hallway will flow in and disturb the entire gravitational field. Besides, here in the dark, it is easier to pretend my room looks the same as always and that it is not angry at me.

I can hear its grinding teeth, my empty drawers closing and opening. If I get to my magic slippers on time, maybe I can prevent the future I already saw, the future me I have already been, from happening.

My arm stretches out all the way through the Milky Way to another galaxy. I try to reach the heel of my house shoe, but instead all I do is push it away. I try again, but the tip of my finger nudges it further. I have to get to it somehow before I find myself on the floor of some place I don't know.

But I am getting sleepy.

I am getting sleepy and my shoulder is hurting. I stretch out my arm trying to hold the stray dog's paw, but my finger flows through it the same way as through the fog before opening the car's door on the morning we left.

I hear the sound of a door close, how strange. The one here in the apartment hasn't moved. I am sure of that because there was not a dash of a draft. Yet, somehow, I reach for his paw again, but nothing is there except the trace of my hand's movement in the air. A loud emptiness resounds. I think that someone forgot to tell me that passing through an endless hollow is louder than the impact upon hitting an unexpected barrier. There is nothing there. I am falling through the air as I often do before I drift into sleep. Not even my dusty pyjamas can help me. I try to grab onto something, but only emptiness takes my hand. The nothingness is so loud. I can barely hear.

My father slams the trunk of the car shut. Maybe finally the grownups are listening to me. Maybe they are finally admitting they don't know the way at all. The driver stopped the car after I told them that I am sure if they give me my grandfather's lamp from the back, the street will be easier to see. I don't know if they really believe me or if the driver is just tired of me still constantly pushing his seat.

I think he should be happy that he is getting a back massage. I can't say the same is true for me. All I know is the more I push, the more of my bare footprints I can see in the old leather seat. More footprints appear on the hallway floor of the apartment. The grownups are mistaken if they think just because they are getting the lamp for me, I will stop kicking.

The driver asks me where I would like to plug the lamp in. I don't know why he is asking me such a silly question as this. He knows very well there are no outlets in the car. I tell him not to worry about that and to leave it up to me. It is best you stick to what you know, I say as I take my foot away from his seat. My mother nudges me with her elbow. I admit that was a little rude, but I just didn't like the way he winked at me when he asked me about the lamp. I think he should take me more seriously than to do that.

Besides, I don't think he knows how to wink. When he tried, both his eyelids closed, only one opened sooner than the other. I shouldn't be so hard on him, maybe he is just sleepy. Maybe if he wasn't too tired, he was lucky enough to see the world twice in that moment. He can pick out the one he likes better, because even the same moment has many worlds inside.

My hand circles around the same axis in a spiral. I am trying to tighten the loosened lampshade, but it just spins without end. I think it broke when the man at the border, who checked our passports took it out. It's okay. Even though my wrist may start hurting from all that turning, I like it even better this way. The moon spins without end, too.

I wonder where the light bulb went. It could be because of the missing bulb that the lampshade is not tightening. I think the man at the border took it, because he looked sad. Maybe he needed it to change the neon lighting. This way next time a car like ours arrives, he can let them go more easily. Yes, this must be it. I am glad he took it away, in that case.

The driver's seat squeaks the moment he pulls it forward a bit. My bed makes the same sound as I crawl in while the lampshade spins. Little grey clouds are descending from my dusty pyjamas all over my bed-sheets. Inside, a dark morning slides down my eyelids. I keep turning faster and faster, like the lampshade around the empty socket. We might be turning at the same speed. Then, all of the sudden, a standstill.

I am hovering in the air tied to a balloon string. I am rising up with my back towards the Earth. I wish I could take a good look at it from up here, but for some reason I am unable to turn. I keep floating up and up towards the torn sky, the one you told me looks beautiful as it comes apart.

The air glides through my fingers like the fresh spring water from my grandparents' garden. I washed the marbles there, too, the way one would wash grapes. The boy always thought that was silly. They could just stay gritty, filled with whatever they pick up, he said. It's not that I don't agree with him. I do. It's just that I like to feel the water run over my hand. I won't wash your favourite marble, I said. That way it will always be the only one that remembers everything. He ran his hand through the air as if to tell me it's all right, I can do whatever I like, he doesn't mind. Then he smiled and the sky tore some more.

If my fingers are leaving a trail in the air like all these airplanes, I wonder if you will be able to see them through your window when you wake up. By the time you get up, anything I left in the sky may be gone. On the off chance that your sleep this time wasn't so deep, because you and I are supposed to meet again, you may see something after all.

You could watch the trail I leave grow like a never-ending balloon string. Just let it go, don't reach for it yet. I want to get closer to the orange, red and purple light peeking through the broken sky. If you would like, you can fold your fingers gently around the string, just in case, and let it slide through your palm. As long as you let me float up as high as I would like, I promise to let you pull on the string another time, just not now.

The night before we left, a button fell off of my pillowcase. I think a star fell out of the sky, too. God slightly lifts his eyelid as the sleeve of the person's coat touches his cheek before it wraps around the empty chair with a movement familiar to me. The hole in the sky expands.

The bright colours are seeping into my iris. The spring water is filling up the empty canisters. I am almost there. I am almost there. The colours are getting brighter. Light is bouncing off the water in the canisters and into my eyes. The next person in line comes in. The gate in front of my grandparents' house makes a screeching sound as a gust of wind bumps it against the side. A vibration flows through the ground and tips the canister. The wind circles around its opening and whistles in a melody that sounds a lot like the sound the cylinders with the children's names made.

The ground is vibrating again and something is pulling at my back. My eyes are opening, but it is getting darker instead, there is no more space in front of me. My eyelashes are brushing against some kind of ceiling. Dust particles are falling into my pupil.

I feel something vibrate near my thigh. Maybe the person next in line is opening the gate a little too hard. Maybe they are in a rush to get back home in time. I blink one more time before I realize the vibrations are coming from my phone I left inside my pocket last night.

A ray of daylight shines onto the ceiling like our winking car. I remember again where I am, but what happened to all the little footprints? The ceiling moves away as I reach for my phone. A cold, wooden floor is pressing against my cheek and I can't see a single step anymore. How can that be?

My palm on the hardwood floor sweeps away the fog on the inside of the car window. How much longer is it going to take us to arrive? How does sometime this afternoon sound to you? A light, faded moon appears behind the window. My finger swipes over the phone screen. Would 3 p.m. work for you? There is this café called Toi et Moi. I thought we could meet there, because it has just the right name. We could meet out front, then take a walk in this nearby park where we can watch the falling dark. Let me know if you would like that.

Of course I would. Maybe part of me is hoping we will just run away. Maybe I am hoping this is what we already planned. Even before I am fully awake, I let you know that I will be there, that I have the perfect lamp for that. If the moon does not come out when we are in the park, we will have our own as a backup plan. My phone screen lights up and throws fragmented light rays across the ceiling. If this is the lamp you told me about in your letter, we could potentially even skip the real moon altogether, yours may be even better.

Sweet of you to say. The light scattering across the ceiling looks mesmerizing. The driver sprinkles soapy fluid over the windshield. The colours of the rainbow inside the little drops disguise that it is not as beautiful outside as it looks. Behind the clouds of light your text message has created on the ceiling, the paint is peeling. I don't mind.

I don't even mind that I know any time now the windshield wipers will get stuck. The outside air is just too cold. It is just too cold. They freeze in the position of frowning eyebrows and I can't quite decide.

I can't quite decide if I think the car looks more like it is sad or if it is expressing its disapproval, signalling we are still going the wrong way.

Of course we are. I have not activated the lamp yet. I stick the plug into the torn car seat. Soon it will charge up with all the things left unsaid, hiding between the seats. Another cloud of light appears on the ceiling. It must be a message from you.

Remember how I wrote to you that in this city I feel out of place? Remember how I told you about the little bird that came to me at Russell Square? Remember how I said I wished I could follow it and go somewhere else? I lost it then, but maybe I will see it again when we meet. Maybe it will come when you turn on the lamp and I place my hand on top of the lampshade.

What a cute message. Your messages are getting sweeter with every next one you send. I am usually not really into that, but I am on a morning with the shade of blue it has today.

Maybe you will wrap your coat around me again when I take out the lamp. Even though it has the same colour reminding me of the war over and over, from you, I want that. I could scratch its inner lining with my hand. A feather may come out and I would draw a tiny line on your cheek with its tip. It's God's eyelash, I would say to you. See, he remembers what happened, he keeps plucking his eyelashes, making a wish that someone would tell him how to get better after all this.

Then I could blow on your cheek and ask you if this is what you felt like when the little bird found you on that day. If you move your fingers above the light in just the right way, it may come back. I wonder if it looked anything like the bird sitting on the street lamp that night when I waited for the boy and the stray dog kept tugging on my sleeve until I followed him.

I should spread my fingers slowly over the bulb until four light rays are beaming into the misty air, you answer. Maybe one of them will fly beside the bird's eye and it will turn around.

The stray dog's paws spread across the pavement as he runs. Drops from the puddles he is stepping into splash onto my cheek. I don't know how because he is getting farther and farther away from me. I have to run faster, but a plastic bag is stuck underneath my shoe. I can't stop now. I have to follow him. I think he knows where the boy is. If I knew where I am, I would not have to search for the moon to tell me. I know I am far away from our bench, but I don't know anything else. I lift my head up to ask the stars, but there is nothing there this time.

All that surrounds me now are unfamiliar windows looking at me with droopy eyes. Their curtains are moving in the breeze the way eyelids open and close, someone's who is very sleepy and trying hard to stay awake.

I know I am on the wrong street, because I don't recognize anything, but the boy would blink the same way every time before he looked at the moon. Before I knew better, I kept asking him if he is sleepy. He said it is nothing like that. If I open my eyes, then close them again, I can see the moon afresh, as if I have never seen it before, he said. Every time you do this, it will look slightly different. Every time you do this, the world is slightly retuned.

I think I was doing something wrong. Maybe I just blinked too much and now I made it disappear. I can't see it at all. I wish the boy was here to tell me what it is that I am doing wrong. I am sure he would know and then I wouldn't have to worry anymore that the moon is mad at me now and won't talk to me anymore.

Maybe if I manage to run just a little bit more, I will manage to find him. Just a little bit more, just one more street lamp I need to touch as I pass it and maybe it will be the one that lights up and shows me where I am.

My foot is dragging against the sidewalk. It is getting harder and harder to run, because with every step I take, the plastic bag wraps tighter around my ankle. I don't think I will be able to take it off, because my soles are sticky now. It took me a while to scratch off the sticker showing the shoe size. Without it I can pretend they are just right, while flakes of glue remain at the bottom, picking up evidence of the Sarajevo street.

I don't know where all the shadows on the pavement are coming from, the moon is gone and all the lights outside are off. I am splitting apart at my feet. It feels like something inside my soles is turning into a seed. I think I broke the bottom of my shoe when I took off the sticker and now all the different versions of me are seeping through. They wobble in the form of a shadow on the ground showing me all the different people I have become. None of them look the same, but they all shake at their knees. If I bend my head a little bit, I can imagine they are all trying to break away from me, but they can't. I am not sure if they want to leave, because they can sense I don't know where I am going or because they know if we all walk down a different street, we have a higher chance of finding him.

I shake my foot to try and separate them, but it's not working. They are entangling into each other even closer, the plastic bag is pulling around my ankle even tighter. It holds all the mes together even more. Maybe if I ask nicely enough, it will let them go. I don't know. It may be too late for that now, because I have walked for too long and made too many turns without finding him. There are too many knots now squeezing around my ankle. The longer I walk, the longer the shadows are getting. I think they know it is too late for them now to each turn their own way, because I didn't know sooner where to go. The grip of the plastic bag around all of their ankles is too strong for them to separate.

I stretch my arms up and try to grip all the clouds. Maybe the moon is sleeping somewhere inside one of them. All the shadows on the ground that grew out of me do the same. They seem to be stretching out until eternity, because I can't see their end, but I can feel they haven't reached anything they wanted to reach. I can feel their restlessness shaking my feet. Underneath me, the Earth is breathing irregularly. It must be having some kind of bad dreams. Somehow, I am feeling a bit dizzy, either I am getting taller like the shadows or I am floating up above the ground. This is making my head spin. The Earth's big belly is rising and I am standing right in the middle of it. My knees feel soft as jelly.

The soft bedsheet lifts towards the ceiling as my mother shakes it before it lands on my bed. It looks like someone breathing in. Warm and fresh, right out of the laundry, so you can get proper rest before our big trip tomorrow, she says to me. A breath of fresh lavender comes out of the now flattened belly. I want to tell my mother that it doesn't smell like that outside anymore, that I won't be able to fall asleep like that: with lavender fields that don't exist coming out of the bedsheet. But I don't say anything, because I don't want to make her sad. Besides, I feel bad that on our last day before leaving, she had to do laundry, just because of me.

A whiff of burnt lavender enters my nostrils. I am descending again. The Earth is breathing out in shallow breaths. I hear some kind of crackling sound, like someone is smoking a cigarette in the cold. I guess there is just too much smoke all around. No. It's just clouds. It's just clouds, I tell myself as my feet touch the pavement. I am shrinking again and the other, darker mes, are growing.

They are spreading out flat on the ground. In a way, I could almost trick myself into thinking they look peaceful. They are just lying down and stretching out their arms as they yawn. Maybe this is just the moment right before falling asleep, nothing more. I have fallen asleep that way often, after all. They stretch again as another wave of burnt lavender comes their way. God spins the wheel on his lighter. There is no more flame. I guess he used it too much and spent it all. Nothing comes out, except more of the same smell. My ankle is hurting more. One of the shadows must be pulling harder now. One of them is trying to reach all the way back to my bedroom. I don't know how to confess to it that the old lavender it is looking for between my Mickey Mouse comics pages is long gone. I burnt it over one of the candles the kind man gave me. I did that to check and see if the smell sneaking in from the outside through my closed window smells anything like it. I watched the stem of the lavender turn into a red planet sliding along the given path while part of my curtain waved on the other side. This is how I knew there are no more lavender fields outside.

If I cover the shadow's nose it might calm down. I don't think it is ready to hear any more bad news, so I will stay quiet, while I watch it climb up a building and reach into a window across the street that isn't even mine. I don't know what it will find there, but it won't be the lavender.

The lavender is tucked away behind God's ear. It peeks through his long dirty hair like a hidden barrier. I think he should use it for something better than to help him carry the weight of all the soaked strands of his hair. Maybe it's not even anything like that at all. Maybe none of the lavender fields mean that much to him. Possibly, he simply plucked one lavender sprig from the field without paying attention or he needed it to scratch the tickling behind his ear. Now it has been there for so long, he doesn't even notice it anymore. I wonder what the one he has smells like.

I don't know, but he keeps spinning the wheel on his lighter. With every spin, one of the shadows pulls again. I pull, too, but in the opposite direction. There is nothing left for me to do, but to drag them along the pavement like a bouquet of deflated balloons.

The shadows are leaving a wet trail behind them as I drag them through all the puddles. I am not trying to hurt them or be mean, but I have to keep moving. I wish the stray dog would stop running so fast, but he won't. The shadows' hands flow through the water reluctantly. One shadow tries to hold on to one of the puddles not realizing it is impossible. The one that managed to climb up to a window is still there, while the others form crossing wet lines on the ground.

The lines on God's thumb are wearing off from all that pressing on the lighter. I hope his fingerprint will disappear faster than my shadows merging into the ground. Why is the night already leaving? It is only a little past midnight. At least that is what it feels like, because I haven't been running after the stray dog for that long. The daylight is appearing way too soon. The shadows are fading. The daylight is trying to swallow them, but I know that is of no use, because they are too strong to chew through.

The day still embarks on this attempt, however impossible. The squeaky sound reveals to me its stubbornness. It must be the day's teeth trying to slice through the darker versions of me spread out on the ground.

Nothing happens, its teeth are too weak. It tries to sharpen the edges by pushing forward the outlines of objects around me. It is getting brighter and brighter. The day is getting closer, revealing the present to me as slowly as it can. Still, it is going too fast, and only the past is getting clearer. How naïve and hopeful of the day to think it may make the rustling sound of the plastic bag go away by calming down the shadows bound to my feet. It's them. It's them constantly shaking it.

I wish I knew when the boy lost his plastic bag, because maybe then I would be closer to knowing where he is, and if there is any chance you could be him. Maybe the shadows know, but even if they do, I don't think they will tell me. They just won't speak.

If I knew what the boy's plastic bag was doing on the street maybe the sounds it makes around my ankle wouldn't pierce through and into my being, dividing me, the way the sunray smuggles itself in through the worn curtain, splitting my dreaming into two.

The boy's hand is appearing through the plastic bag. He is pushing the wall beside my bed right next to my cheek. I never used to sleep that tucked away, but when he didn't come that night, I pushed my bed into the corner as far as I could. I needed the world to be smaller, but it grew instead.

The world stretched the way someone would who overslept. The future may have won by crossing the finish line sooner, but at least it is warm and cozy here in bed. That's what the world thought to itself then, its arms stretched towards the ceiling. Still in half-sleep, unaware of where exactly it is, the top of its hand bumped against the chandelier on the way up. I will just go back to sleep, the future thought to itself quietly, while the shadow cast by the swaying chandelier brushed over it softly. It still glides back and forth, back and forth.

The door is pulling back shut again until I stop it with my foot. More contours have been pushed to the foreground. The door is as close to my eyes as the wall watching me try and uncover my foot from underneath the bedsheet. Ever since I was little, I had a problem with burning soles. I don't know if it took my parents too long to figure out to never cover my feet when they prepare me for sleep and that is why they now burn even more. Or maybe I could tell some years down the line God's cigarette buds would be growing underneath the asphalt soaking up the heat.

God's eyelid twitches as I push up the bedsheet with my foot. The door I am standing in front of opens, sprinkling in particles of air into my eyes to wake me up. I am neither in my bedroom anymore, nor on the dark street. I am back inside the apartment I am possibly going to rent. I know I just woke up, but I feel more like I have fallen asleep, straight into the day that reveals its poofy eyes with dark rings underneath.

Somehow, I prefer eyes that look that way. I don't know if that is unexpected, but I think when the world slept in and stretched, it stretched my life with it. Now I am holding on to a doorknob resembling the chandelier in my old bedroom spinning me around. My fingers are getting slippery, I don't know for how much longer I can hold on. I don't know if I could hold on at all without the boy's tight grip still holding on to my hand, making sure I don't fall. I remember his hand and then I remember yours. I feel a little less dizzy than before, but I am still not sure how properly I can walk. I am about to step out of the apartment and onto the street, but the outside stairs in this city are really steep. I am not really used to this. Besides, the moment I opened the apartment door entirely, your street began wrapping all around me.

Three

A slight panic comes over me the moment I realize the branches of the trees on your street bend into the same shape my hair formed itself into when I kept opening the car window secretly. Behind the branches a faded moon peeks through discreetly, softening the pulsating inside my head. I push my forehead against the driver's seat even harder than before the moment I hear him say to get our passports ready again, because the second border is approaching. I push again and again against his seat even though I can feel my mother's warm hand on my neck trying to calm me.

This time, she doesn't say anything to reprimand me. Maybe you won't say anything to me either when I tell you I found the apartment quite dark and desolate, but I will take it. The reason I am taking it is just because I am so sleepy. I am so sleepy. It's not because of you. I know that's not true, but I don't know what else to do. I don't know why I feel I am near the boy when I am close to you. This apartment will be all right, I am okay with the dark. The neon lights in front of our car are getting way too bright and I need some place to hide. Besides, this place looks just forgotten enough for me to want to be here. No one will be able to find me now. I know I said that before, but this time it will work, because even my parents have no idea where I am. If it looked any less abandoned, I don't think it would be anything quite suitable for somebody like me.

Sometime, long ago, before the war, a man with a large forehead was sitting on our bench. I didn't mind, because I liked the way his knees curved in towards each other. I stood still in front of him without saying anything. I couldn't tell you if it was because I was shy then or because he seemed to be from another time, and I wanted to see what happens if I am just silent. Without looking up at me, he turned one of his feet inwards. He lifted his shoe and said: I can see the future returning backwards to me, carrying all the ruins from the past. It slides underneath my sole now. One day it will come your way and you have to be careful what to do with the broken and incomplete pieces it brings. One of its sides may loop up, while the other stretches out. I think the future comes in the way a child is taught to tie its shoelace. One side circles time like eternal beauty, while the other stretches out in a linear grotesque smile. I have seen the future turn them around each other. If you step down on it at the right time, the way one places a finger on a shoelace, a bow may come out. But I didn't know how. So, the world is full of knots now, the man said and laid his shoe against the ground. Then he disappeared.

I pull my finger out just before I tighten both sides. A ray of sunlight reflects from your window and onto the steep stairs I am standing on. The bright line moves a little as you open one side of your window. I hope a cloud comes and covers the sun, because I am not sure I know how to walk down the way things are now. I wish I still had your hat on my head. I guess I should have told you I am afraid of stepping on any lines. The man at the second border motions for us to roll down the car window. You drove your car too far out. The tires are way beyond the chalk line, he says to the driver.

He grabs the car door's handle and pulls. Your window opens some more, takes another sweep of air while recording your fingerprints on the glass. It was just one extra soft nudge, but I guess enough to make your window a little dirty, enough for the man at the border to think it was one too much. He taps on the car window a little too hard. I think someone should have told him that is not very polite. I think I should have just stretched my arm out and pressed that lock even further down the moment the driver reached for the dangling car key to turn off the engine. I could have pushed it down all the way into the car's fabric, so none of the grownups can ever reach it with their chubby hands. I definitely should have done that, because then maybe the man outside would have known not to talk to us that way. Maybe he would have been a little nicer then.

The car key dangles in my ear the moment I move down one step on the iron stair. Crisp metal echoes through the air together with the closing apartment door. I can do it. I can do it. If I am careful enough, I can step over the light without touching it. As long as nothing shakes, I will be all right. My hand reaches for the brass fence. I think I pushed it too much, because the car door opens, a light beam pierces through the silence and lands on my father's eye. I don't know why the man outside is using this harsh flashlight. Didn't he see the little light in the car turned on the moment he opened the door?

Maybe I shouldn't be so hard on him. Maybe he just can't see very well and that's why he needs extra light. But I am not sure about that, because he is not wearing any glasses. Still, it could be that he does not have any time to go get them. Who knows, possibly he is afraid to walk alone too far. He doesn't have magic houseshoes like I do, that automatically diffuse any mines. Whatever his reason is, I want to tell him to turn off the light. It is hurting my father's eyes.

His pupil is contracting too much and his iris is getting too big. There is not enough black in his eyes to hide. I need to do something quickly before the man sees my father's eyes are too brown. At least he has not looked at our passports yet.

The light beam illuminates little grey dots floating aimlessly as though they want to go everywhere at once. Oh no. God has turned one of his pockets inside out, looking for some change to pay for his drink. But there is nothing left in there except these tiny remains floating into our car. God, God is so strange! He must be really desperately looking through his pockets, because there is so much ash whirling around. What did you say? The man outside asks me and redirects the light into my eyes.

I won't let him hurt me. The bright light is just the moon getting closer. My pupil is not closing at all this time. The light is slowly gnawing away my surroundings before it slides them over the edge of my pupil. What used to be around me, falls down into the abyss inside my eyes like a giant waterfall. If I rub my eyes, the air will fill with sparkling stars. It will be okay then. Besides, if everything around me disappears, I can pretend I am on my spaceship. I have a lot of practice. If I concentrate and stop listening to the grownups' voices around me, I know I can get there.

I used to take off the lampshade before bed and stare at the light bulb until my bedroom gets fuzzy. The wallpaper would peel itself away to be replaced with soft white light. My spaceship windows appeared right behind them through which the moon was beaming light rays at me carefully trying to talk to me. All I had to do was place the lampshade over my mouth and it would hear what I had to say. It worked even better than a phone, because I didn't even have to dial any number, it would just know. I think it heard everything I said back then, but I think back then I didn't quite know what exactly to say.

If I try hard enough, maybe I can get through to it now, but I am not so sure. The air is too dense. There is too much fog and there are too many holes in the air. The tree branches are scratching the sky open, my messages to the moon are falling through before they get very far. I wish the branches wouldn't do that, but I am not mad at them. I am not mad, because I think they are just too busy taking care of all the runaway balloons to pay attention to anything else they do.

I don't think I heard you, someone says to me. The voice is way too harsh to be the moon. My mother's hand touches my wrist before she says that it would be better if I move my hand away from my lips before I speak.

The light blinks and in between I catch the man outside of the car looking at me. I spread my fingers apart and say, I think God is looking for something, there are too many tiny flakes floating in the car.

I don't think he meant to do that, but for a moment the flashlight turns off and it is dark. The moon peeks through behind his head. It bends him into a shadow that falls over my father's eyes. The shadow looks very deformed and ugly, but at least my father's eyes are in the dark.

I think whoever came to see God wants to make God more comfortable. He pulls the curtain behind him shut. I think he is a he, because briefly, his frame was in the light. Maybe God will relax a little more now that there is even more dark. Maybe God will feel a little more safe looking up now. Outside, it has long been dark, but maybe he is even afraid of the moon. A cloud of red appears on God's cheek. He must be blushing now that he is no longer alone, now that the person who came is pulling his chair out. I think he should not be so afraid to lift his head, because what he is going through right now already looks pretty bad.

I think whoever came seems very kind. I think he can let God know that his cheeks look pretty sweet right now. A lot of fine little light freckles have appeared. They move every now and then, if someone breathes out too heavily. Every time the curtain moves, they move along, too. Somehow the moon is managing to sneak in through the loops in the curtain's weavings. I wonder once the moon touches God's skin, what it will think of it. I think maybe those are just some of the stars that God collected from the sky, but still doesn't know how to rearrange. Maybe the moon is trying to help him.

Come to think of it, the little dots look a lot like the ones you poured into my coffee. Another strand of hair falls over God's eye. The light ray in front of me disappears. I don't know how, because I do not see a cloud in the sky and, as far as I know, you haven't moved the window. Thank goodness, because now I can walk down the stairs without being afraid. I think it is time for me to start walking to the café if I don't want to be late.

The stairs rattle with every step I take walking down. As if he felt the ground shake, God leans his head into his palm. Maybe he is trying to stabilize the stairs and make it easier for me to walk down, I don't know. I just hope that he is not squishing any stars that appeared on his cheek. He should worry about those more than about me.

I admit, the clouds coming out of my mouth every time I breathe out are a bit worrying. Over time, I have grown to like them. Over time, I have grown to like the fog they leave in my eyes as they float up. One floats past your window as I walk by.

I think I saw you guide one in with your hand. Or maybe you just waved at me to say hello, but I don't think so. I remember you told me how you like quiet streets and often when you wake up, your street is just too alive for your taste, especially in the summer. I think maybe you were happy to see something dark coming your way and tried to catch it.

I am not even sure you saw that it came from me, because a text message from you just came in. The *Akšamčići* flower you sent me just lifted its head a little bit, you write to me. It has been at my window ever since you gave it to me and this is the first time that it moved. I placed it inside the cap of my empty lighter, because based on what you said, I thought it may like the still lingering smell. Sometimes, when I wake up, I dip my finger in the glass of water beside my bed and walk over to the window to sprinkle some extra drops on its stem. I did that today, because my eyes were too dry. Maybe when we meet today, together we can summon the clouds.

Your message reminds me of the boy dipping his finger in a puddle. He did that the day I got frustrated I was kicking all the marbles out of the circle constantly. He brushed over the chalkline with his finger and said: Don't worry. It's going to be okay. Look, I will draw a circle so giant, none of the marbles will fall outside of it again. He stretched out his arm so far that I think his shoulder hurt for days, though he never told me that. He would not want me to feel bad. I could just tell he hurt himself by the way he held his arm when he flicked his marble that it was not the same after that.

Later, when he was putting away all the marbles into his plastic bag, he was moving much more slowly than before, almost carefully as if one wrong move could compromise everything. I could no longer perceive any sound in his steps as though he wrapped it up and put it away somewhere deep inside his pocket. He placed each one of the marbles quietly into the bag. If I didn't know there were already some inside, I would think the bag is empty by the way the silence whirled around. See, they are safe now, he said. After he tied the handles around each other once, he took my finger and positioned it on top of the half-knot. If you hold it there instead of me, the marbles inside won't be as afraid. They trust you more. I don't know that I agreed, but I nodded anyway. I wanted to make him feel that he will be able to take care of everything, even of the unfamiliar sounds pushing through the black sheet in the sky as I fail to fall asleep.

He dips his finger into the dirty rain puddle one more time and taps over mine before tying another knot on top of the one I am holding. I want to be careful not to hurt you, he says. Today feels like it is even worse than yesterday. Today it is even more blue outside when it should be fully dark, so I have to pull tighter than usual. It's better you move your finger away before the plastic edges manage to touch its side. I know you want to wait, but it's better you don't wait this time.

God digs a nail into his cheek. I don't think I did it right. The boy tells me that it was great. But I don't think so, because he dips his finger into the muddy puddle and rubs the water over his favourite marble. He never does that. He looks at it for a while before he says: Hmmm. How beautiful. The wave inside looks like someone's scarf detangling in the wind, about to escape.

I remember your scarf moved something like that when we first met. I wonder if you lost it by now, because a lot of time has passed since. I wish outside it wasn't so warm, because I like the way the scarf loosely wraps around your neck. It makes me think that you are prepared to tell me anything. Maybe I am hoping that you will tell me you remember me now. Not from six months ago when we last met, but from twenty years ago, when we were still children. Maybe part of me thinks you will tell me you are sorry you never made it to the bench, but you are here now. Maybe you would remember we planned to run away long ago, but it is not too late, you would say. I am glad I found you. Maybe all that could happen. Maybe all the stars that fell could return back to the sky.

Sometimes I can't manage to say anything and more often than not I find it hard to breathe, I remember you saying to me as you loosen your scarf some more. Your hand pulls down on its knot. Little currents of pain travel to my neck. I think I am too little for this car, because the seat belt is resting too high above my shoulder. It could be that the driver hit the break too suddenly once he realized he drove too far out. The edge of the belt digs into my neck. I guess I could move it away and loosen it with my hand, but I don't. I don't want the man at the border to know that anything he does is hurting me or that I am not big enough to take care of myself. I don't want him to think I am afraid of him.

He tells the driver to step out of the car for a moment. Maybe he just needs to see him better. Or maybe he wants to help after all and thinks it would be healthy to stretch our legs for a bit, because he must be able to tell by my puffy eyes that we have been on the road for quite some time. The driver's seat slides back slightly as he prepares to get out of the car. I like the way it is pushing against my knees. It gives me a chance to push back and stretch. I will grow now, whether I want to or not. If I am not careful enough, my legs will keep stretching until I have to curl up and lie down on the seat the way I did when the blanket became too small to cover me.

I wonder if this time when we meet, you will be wearing your hat. I know it is summer and not that cold, but it can get too bright and I am not sure if you were able to catch any of the clouds coming from my mouth. I think a lot of them passed by your window the night I arrived.

The man at the border bends down his flashlight to allow space for the driver to leave the car. One last push of the hand on the headrest to make it easier to get out. The seat squishes my knees again. At least now with the driver gone and the light not shining into my eyes, I can see better through the windshield. Straight ahead, a bit farther away, a man in a uniform is holding a balloon. He leans on the window of a booth. I guess he must be talking to someone inside. I am not sure, because he is standing too far away. He is twirling the balloon around his wrist as he speaks. Even though they are far away, I can tell the balloon does not want to be there. It resists every turn of his hand. I push the seat in deeper hoping to stop him. My knees are hurting.

I think I have been standing here for too long. The Sarajevo streets the stray dog is leading me through are flowing into yours. My knees are getting stiff, because the legs of all my shadows are getting too long and too heavy to carry. One of them is stretching towards your front door. Kind of indecent, you could say, but only when you do not know any better. Still, I don't want it to ring your bell, so I think I should go. You are no longer at your window. The man holding the balloon has moved aside. There is nobody inside the booth, but he is still talking. It is time for me to leave, it is time for me to leave.

My shadow is growing taller as I keep pushing against the car seat with my knees. It misses your bell and climbs up all the way to your balcony. If you see it, I hope you will forgive the intrusion. I know it is rude. I just don't want that man at the border to have the balloon. Maybe if I move farther along on your street, the balloon string will twist the other way, so it can at least float higher up again.

My shadow does not want to go. It grabs onto the lavender on your balcony as I walk and drag it back down along the wall. I know that was much too sudden a move. I should have been more gentle. I should have prepared the shadow somehow. My own pull startles me. Even if most would not perceive an abrupt decision to start walking as violent, it felt violent to me. Crumbs of lavender in my shadow's palm make any form of comfort seem very far away. Fear. Fear I am becoming just like the man hurting the balloon, of becoming one of the grownups. Fear. Fear on both sides. The grownups' shame is subtle, but noticeable. The naked lavender stems on your balcony move left and right and back in the outside draft. They bend. The grownups' necks are slightly hunched, even if they are standing upright. Just one of the telling signs.

I don't know what to make of my neck hurting. If I am lucky, it is only from leaning forward too much during the drive. After twenty years, you would think I would be all right.

The aggression in my own shadows towards me is getting more obvious. The one I pulled down from your balcony is tightening itself around my ankle. I don't quite know what to make of its behaviour. Maybe it thinks it has seen the boy and doesn't want to leave. Should I be mad at its intemperate plead, threatening to wrap around me too tightly? Or should I place my hand over my heart in grace as I watch it bow underneath me in quiet, humble, apology? If my knees did not hurt so much, maybe I could kneel before it and ask for forgiveness. I don't know what it is exactly that I did wrong, but I must have done something.

The car door slams shut. It makes the same sound as my palm against the balloon. It was one of the man's balloons, who used to sell them in the park. I think I already told you he does something else now and wears much uglier clothes for that. I pushed the balloon in passing, just to see it billow backwards, its string bent in an arc, not entirely pleasant looking.

My body curves just like that as my shadow pushes its hand against my stomach. I think it is angry at me for pulling it away from your balcony. It pushes me again. I gasp for air and open my lips, my feet giving in, maybe too willingly. It feels like some stranger was walking by, decided to punch me, and is now dragging me away along your street, his arms underneath my armpits, the heals of my shoes limping over the cobblestone. I could imagine the man at the border doing that, because I noticed his knuckles are red. But I know it wasn't him.

I push the balloon again. My shadow is pulling on me harder now and my legs are dragging along your street. I guess you were not exaggerating when you said the Montréal streets are broken, and the city likes it that way. I am starting to think if I hit one of the cracks too hard with my heel, your street will bloom too, like the ones in Sarajevo. My street is in an especially bad shape, you said, but you may like its brokenness.

Maybe I do, but the dragging is becoming just a little bit too painful. The shadow seems in a hurry to get me farther away from your balcony. I don't know what has gotten into it. Maybe it saw something it didn't expect to see. My mouth opens some more. I don't know if it opens in order to scream or to ask the shadow what is going on. But there is no time for a single sound, my shadow places its hand over my lips almost immediately. I can barely breathe, but it's okay, I can understand it. I think it is afraid I may scream and it does not want me to cause a scene.

I would not do that, but I guess the strange creature in grey does not know me as well as it thinks. I can barely speak, especially now with the lavender pieces falling from my shadow's palm into my mouth and underneath my tongue. I don't know if all of them are from your balcony or if some are from the long-gone lavender fields. A message from you comes in: I forgot to tell you that the café we are meeting at serves coffee with lavender taste. I am usually more of the traditional type when it comes to coffee, but with you I feel a little more daring. If you will drink it with me, I may actually discover the courage to try it. Even though I find your message endearing, it does not seem so much coincidental as it is cute.

At least there are a lot more clouds in the sky now. With every squeeze of the shadow's arm against my stomach, another cloud comes out of my mouth. I guess it must be really upset. A cloud slides between the shadow's fingers still covering my lips. Between them, there is just enough space for a cigarette. If I look through the opening, I can see the moon. In the daylight, it looks like the tip of an almost finished cigarette, about to go out. Meeting you again seems like a good time for lighting my first cigarette. The boy and I said we would light one once we managed to escape. Yes, I think when we meet is the time. I think smoking is pretty gross, but just one to celebrate not having the grownups around telling us what to do, is okay. The boy thought so, too. I am not sure I know how to properly inhale, but it seems the burning would go well with the lavender coffee.

Lavender coffee, yes. This one sentence is all I manage to write to you while the shadows are taking me away. Your window is becoming only a tiny dot somewhere far away. The corner of my mouth bends up into a deformed smile at the thought of what all I could say to you in the span of that one cigarette. I wonder if I would feel anything close to free, the way the boy and I imagined it. All the moments that happen within its duration would be memorized, while the others become so distant, they are almost forgotten. Maybe you would even ask me if the smoke I am exhaling looks anything like the one I saw from my window. That one came from the lavender fields right after a loud sound.

Another sound finds its place inside my head. I imagine you with a lighter in your palm the way I imagined the boy. Your wrist moves upwards in a commanding way, yet bends back down slowly, not sure of its command. The lighter's cap is open now, even if we have not met again yet. The moment has already begun on its own schedule. Sometimes it repeats again like the sound of the metal still echoing through me, even your hand can't dampen it.

I remember again you told me you can't hear so well on your left ear. I want to tell you that the imbalance will help you hear the frequencies you could not hear before, the ones stored around us from some other time. At least that is what the boy told me when I asked him why ever since the war began, I keep hearing sounds that have long passed. The boy told me not to worry about anything, because it may be true that these sounds sometimes don't make it easy to fall asleep, but the special hearing is one of the things that makes me better prepared for the moon.

Maybe today, at the café, we will be able to figure out how to get to the moon, especially if you brought your hat. Every time you slide it over your ears, it becomes quiet enough to hear. The boy never said this, but I saw him pull down his hat before running down the stairs when we were practising our escape. That must have been why he did that.

I misjudged the size of the steps on one of our practise runs and fell. Lying down with my elbow scratched, I looked at the ceiling from a strange, somewhat slanted angle. It could be that I never looked at it before, because I can't tell if the chandelier was never there at all or if the wire grew out of the ceiling recently and pushed out a bud in the form of a black bulb. Someone is watering it as though somewhere in this lifetime, there is a chance the light may open and unfold. That much I can tell, because the ceiling is filled with water stains.

This morning when I woke up on the floor of the apartment beside yours, they appeared again, forming every time I tried to get up. When I turned my neck, I saw the moon through the window. It looked different than usual. Maybe someone is already there. If you are not the boy, I hope he is up there taking a walk. I imagine him taking his steps, turning the moon, with my bedroom curtain around his shoulder. I wish I had better ones to keep him warm. The ones I have are filled with holes.

My own walking is rather on the wobbly side, not entirely to the credit of one of my shadows pulling on me. I think it has something to do with my leaning too heavily on the nightstand to help me get back out from underneath the bed the night before we left. I should have been more careful with that. One of its legs wavered as I pushed myself up with my dusty hands. Maybe I shouldn't have pulled out the sock the boy had placed underneath one of its legs. I took it out before I crawled down into the universe underneath my bed. I knew it would be even colder there than in my room and I remembered the boy say to me that this is the perfect sock to even out the floor. Then it must also be the perfect sock to keep me warm. This is what I thought to myself, but I forgot to think about much else.

I think I am pushing down too hard. The large candle leaning on the nightstand slides down. God's shoulder nudges against the table. He is still going through his pockets trying to find something. He must be frustrated by now. The table slants a little bit towards the other side. I hope the person sitting across from God will be all right. The candle that used to be part of the kind man's leg rolls down the uneven bedroom floor.

I can see the floor extending through the walls. The candle is rolling faster and faster. The shadow dragging me is speeding up, too. I think it is because it can hear the stray dog's steps getting closer. I want to tell the shadow to slow down, to stop, that I have been wanting to find the stray dog again, but it is hard to speak. Its hand filled with lavender is still covering my mouth. I don't like that, at the moment, I feel I am somewhat at the mercy of this creature that came out of me. Maybe I can trip it with my foot, but I don't want to hurt it even more. Even though it is frustrating to see it running away like a hasty, hunted child, I want to protect it and let it do what it thinks it has to, regardless of where it takes me.

The faster it runs, the louder the rustling of the plastic bag around its ankle is becoming. The reminder of more than simply emptiness will likely exhaust it soon. At least that is what I am hoping. Hopefully it will stop running, because it is becoming harder and harder to detangle the plastic bag. The boy needs it back. I have to return it to him as quickly as I can, because there are just too many. There are way too many marbles for him to carry them all by himself in his hands.

I hope the stray dog won't give up on me or think that I want him to leave me alone, just because one of me seems to be afraid of what he has to reveal. I don't think I have ever seen this me before the plastic bag appeared underneath my feet that night when the boy didn't come, when I stayed sitting on the bench for too long. Maybe I wasn't paying enough attention to the colour of the sky. I think my steps were too small, and I wasn't running fast enough. The stray dog barked then.

He is barking now. We have to slow down. I hurry to grab onto something. My arm stretches out and my fingers curl around the first object they can reach. A tree branch lands in my hand. With every further step the shadow takes, sharp edges dig deeper into my palm, disappear in its pillow, not unlike my head I covered underneath my bedsheet after climbing back into the bed. I keep pulling on the branch without wanting to. Part of me feels bad about resisting, a little bit because I am making it harder for the shadow to run and a little bit because the entire ground is now trembling. I am definitely pulling on the branch too heavily. I feel I am pulling something out, but I am too afraid to let go. I don't know where my shadow wants to take me. I don't quite know what is happening, but I can't open my hand.

The asphalt on your street is opening instead. I think I am lifting everything up. This is not how Sarajevo Roses bloom, but the cracks are widening. Even if I wanted to open my hand, it would be of no use. What I want is irrelevant, because my hand holds on tightly to the driver's headrest as I watch the balloon around the outside man's wrist trying to escape. To no avail. He is walking towards the other outside man now, the one who told us our car drove too far out and crossed the line, that we shouldn't have done that without first having asked. I don't know what is so special about him that he gets to be the person to decide something like that.

Neither of the outside men seems very kind. The one with the balloon is spinning his hand. I don't know if he is nervous about talking to the other man or why else he would be doing that. Doesn't he see the balloon is afraid. Its string is getting shorter and shorter. Doesn't he see the balloon needs more space. It is shaking by now and so am I. I pull myself in closer to the car seat trying to see better what is going on. I lean my forehead on the headrest and look over to the side, but it is difficult to see anything through all that fog. More and more of it is filling up the outside.

My other hand grabs on, too. It is just a branch. It is just a branch. More of the street is lifting up now as I keep holding on. Maybe the street is blooming after all. I have no idea where I gathered all this strength from, but a line of blooming asphalt is forming on your street as I keep holding on and the shadow keeps walking. It feels like I am pulling on a loose thread, the inside roots are coming undone. The balloon is crackling from all the moving. The rain pipe along my grandparents' roof is becoming loose. It continues to unravel all the way alongside the wall, all the way to the pipe going downwards to the ground. Oh no. I didn't mean to do that. How did the metal pipe get into my hand?

What is it doing all the way here in this city so far away from my grandparents' house? When did it get so long? It just continues on and on the farther we walk. Even though it is not so kind of me that I am ruining the street, I get the thought that maybe whoever walks by here will find it nice to know what all is hiding down below. I have to admit it may not make much sense to find a rainwater pipe from somewhere faraway, and I hope nobody feels too surprised or estranged. After all, I still want them to be able to find their way home.

Little white flakes are falling all around. I know this can't be snow, because we are nowhere close to winter. I know my sense of time is off and it feels like I have been walking for very long, but I still remember it is supposed to be warm now. I know this, because you wrote to me it will be nice to see me in the summer when the atmosphere is light and the sheet over the sky is thinner than in the wintertime. If you look up in the right moment, you can even briefly see some silhouettes moving subtly on the other side, inside the space behind the sky. There might even be a bar.

I wonder if it's them or me filling up the air with all these tiny little white things. A lot of them are ending up inside my eyelashes. One or two fall onto my upper lip and now I can see that it's probably me. The little white things taste the same as the walls of my grandparents' house. I know exactly what the outside wall tastes like, because of the grenade that fell not too far from the window. Maybe it fell on one of those days when the sky was just too thin, I don't know.

All I know is the day before is the last day the boy and I played our marble game. An ugly flower opened now in the spot where our circle used to be. Its asphalt petals opened in an unruly way and looked nothing like what my grandfather built just so the boy and I could play the marble game. I think my grandfather saw through his bedroom window that I was always sad all my marbles kept rolling outside of the chalk circle, so he decided to pave more of the back garden. I know you like these *Akšamčići* flowers along the edge, he said to me, but they will understand you need a little bit more space.

I don't know what they would think of me now if they knew that even though they died, the circle was still not big enough for the marbles to stay inside. Knowing them, they would understand, but I still feel bad.

I plucked them all myself, because I wanted them to die a gentle death. The night seemed like the best time for something like that. Even the moon peeked its head entirely from behind his pillow cloud. I told my grandfather I wanted to do this alone. He never asked why. If he had asked, I don't think I would have known the reason, other than it felt right. I felt happy the moon was there to witness my crime and comfort me at the same time. I did not want to get away with something like that without anyone knowing what I have done. None of the flowers opened that night. All of them pretended to still be in deep sleep. They looked so peaceful, almost relieved. I understood they are aware that I know they are only pretending, but we all play along. Both my mother and I knew I wasn't asleep when she came into my room to check in on me the night before we left. Yet, there wasn't any way to live through this last night other than to pretend. The only chance to survive was to keep my eyes closed while my mother placed her hand on my head. The pretending, too, was probably not enough. Sometimes I still ask myself what my mother did with all the dust my hair left in her hand from underneath the bed.

Sometimes I remember all the *Akšamčići* flowers filling up my pockets. They like it dark. I will keep plucking only until my pockets are full and there is no more space, I told myself. I can't stuff them too much, because I don't want their petals to break, I don't want them to hurt more than they already have to. I even wore an extra coat just to fit in more.

One row remained. I never changed into my pyjamas that night, but slept just like that, with all the dying flowers as close to me as they can be without squishing them. I lay down on my back.

I can sleep without moving. Ever since the beginning of the war, it happened all the time that I would wake up in exactly the same position as I fell asleep in. Before the war, it didn't happen even once. I guess the war teaches you it is best to not make any sounds. That night I made no sound at all, but I could hear the *Akšamčići* talking to each other as I drifted into sleep. I have no idea what they said, but their whispers lulled me into sleep almost instantly. The last time I fell asleep that quickly was before I knew something like the war existed.

Today, I sometimes still have trouble falling asleep when I remember the best sleep I had during the war was the night when the moon convicted me of a crime.

One of the flowers slept inside my closed palm. If I opened my hand at all during the night, I wouldn't know. I am not sure why, but the next morning, the flower that slept in my hand looked worse than all the others. I could sense it was dying even faster, something must have made it sad. I have been trying to revive it since, because I don't think I managed to give it a beautiful death. This is the one I sent you. When I see you, I have to remember to tell you that. I want to tell you everything about that night and everything about the next day and the day after that.

The next day my grandfather had already prepared everything for the big circle. That was the day the boy stretched out his arm as far as possible and drew the biggest circle he could, while the flowers that still remained outside slept.

All the marbles I flicked ended up in the grass, somewhere between the remaining *Akšamčići* flowers. The boy could see how sad I was, so he stayed beside me and placed his hand on my head instead of picking them up one by one as I miss, the way he usually would. It's okay that you missed, he said. I think the fog is making it hard to see. It's about to rain. Let's go inside and we will pick up the marbles tomorrow, he added.

Tomorrow the grenade fell into our circle, together with the rain.

I have to tell you all this, I repeat to myself over and over again as I hold tight the drainpipe between my hands. Many tiny little holes are covering it. They look like stars God decided to blow out. One big hole is hiding alongside the downwards flowing pipe. This one is big enough. Your favourite marble is smaller than this. It escaped. It escaped, I know it.

I pull some more to bring the hole in the rain pipe closer to my eye and make sure. The street I am walking on breaks some more. The final bloom. Everything comes to a standstill. I guess the shadow wants to see. I want to see, too, and look through the hole: Toi et Moi Café. I am here. I hope I am not late again.

THREE ☆ DAYS

One

Strange. I am already sitting at a table inside, but I don't remember walking in. I suppose the shadow must have opened the door. At least we both agreed on coming here. Thank goodness, because the shadow could have taken me anywhere else. It is comforting to know that the shadow can be gentle like that. I wonder what it is about this place that made the shadow be more careful than before.

The clock is one of those without any numbers on it at all, but as far as I can tell, it is exactly three o'clock. Good. I made it on time. The grenade made it on time, too. It was around three in the afternoon when the grenade fell, my grandfather told me, give or take. A few hundred lives that day. Maybe a thousand. Maybe more than that. Give or take. The news changed the number with every minute that passed.

The minute hand moves. I slept for way too many minutes that night when all the flowers in my pockets were trying to get used to dying. Usually, at least ever since the grownups outside started fighting so much, I would wake up early and walk over to my grandparents' house for breakfast. That day I slept so long, when I woke up, it was almost already dark again. You are lucky, my grandfather said. If you had come here, like you always do, who knows what would have happened then.

I don't have the heart to tell my grandfather that I left all the marbles outside. Maybe he knows, because he places his hand on my shoulder and tells me he is sorry my and the boy's circle is gone, that he is sorry he isn't able to build something for me strong enough to withstand all the ugly things falling from the sky.

I wish I could comfort him, but all I can think about is how I am going to tell the boy that all the marbles are gone. I know he won't be mad at me, but I don't want to make him sad. I am still trying to find a good way to let him know.

When I started hearing loud sounds in my dream, I should have known they were sneaking in from the outside. In my dream, marbles were falling instead of rain. I should have known then something is wrong with the sky. Maybe I just wanted to prolong finding out that the flowers I thought I managed to leave in the garden and save from death were not saved at all. They could have died a peaceful death if my pockets had been bigger. Ash from God's table slides down. The table is still slanted, because someone's coat is stuck underneath one of its legs. That is all that is left of them now and it is all my fault.

My grandparents' house tasted something like that. A lot more white little floating things filled up the sky that day when the loud sounds just would not stop. I guess a lot more houses fell apart, their walls turned into snow. It is true that the sun was shining much brighter that day than in a long time, but I don't think that is the reason there were more white things in the sky. Part of me thinks it was a little insensitive of the sun to come out at almost the exact same time as all the ugly and violent things falling from above. It was not a happy day, so it should have stayed away. I think I haven't liked the sun much since then. On the other hand, maybe it just turned the air inside out, God's pocket pulled out. Maybe the sun just wanted to help reveal better what the world really looks like now. All the rubble is falling out. Or maybe it thought with some more light, God will find what he is looking for and he will stop turning his pockets inside out.

I don't even know that I trust he is looking for anything in particular, but a lot more rubble is falling through the air now. I hope he stops going through his pockets soon, because it is getting hard to see from all the falling things. He is at least somewhat drunk after all. His mouth must be dry, because he is licking his lips. Mine is dry, too. More strange things are happening. Drops of water are falling on top of my head, the wallpaper in the café is pealing, exposing brick from my grandparents' house underneath. The grenade was just too strong. Pieces of concrete appear under my tongue. The more I chew, the more the wallpaper rolls down. Behind it, the day I arrived at my grandparents' house too late is revealing its sleepy head with hair so out of order, a sorrowful mess.

I remember very well the first time I saw the house that way. I walked over as slowly as I could and leaned my cheek on its open wound. My arms spread across the wall. If anyone had seen me, it would have looked like I was hugging it. Even though that sounds rather sweet, I was simply trying to cover it more than anything else. It must be cold with the brick revealed, I thought to myself, and remember the way I woke up the morning we left. My bedcovers were crumpled up on the floor and I had goosebumps all over my skin. I just didn't want the same thing to happen to the house.

There is nobody here, except me. I hope it stays like that and nobody shows up except you and maybe the boy. Besides, the wallpaper is continuing to roll down. I feel the walls are changing clothes and they need more privacy. Not everyone has the sensitivity to be gentle with intimate moments like that. I look around again, just to make sure I haven't missed you. Your pyjama tag is showing, my mother tells me as she comes in to wake me up. It is time for you to get up, she says. The taxi will be here soon. No, I am not going. I just got here and want to wait for you. I am not going to listen to them again and just leave. I missed the boy once and I won't miss him again. As I reach behind my head, I realize my shirt is inside out. I don't think you'll mind, because when we met, you told me you know what it is like to have to leave suddenly. I don't know if right now I am choosing to see only what I want to believe, but you saying this gives me another bit of hope you may be him.

I think I hear the door opening. My fingers play with the tag and tickle my neck. It feels pleasant this time, instead of like a harsh scratch, because the person at the door might be you. It might be you. The little hairs on my neck stand up curiously. It is just the outside man with the flashlight again. I thought by now he would have realized that he doesn't need this much light to talk to us. I guess I was wrong, because this time it is even stronger than before. It glides over my arm the way a hand would flatten a wrinkled bedsheet, only it is too late to hide the disarray. The light lands on my father's eyes again.

No one says anything at all, but somehow my father understands that he is now supposed to leave the car, too. The light floats across the car's ceiling in an arc. A wave of the man's hand confirming this is what he meant. Don't worry, my father says to me, I will be right back, a little fresh air will do me good. Inside my head I answer him that the outside air is not fresh and he should stay. I nod instead.

The sleeve of his coat brushes my cheek as my mother passes it over to him. It almost appears as if the coat tried to comfort me, but I guess coats are not as good at that as people believe. Now I am even more worried than before. My mother places her hand on my shoulder.

Would you like anything? I realize the hand is someone else's, but I am having trouble seeing. All I see is a silhouette as I look up. Maybe my eyes are still adjusting from the flashlight. It is just too bright in this café. I didn't quite realize I said that out loud, but I must have, because the silhouette tells me she is sorry she can't do anything about that, but she can bring me a coffee. No, that's okay. I am waiting for someone. I will wait. I answer to my father, but I think I said that too late, because the door is already closed.

A few seconds later the light in the car dims. I notice my father's seat belt is stuck between the door. What are we going to do now with all the outside air getting in? The door is opening again. Maybe this time it is you. Either the silhouette did something about the light after all, or outside it is getting darker, because it is much dimmer now. I still see only silhouettes. This person walking in can't be you. It must be a child from what I see. The child is holding an opened umbrella above its head. The umbrella looks like yours did on the day we parted and when it turned into a giant chalice. Its arms are facing upwards towards the sky. The strange thing about it is that I don't really find this all that strange. I know it is not raining outside and I know there is no wind. I think the child just knows. It knows. From the way it walks past me, I get the sense the child knows everything. Another drop falls onto my head.

I just wish the wallpaper wasn't pealing so fast. It would have been nice to see what kind of café you picked for us to meet in. I think I manage to spot a little terrace outside the window. Little lights line the top of the wooden fence, some flower pots hold on to the edge, but I can't see what kind. Judging by the outside space, the place looks a little rough around the edges with a special charm. Something like one of those sweaters worn for so long, it looks so frumpy by now that someone who didn't know may think it was older than the world. Still, it looks better than all the other clothes. Probably exactly because of that.

In a way, it even looks a little bit like my old pyjamas worn inside out. The seams are showing the edges of the fabric. The sides of the wooden tables are somewhat chipping off. I like you more already because you picked a place like this. As you know, I think it is okay to sometimes pretend, but not when it comes to pretending that outside, everything is okay. The inside of this café reminds me of that. If only I could find a way somehow to stop pealing the wallpaper. I think this place must be so cozy, being here would feel something like putting on pyjamas from the night before, ready to continue where one left off. They would still feel familiar and warm.

At least for a moment I do feel that way, because the light dims some more. I enter the dark before my head peeks through, my arms journey through the sleeves, my fingers come out on the other side. The tips of my hair are still held inside the pyjama top by the collar and I keep it that way. I like to feel the slight pull on my hair, a subtle pain, sometimes when I turn my head while asleep. Mostly I like it because it wakes me up every time. Then I get to experience the feeling of being in my warm pyjamas in my bed all over again, yet while not fully awake.

In between waking life and sleep, sometimes I manage to see better what is really going on, but I always forget. All I manage to remember is a sense of peace. At least it reminds me that something like peace may still exist.

How silly that Snoopy enters my mind now. I imagine him outside on the patio with you. He is telling you everything about my life that you want to know. Embarrassing to admit, but he knows how to tell you these things in a much more accurate way than me. He would tell you everything exactly as it is and in the simplest of ways instead of through part imagination and part overlapping memories. He may be a bit crude and without tact, but you would forgive him for that. He would also ask you about you. He would do all that while snacking on the flowers inside the pots, so it would be difficult for you to take him seriously. You would take him seriously anyway. I know, because I see the two of you out there right now and neither of you is smiling.

I admit the windows in this café are foggy, so I can't be sure of what I see, and I admit someone is placing all the chairs on top of the tables. It seems that the patio is being prepared for closing. It's okay. Snoopy will still stay. He told me in my sleep yesterday while the marbles were falling around me that he thinks I should know more about you, but he thinks I may have forgotten how. I think at least that is what he said. The marbles were very loud. All the chairs are up. I think the outside is closed now.

I think everything outside has gone so bad, I am just going to close the entire outside down, I tell my mother the moment the light on the ceiling of the car goes out a few seconds after my father closes the door. I think the seat belt is stuck, the door is not fully closed. I guess it is closed enough for the light to go out. Before it leaves, it waits for a bit just to give some time to adjust to the new life. I guess it thinks a few seconds is enough.

See this switch, I tell my mother while holding the string on my grandfather's lamp. There is no light bulb here right now. The way it works when the socket is empty is that if I pull on the switch, the entire world outside will go out. When I pull on it again, everything will be reset. That was my last-resort plan if things started going wrong. It is a little bit dangerous, because you never know if all the people will still be here after that. Some people, once they are gone, never come back. Now the very uniformed man ruined my plan. Now my father is outside with all the outside people and I am just too afraid to pull on the switch like that, while he is together with them. He may disappear and I may never see him again.

With only the two of us left in the car, it is almost calm. All the little falling white things along with all the sounds are gone. It is almost too quiet, so I spin the lampshade just to hear something. If the Earth could just spin with it as quickly, maybe then the war outside will just have passed the next time I look out the window. A few years could just go by in a few seconds and everything will just be over.

My mother places her finger on top of the lampshade. I guess the world won't spin faster, after all. I guess the war will go on just as before. Hold on, my mother tells me, try not to play with the lamp. It is too loud and I want to try and hear what they are saying outside. I understand why she would want to do that, but I wish she would have just let the lampshade spin anyway. Maybe there was a slight chance the world would have changed its pace.

I think something happened when my mother stopped the lampshade or probably even earlier, I just didn't notice until it was completely silent. The clock in the car is blinking now and showing all zeros. I feel a little bit worried, because how am I going to know how long they have all been gone for. I think something is wrong, I tell my mother. The clock is confused and doesn't know what time it is. It needs some help. If I push some of the buttons beside it, maybe something will change. I stretch forward and push one.

A loud rustling whirls around my head much like the time I tried to talk to the moon after the grenade fell into the circle the boy drew, but it didn't work. I asked the moon if it could stay a little bit longer with me that night, but instead it went to sleep behind a cloud that covered the entire sky. I think maybe it was selfish of me to ask. I guess the moon is sometimes sad, too, and needs to be alone first after seeing something as horrible as that.

That night the moon sighed so much, its breath combed through all the branches, until it found the one with the boy's plastic bag hanging onto it. The moon shook that one the most. I think it wondered the same thing I did, why isn't the plastic bag with the boy. I don't know if it heard any answer. I just know it became as loud as it is now.

Two

The plastic bag rustles again. This time through my phone. I must have pushed on it, because you are on the line. I have no idea who called, you or I, but all I hear is the branch shaking. Your words are getting trapped in the hollow of the empty bag. Hello. Hello. It looks like they prefer to stay inside. The crackling is only getting louder with something like a whoosh every once in a while. Water filling the canister. The whoosh of the water is loud. The pressure high. The faucet is turned all the way. There is no time. The sound of a fired mortar shell. They make no sound while they fly. They like to surprise. The sound comes at the end and at the beginning. In between, silence. In between the borders: our car. A car passes the other way. Away from the uniformed men. The whoosh of a balloon untied. Unlike the mortar shell, it whistles during the entire flight. It flies with its back towards the world, a final beautiful spiral before it bows one last time to humanity and says goodbye. Hello. I can't hear you still. The balloon lies wrinkled on the floor and won't get up. More rustling echoes through the phone. More whooshing balloons. The bird you told me about that you saw at Russell Square could be here, too. I think it is the same one that sat on my window ledge and looked over at the lavender fields as if they were still there. Sometimes I feel I am doing the same. The sound it makes is not the same as before, because it is just a little injured now. The crackles in the phone are loud. Another whistle. If it is the whistle of the mortar shell, it has already hit the ground. The mortar shell itself travels faster than its sound. Sound covers its blushing cheeks trying to come to terms with its guilty conscience. It is just too slow to warn. By the time it comes, the future has already long arrived. A water canister pops, returns back the strange air. Red feathers are falling from the ceiling of the café with lavender ash inside.

All these feathers are getting caught inside my hair. I am trying to get them out, but I can't, they are falling too fast. I am only making things worse now by flipping my hair upside down, trying to get them out. Lavender ash is falling into my ear. It is getting even harder now to hear.

I manage to pull one feather away from near my earlobe. I must have simultaneously pulled on my father's seat belt stuck inside the door. My pulling on it cracks open the door. Voices mix together with the rustling. I still can't hear your voice coming through the phone. The outside border air fills up the car. The rustling of the balloon is getting louder as the outside uniformed man talks to my father. He is waving his arms a lot every time he speaks. I think he is making the balloon he is holding tired by doing that. I wish he would stop. Maybe he knows this way it is harder for anyone to hear what he is saying. This way if he says something wrong or something that could hurt him some day, he can claim he never said anything like that at all.

I think the balloon noticed I am listening, because it is trying to move as quietly as possible. What happened to your eyes? The man with the balloon asks my father and waves his hand at my father's passport photograph. The phone crackles. Are you there? I am a little bit afraid of this sound now. The balloon is a little bit afraid, too. It can't hold in the noise it makes. I don't think your eyes are the same colour anymore, the man says to my father. In the photograph they are clearly blue and now, when I look at you, they are brown, the man says, and waves his hand again. I hope my father can think of something to answer to the man. I feel bad. I should have prepared my father more. How could I have forgotten to tell him what to say. There are so many answers I can think of to give to the uniformed man. Maybe my father will remember. Maybe he will remember I told him I am sad, because outside all the rivers are turning brown. On some days, even the one in the boy's favourite marble changed. Everything is different now.

He will think of it. He will, I know. I see him move his lips, but I can't hear a single sound at all. The uniformed man is waving his arms even more now. I can't hear my father, but I can hear the balloon. It looks upset that it can't stop the man's waving hand continuing to point at the passport photo. The hand taps and taps and taps until I hear nothing at all. I was afraid before. I am terrified now.

On the phone: a sudden silence, too. The silence stretches in the in between space between throw and land. The launch has already happened. I don't know how much time we have until we reach the ground. If we reach the ground before the silence comes to an end, it will be too late. Maybe I can break it off somewhere mid-air. Hello. It goes on some more. No sound comes out of the phone. My father's lips are moving. Silence. This stretchable silence.

I push the car door open some more in the hopes I will be able to hear. The uniformed man turns his head towards the car. Our phone line breaks. Oh no. You are still here. You are still here, I know. And so is the boy. I think I just made the silence expand even further. The uniformed man says something to me, but all I hear in my ear is water. The canister is overflowing. The person waited for too long. I guess the person missed the first sound. Where are all the other people, who were walking to the water across the metal framework bridge, with canisters in their hands. I hope some of them didn't wait. Where is the boy?

I don't know how long I have been waiting here for you, but my phone battery is dead. All these sounds are making me afraid. I think when I see you, I will just ask you if you are the boy. After all, sometimes I feel I don't have much time left. The worst that could happen is that I scare you away and you disappear. Time is already disappearing. The clock in the café says it is still three. This cannot be. I must have been here for quite some time, because the day is about to leave to make room for the night. They touch shoulders briefly at the door. The outside is putting on its deep blue coat. It is just about to pull the coat belt through the first loop. Three o'clock has long passed. I can't tell if I am living in delay or too fast. I guess this is what happens when the present goes missing. I wish someone would find it and send it back to me. I don't know if you were already here, but the moment for us to meet in this café is long gone. All the walls of this café have turned into the brick walls of my grandparents' house that were exposed the day the grenade fell. More drops are falling from the ceiling now. They are accelerating as quickly as the uniformed man's taps against my father's photograph.

I wish everything would stop, but I know it won't. I know the drops will continue to speed up, because the roof is leaking. The problem is getting too large to fix. It is more than just that one loose tile. The entire drainpipe is missing now. I didn't mean to rip it out on my way here, but now it is too late. It is still in my hand while I wait. I think I should get out. Water stains are appearing around the chandelier. Little water pillows have formed throughout. Not too many more taps and the entire ceiling will collapse. I just know by the sound. The uniformed man taps again. The balloon around his wrist tells me I should no longer wait.

I know I should go, but what if my grandparents are still inside. I need to tell them what I have done and that now, because of me, it is also dangerous inside. I need to tell them to leave the house before the roof falls down. I look around, but they are nowhere to be seen.

Instead, more silhouette children are coming in. I don't know how to leave them here alone. They look like they are prepared, because they are all walking in with umbrellas turned, ready to collect the rain. I don't know if they are doing this, because they know what is about to happen and are here to help. Or maybe they need the rain for something else. They must have heard me that time when I said I need more rain to help push down the boy's favourite marble from the drainpipe. I don't know how to tell them now that the marble is not there. They probably know. They probably also want me to go.

I guess I should, because outside, the day is pulling its belt through the next loop on the coat. Another, deeper blue knocks on the windows of this café. The day is getting ready to depart. I should leave before the night gets here, before the outside pulls tight on the coat's belt and I can no longer escape or try and let you now that I came. If I leave now and gently knock on your door, maybe you won't be asleep yet. I hope you won't ask me to explain.

The moment I get up, the door slams shut. It looks like the uniformed man really does not want me to know what is going on. I try to open the café's door, but I can't. The uniformed man can't stop me from escaping and going back to the boy. He also can't stop me from leaving the café, from letting you know I came. I won't let him. I roll down the window a little bit, the one on the other side that he can't see. He will never notice I did this, just like he will never be able to see what all exists on the other side of the moon. I hear more tapping. My mother is tapping on the car's window to let me know that's enough now, it would be too risky to roll down the window more.

Someone is tapping against the glass of the café's entrance door. What is the stray dog doing here? How did he find me? I have no idea, but he came at the right time, because it is starting to pour inside. He will know how to take me to where you are. After all, he knows everything. I lift my hand to say hello to him and pull on the door. All the rain and the lack of air are making the windows fog up. I pull on the door handle again, but nothing happens. The stray dog lifts his front two paws up trying to help. Maybe I need to push instead, I don't remember. I lean my forehead on the door and push as hard as I can. The car seat moves forward, but the door is stuck. Now that I am closer, I can see the stray dog is also just a silhouette. I don't know why everything is appearing that way here, but I am certain it is him.

My breath is fogging up the door even more now. I don't see anything outside except the stray dog's nose leaning against the other side of the door. He sticks out his tongue and licks the glass. The fog is still here. He tries again. Nothing is going away. It can't, because the fog has formed on the inside. By now the stray dog knows, yet he licks the glass again. Maybe this time he just wanted to comfort me, because I can feel his tongue on my forehead.

Something wet slides across my eyelids and over my forehead. I recognize this smell. It smells like wet earth, mixed with the drops dripping down from my upside-down sleeves, fresh laundry detergent added to the dark rain. I remember the stray dog drinking from the puddle underneath my favourite sweater. He is waking me up now. The air outside is much more blue than the black that was around me when I first left the bench. Oh no. How long have I been sleeping for? Have I missed the boy? The last thing I remember is waiting for him on our bench.

The stray dog licks my eyelids again. I remember now. He didn't come. I remember the candle man and the sparrows. I remember the boy's letter that was crumpled into pieces and washed away by the washing machine. I remember trying to piece it together. I remember the stray dog scratching my knee. I think, after that, he was pulling on my sleeve. I think, before that, I should have known he was telling me to get up and follow him. I remember running after him. I couldn't keep up. I remember the boy's plastic bag rustling and all my shadows multiplying. Maybe I was already tired then. Maybe life would have turned out differently if I had listened to the stray dog sooner. I remember he was just too fast. I couldn't keep up. I remember the outside being black. I remember a uniformed man with a helium balloon around his wrist. I don't know where he came from, because at that point, I hadn't lived this yet. I didn't know then that soon after the boy didn't come, my parents would decide to leave. Yet, it still all came to me before it happened: the border, the shot, the escaping bird. It must be just a dream. It must be.

His paw is touching my stomach gently almost as if to check if I am still breathing properly. His ear twitches as I breathe out. When I breathe in again, I realize I have fallen asleep on the boy's street. I recognize it by all the waves in the asphalt. The trees' roots are pushing it up. It was like this long before the war, too. Maybe the trees sensed what was going to happen and they tried to leave before the beginning. One of the asphalt waves is below my head. I guess I must have used it as a pillow. With my eyes so close to the street, I can see there are a lot more cracks in the waves now than there were before.

I remember being on the bike with the boy almost every day. We were riding over the frozen waves on the street. It felt great to sit above the back tire holding on to the seat while the boy navigated the waves. We were on our way to my grandparents' house to play the marble game. All of the marbles were inside the plastic bag hanging around one of the bike's handles. Listen, the boy said. Every time we ride over a wave, the marbles talk to us. They tell us all the secrets the grownups have forgotten they know. I know we won't forget.

I need to get to him now, so we can ride over to my grandparents' house. I know there will be silence now.

Something soft and warm pushes against my forehead. I haven't felt a tender nudge like that for a while. The stray dog is helping me get up. The car seat squeaks as it gets pushed even closer to the steering wheel. A rotation happens in the sky as I lift my head up. Familiarity. Or something a little less than that. I recognize the windows on the buildings lining the street. They seem happy to see me. All the curtains are waving at me. I am sure it is not all about me, there must be another reason for their subtle gesturing, because there is no wind. Still. Something on the boy's street isn't the way it used to be when I was here last. Too many windows are open. Too many curtains are outside.

Behind them, a quiet darkness sends its signature to the unknown. Maybe everyone is only still sleeping. It is still early after all. I must be still somewhat asleep myself, because the asphalt waves are moving. While I balance, it comes to me that my parents must be very worried. After all, last night I didn't come home. When I explain what happened, they will understand. I can't go home without the boy. I have to walk to his apartment and get him. Standing up without feeling slightly tipsy is somewhat difficult for me. I think it will help if I stand only on top of the waves, instead of in between. If there is any movement, I will notice much less of it. Thank goodness in school we had a lot of practice balancing. Our teacher said it will come in handy if we ever have to walk inside shelled buildings or if we have to escape from strange places. She forgot to mention walking over skeleton bridges. The exercises would help with that, too.

I never had to walk on any myself, but this seems just as hard. It never seemed so hard when the boy was with me. Soon I will see him. Soon I will see him. All I have to do is keep walking without falling.

It helps that the stray dog is not walking as fast anymore. I think he knows if he speeds up, I won't be able to make it. He is letting me set the pace this time. I step over to the next wave. This wave is bigger. I guess this tree is older and wiser. Its roots are pushing up the asphalt even more, having learned from experience, not from history. This one carries me over to the next building. A few more are left to walk past before we reach the one where the boy lives. His is the last one on the street. These kinds are the best kind, the boy said. They help you see what lies beyond the end. Right now I am having trouble seeing much beyond the next wave.

My eyes are still tired. I close them again, just for a little bit. It will be okay, because I think if I stand still, the asphalt wave will carry me at least to the next building. And with the stray dog here with me, I feel safe enough to do that. He won't let anything happen to me.

My eyelids are falling down over my pupils, but it is still not getting any darker. I think my eyelids have become worn out. I guess they were not designed to be opened and closed that often. I know when the marbles were falling inside my dream, my eyelids were fluttering heavily. Ever since then, I think they have become more and more see-through. I am afraid if it goes on like this, closing them won't help keep the outside away from me. Right now I am not even sure anymore whose street I am walking on, yours or the boy's. Maybe I am walking on both.

The deep blue wasn't like this before the war. It didn't have the habit of staying very long. It came unnoticeably after the night and departed shortly before the day or the other way around. Keeping its distance, it always left without saying goodbye. Now the deep blue is one of the regulars, who does not want to go home. It is still here on the other side of my eyelids, the wheels of the suitcases are rolling.

My eyes roll up as the eyelids lift. The deep blue sky is still here, but the familiar buildings I recognize on the way to the boy's home are gone.

Buildings I don't recognize are observing me. It looks like I am back on your street. I think the streets are overlapping. Maybe this means the boy is here. I don't know, but on your street, all the windows are closed. Their elongate, narrow physique gives them a somewhat suspicious look. It is not surprising. After all, I am just a stranger walking by. The many steep stairs outside give away that I am getting closer to your apartment. I feel guilty that I left all of those silhouette children alone in the café. Who opened the door café door anyway? How did I get out? None of my shadows are here with me, so likely it was me.

It is not too late. The night is not here yet. It is not too late. You might still be awake. I am not sure what to make of the way the buildings here are looking at me. Maybe they don't want me here. But I can't go. I have to keep looking for the boy.

The stray dog is gone. At least the waves are still underneath my feet, so I won't get lost. If I follow the cracked open street, I should end up a few buildings away from your apartment. You were right when you said I would like the fact that your street is broken. After all, it looks just like the one leading to the boy's home. Only a street like this could make me stay. I have to be careful though. The cracked open holes are expanding. Your street is in full bloom. If I am not careful enough, I could fall through. There is no red resin yet filled into the holes, like there is back at home.

I imagine myself pouring in the red resin. It might be too dangerous to leave the street opened up like this. I am not sure that most people who live here know how to balance this close to an abyss. I don't even think I know how to, either, despite all the training at school. The holes are just too big. I pour in the red as I walk. A chain of roses is forming behind me. Their scattered petals reveal a gentle sorrow behind unrealized beauty. A rose with only one petal appears next in the chain. Alive. Not alive. Alive. Not alive. When the war began, some people started counting like that, instead of wondering about love. I think it all comes down to the same. As for me, I don't remember anymore which one I am at. I make sure to step over the petal while the resin is still freshly in its fluid state. The wind will dry it fast. Its disrupted beauty will be permanent then. Its sorrow memorized. In a hundred years, a stranger will accidentally turn into your street and know nothing about it until one of the petals sticks to the shoe.

I must be getting even closer to your apartment. Lavender pieces are floating through the air almost playfully. They must be coming from your balcony. I could smell the same lavender scent when I was on my way to the boy's apartment after the stray dog woke me up. Something is on fire. Something is on fire, I thought while I walked on. Come to think of it, maybe the rustling on the phone came from some of the lavender burning. Some of the pieces could have landed on your phone, together with the boy's torn-up letter. Maybe you are trying to put it back together. The more lavender I smell, the faster I am walking. I need to get to you fast. I need to find out if the boy is alive.

I also simply want to tell you that I like the apartment beside yours. It is dark and hidden enough for my taste. All the water canisters behind the door make me feel prepared for what is soon coming. It is already starting. The wave beneath my feet grows. This can't be good. There is too much water. I think the ceiling in the café has collapsed. There is too much rain seeping through the roof of my grandparents' house. Regardless of how hard the silhouette children try to catch it with their umbrellas, they can't. Only marbles are falling in. I hear them spin inside the umbrellas. Faster and faster. I feel myself, once again, moving forward slower and slower, yet somehow I am already at your front gate.

Three

One rotation after the other. I don't think that there is any end to this. The marbles are looping inside the umbrellas with sounds that are scratching God's emptied pockets. The stray dog is scratching at the boy's apartment building's entrance door. I push open your front gate. The boy is here. The boy is here, I think to myself. Usually I ring the buzzer to the right of the apartment door and the boy lets me in. First I have to live through an ugly screeching sound, but then the door opens. Your front gate pushes aside some fallen branches. Now that there is a war, the ugliness of the sound is even more pronounced. It didn't take very long to realize that war makes ugly things uglier and beautiful things more beautiful. It took a bit longer to realize that pain became an element of both.

I am happy at the thought I may see you soon. My hand reaches for the buzzer on the side of the boy's building door without looking. Nothing is there, except a barely standing wall. Rubble is crackling beneath my shoes. I guess I couldn't hear it, because of all the spinning marbles. The stray dog continues to scratch with the same speed as the marbles spin. He has to open the door. I know the boy is there. I hope it is okay that I am coming to see you at this time. I don't know if it is too late or too early. I think it is still the early morning. The boy must be sleeping. But it's okay, he won't mind if I wake him. He made me laugh the other day when he said he couldn't imagine a more beautiful way to wake up than to the ugly sound of the buzzer if it is me. I don't know how he remained so sweet, despite everything.

A flake of ash falls into my hair. I lift my head to see where it came from, your balcony or the rubble from the boy's building. Between the branches I can see the boy's bedroom window is open. He must be there. Ever since I have known him, he never liked to leave his window open if he is away. This was even before the war. This was a preference entirely of his own. A rare occurrence. I don't think there was any reason for it at all. Sometimes it is nice to have none, he said.

Another flake falls into my hair. This time it is lavender. Behind the lavender strands on your balcony, a light has just turned on. I am glad, because the boy's building seems darker than it was before. The hallway light inside seems to be off. With your light on, I will see him, I know. The car is not completely dark anymore. No one will tell me what to do, especially not the uniformed man, who closed the door. I am not afraid of him. The car door squeaks a little bit. Maybe I pushed it open just a little bit too much, but it doesn't look like he noticed anything. I am going to find him. I won't let the grownups tell me where to stay and where to go.

Maybe you noticed I am here and that is why you turned on the light. The light in the car is a little bit dimmer than usual. I think it is because your curtain is covering it. Could be just the shade dark enough to hide from the outside man. He won't know now that I have opened the door. If I opened your front gate too loudly, I hope none of your neighbours were sleeping. I wouldn't want them to be mad at me. I wouldn't want you to be mad at me, either. The sky is not fully black yet. There is still some blue left. But maybe that is not enough. Maybe it is too late. Maybe it is better I leave you a note, so that you know I was here. I don't think I have a paper or pen. All I have is the piece of paper I found inside my pocket when I woke up at the hotel Chateau Versailles. Back then, I didn't remember yet that the time and place on the paper is the same one I wrote on the boy's shoelace. Back then I didn't know yet that I would be standing here in front of your door, hoping you are the boy. I could slide the piece of paper under your door without having written anything at all. Maybe silence would say more, anyway. Maybe you would remember the shoelace was yours. I don't know if these are just my wishful thoughts. I guess I could ask Snoopy the next time I see him. I feel like folding the paper into an airplane and throwing it by your window. I just don't want you to think it is meant as a goodbye, so I decide to only look up.

I look up to see if you are standing anywhere near your window. Rubble from the boy's window falls into my eye as I lift my head to see if you are there. The stray dog has managed to open the entrance door of the boy's building. I am somewhat surprised, but prepared, when I see the state of the hallway stairs. Every few, a step is missing. I can do it. The boy lives only on the second floor, after all.

I can sense the stray dog wants me to go first. He has been that way ever since he found me sleeping on the boy's street after I spent the night running after him. It seems very important to the stay dog that this time I go at my own speed. It was not like that the last time, the time when he was trying to drag me off the bench in a haste.

I step very quietly onto the first stair. My toes are the only part receiving any pressure. As I climb a bit further up, I can see a helium balloon through your window curtain. You nudge it with your hand and simply watch what it does. I can't see much, because your back is turned towards the window. I wish I could see the lines on your neck, but you are too far away. Maybe you prepared the balloon for us to go together to the moon.

I think my walking up is careful enough. Nobody will know I am here. The steps are shaky. I manage one more. I better hold on to the railing. My hand scoops through the empty air as I realize the railing is not there. How can it just be gone? This can't be. The boy and I used to slide down on our stomachs, folding over it softly. Sometimes the railing would push down the button on my pants. Later, there would be a circle left on my stomach. Later, the boy grew and became too tall for that. He started sliding down sitting on top of the railing instead.

Eventually he knew how to slide down with his arms up in the air. He would stretch them out in exactly the right position. I liked to run down the stairs as quickly as I can beside him, while he did that. He always arrived at the bottom floor first. Even though it was meant as a race, he knew just what to say, since he couldn't slow down and let me get there before him. It is better this way, he said. A gentleman should always arrive first. I might be old fashioned that way, he added, but I would never let you wait for me.

I manage to climb up one more step even though I am still shaky. I am finding it very difficult to keep my balance with everything around me crumbling. Almost there. Almost there. At least now I can see the boy's door. What is his photograph doing there? This is not making any sense at all. More marbles are falling inside my head and into the umbrellas. Part of the stair I am stepping on falls away. My left hand reaches for the railing again. My right hand stretches out, touches the wall. Something is written underneath the photograph, but I am too far to see. Just one more step. One more and I will see the boy. I think I am getting closer to your door.

My knees are hurting again. I need to climb up. The stairs are steep and trembling. I can do it. My leg lifts. Mid-air. More marbles. I should have listened to the boy when he said I am big enough now and I can also start sliding down the railing the way he does. He called it the Swerving Plane. If I had, I would know how to fly now. My arms would know where to go. I would know how to move them, because the boy and I saw each other every day. I would have been a plane already so many times by now.

The stray dog barks and he rarely does, but he barks now. Just once. He is trying to tell me something, but I have no strength to decipher what, because I am having more and more trouble staying afloat. I don't know why I didn't listen to the boy. If I had, I would have been a lot more prepared to save myself if I fall. I shouldn't have been so afraid back then. My arms are not doing what they should; the wings are failing. More pressure in the knee. I am pushing on the stair too strongly. It is beginning to crumble even more now. Oh no. More of the stair dissolves onto the stray dog's back. He is standing underneath the stairs, looking up at me with concern. More and more lines are forming on his neck as I try to climb farther up. More and more rubble is falling into his hair.

I am afraid again. I am losing control. It feels like the entire staircase is about to fall apart. I try to hold on to the wall underneath my right hand. Futile attempt. My arm has flown too far away to reach it properly. One of my nails scratches it and breaks. The stair below the one I am standing on cracks, too. And the next. And the next. The stray dog is not barking anymore, but I can hear his paws sliding, tapping frantically around the floor. He is going back and forth trying to predict where I will fall. I think he is hoping I will fall on his back. The fall will be softer then. God's table slants more, now that God is bending down. I don't know why he is doing that. His shoulder is lifting it up unintentionally. Maybe he is leaning in closer to the person in his company. Maybe God can't hear so well anymore, either, after all these loud sounds. He must be leaning in. I think this time, he wants to make sure he hears what the person is trying to tell him. Maybe this time he doesn't want to miss anything. He leans some more. His drink is sliding down. The glass breaks. Left over ice cubes slide across the floor. My stair is too slippery. The entire table tips. It should be loud, but I hear no sound. The sound of the table hitting the floor never arrives. I am falling through the air now. I guess all the stairs leading to the boy's apartment are turning into rubble. Any time now I should feel the impact of hitting the ground. My left arm tries one more time to grab onto something, but my fingers fold around nothing. Something rings in my ear. It sounds like a doorbell. I can't hear the stray dog anymore, because the ringing is too loud. Any time now the fall should be over. I feel the air against my skin. The little hairs on my arms lift up. The boy's hair lifts up, too, as he reaches the end of the railing, jumps up, his feet hit the ground.

The ground never arrives for me. Darkness gets here instead. Only black is in the bar God is sitting in now. It looks like the electricity is out. Maybe an ice cube slid out far enough to cause a short circuit. Maybe a wire somewhere was loose.

God's hair has fallen across his face. He is still bending down. The ringing is still in my ear, but I am no longer falling. Where am I? It is completely dark here. I have to get to the boy. Where did the stray dog go? How come I am sitting down on the ground, yet none of my body is hurting? Why is it so dark? One of my arms is still up in the air, the other firmly on the ground. I think I have no idea how to turn myself into a plane, like the boy. It is futile now to try, so I let my other arm slide down. The moment my fingers glide over the wall, the ringing stops. If I rub my eyes, maybe they will adjust faster to this complete dark. As I brush my fingertips over my eyelids, I realize I must have just pressed someone's doorbell. Did I make it up the stairs after all? The bell sounds nothing like the boy's. Maybe his parents changed it.

It looks a lot different up here than it used to. Complete black still surrounds me, but I see a streetlight flicker. Wait a minute, I think I recognize the park now. I am in front of your door and outside it is completely dark. It looks like it is your doorbell I pressed. Yet, I am still hoping the person opening the door will be the boy. No one is coming down. Maybe it is just a little bit too late. The more I look at the streetlight, the more tired I get. I lean on the wall beside your door. My shoulder is touching the exposed brick, rubble rolls to my elbow. I am so tired, my legs are giving in. I slide down, too, until I am sitting down. The streetlight is glaring into my eyes. I should look away, but I don't. Instead, I wait for it to flicker, while I lean on your door with my back.

I can feel my knees now. I know the stairs to the boy's apartment have collapsed, but I need to go up somehow. I stretch my legs just to see how it feels. They stretch all the way underneath the car seat. My magic slippers are here. With them on my feet, I can do anything. I stretch again, but I can't even get up. I don't think my legs are working anymore. If I stretch my arm out again, maybe this time I will have done it the proper way. The boy always said I can do anything. I just need to try often enough. Your bell rings one more time. I am sorry if the black is too black. I am sorry if it is really late. Maybe you are already in your pyjamas getting ready for bed. I am sorry, but I can't move and my arm can't go any other way. I didn't mean to push your bell again.

Something is happening. I hear steps above my head. Your hardwood floor squeaks. Maybe you are coming down. Maybe you heard the stairs collapse and are coming out to see if I am okay. The rubble in my hand makes me think this was a mortar shell. The grain of the brick spreads around in my hand. I know with his special hearing, the boy escaped. I know he did. I still feel he is here. Maybe he came back to his building, because he knew I would be looking for him. I hear steps moving again. Maybe the boy is moving down the hallway. Something squeaks.

The uniformed man's shoes are squeaking, too. He is walking closer to the car now. The door is opening. Madam, he says to my mother, I don't think your husband has the correct coloured eyes. The balloon around his wrist beats against the car window.

My elbow knocks on your door as my arm slides down. Another unsuccessful attempt at getting up. The darkness around me is getting even darker. My eyes are having trouble adjusting. Your steps are getting quieter. Even though I did not even mean to ring, I wonder why you are not opening. Maybe you are mad at me that I am late.

I look at my watch just to see what time it is. I turn my wrist somewhat automatically, like from a distant memory. It occurs to me that all this time, I even forgot I had a watch. When I left this morning, I don't recall having one at all.

What. How can this be possible? My watch says it is April 5. April 5, 1992 marks the beginning of the Sarajevo Siege. It was August just this afternoon at the café where we were supposed to meet. Am I really half a year late? Wait. What year is it now? How can I possibly forget something like that? I look at the watch again to check the year, but it doesn't say. I guess everyone is supposed to just remember. I am scared.

There is just so much rubble in my hands. There is just so much rubble everywhere. It is falling onto the already thick borders, making them even harder to cross. Through your door I hear your steps. You are moving away. The uniformed man and my mother are walking away, too. I am completely alone now. Oh wait. The balloon's string is tangled around the car seat's headrest and leads outside. I guess it tangled itself and then got stuck between the car door. I don't know if the uniformed man left it on purpose or if he accidentally lost it. Or maybe my mother convinced him somehow to give it to me before they left the car. I think she didn't want me to be alone and she knows how much I like balloons.

With fewer and fewer people here, the inside of the car feels like there is barely any space here at all. With my mother gone, I can see the door on the other side of the car. It feels much closer now than before when I couldn't see it properly. There is no light in this car anymore. It is so dark here, I can't see anything. I want to see where the uniformed man is taking my parents, but all I see is the streetlight underneath your window.

The bench where I used to wait for the boy appears beside the streetlight. I don't know how it got here, but maybe that means he will finally come. Maybe you will walk down your stairs and open the door. Maybe you will come out with your arm bent, ready for mine to slide through and lean. I could do that as lightly as the string of a helium balloon swings. You would walk me to the bench and say: I am sorry I wasn't there. The moon would spin an entire circle around itself in the time it takes us to sit down, to make up for lost time.

This is the first time I lift my arm with the intention to ring your bell. I don't want to bother you too much, but I want to tell you how excited I am about the bench that appeared beside your apartment. If you are too sleepy, it's okay. We don't have to go to the bench now. Maybe you can only come down to tell me which year it is, so that I know which way I have to turn to go back home.

I push your bell in. The ashtray in the car flips. Now it is even harder to breathe. This time I hear nothing. There are no steps coming from your apartment. I don't see anyone through the car window anymore. They have walked too far for me to hear anything. The smoky air is making me tired. I don't even think I heard your bell ring this time. Maybe it made no sound. Maybe I was just trying too hard to hear what is going on outside of the car.

The silence around me is making it even harder for me to stay awake. I don't want to fall asleep here. There are too many broken bricks around me. Besides, maybe you are also ready for sleep. I feel a little bit bad about ringing your doorbell. I hope you'll forgive me if you are mad. I am just so sleepy. It is getting darker again. I hope even though I didn't manage to walk up the broken stairs to his floor, the boy will still know I am here. But I don't know, because it is just so dark where I am.

I lift my arm to turn on the light switch in the car. Nothing happens. It is still dark. The balloon is knocking harder at the door. I pull on the balloon's string. The car door opens. The ash from God's table is scattered all around. I think some of the lavender from your balcony is mixed in. I think this is a good time to get out of the car. Maybe they won't see that I left.

The balloon just looks so sad. I want to bring it across the border, then let it go. I will be back. I will be back. We are just going for a little walk. Besides, I have my magic house shoes on, nothing can happen to us.

The car door makes a quieter sound this time. My gentle push is still not gentle enough to make you come down the stairs. If you come down, maybe we can drive across the border together, instead of me deciding to walk. Maybe the stray dog is telling me to drive the car myself and this is why he pushed the driver's seat closer in. I can reach all the pedals now, but I don't think I want to take the car, unless the boy is in the car with me. I would rather step outside into the air that secretly lets me know I am running out of time. I can no longer wait.

Moving is still difficult, if not impossible. I am still in front of your door, because my knees just won't bend. The chalk-line around me is turning into a giant wall closing me in. Hundreds of men in the uniform clothes are behind it. I don't know how they all fit in front of your door, but they are here. All of them are holding deflated balloons. Maybe if I think of the little bird you told me about, they will go away. Red feathers begin to fall instead. The marbles are spinning inside the umbrellas. I turn my hand just to forget that I am unable to move. The balloon string wraps around my wrist. I am glad the balloon is with me now, both for the balloon and for me. I know I will take care of it better than the uniformed man. Besides, I think this is the one that will help me leave, the one that showed up at the right time.

One house shoe is touching the street now. The other follows. I have left the car now. I will be so quiet, not even the moon will notice that I stepped out. I bend down to adjust my magic slippers the way I do every time before I practise the slide and take off to the moon. Maybe this time, it won't be the practice round. Maybe this one is the final one, I think to myself as I stretch my arms towards the border.

God stretches towards the floor to pick up one of the ice cubes he dropped. The ice cube slides through his fingers instead. He watches it slide towards the electrical socket. For the first time he moves a strand of his hair away from his face. If only for a short time. Buzzing. The strand falls back across his eye again. Little sparks fly up. The neon lights at the border all go out. More of God's hair falls over his eyes. No one will see me now.

With all the neon lights gone, the border barely looks like the border anymore. I have done the Moon Slide so many times at home in the apartment we left, I can do it now, too. It is true, the hallway there was better than the street here near the border. Regardless of all the cracks, I know I can do it anyway, especially now that everything around me is dark. If it works, I will feel a little less guilty for breaking my parents' curtains the time I ran towards the window too fast. I can do it. Concentrate. In my head I count: One, one one, one one one. I do it that way, because it is more precise. It also makes it sound like everyone is still together. A few smaller, faster steps now. Preparation. Sounds are coming from the stairs. I don't know if they are yours or the boy's. Oh. Wait. The stairs in the boy's apartment building are gone. Concentrate. Again. A few smaller steps. Faster steps now. This is getting serious now. Another smaller step. I am running closer towards the border. The balloon around my wrist is rustling the way the boy's plastic bag did when he was still here.

It is working. It is working. I am sliding across the asphalt as smoothly as on the hardwood floor. When I lift up, I will see the boy. I will be able to see the floor of his apartment from above, before I get to the moon.

My arms lift up. In the deep blue air, I know how to use them better. Or maybe the balloon is helping me. I am accelerating. The grownups must be around somewhere, because I can hear their voices again. Distinguishing any of their words is difficult. Air is fluttering against my ear heavily. I imagine this must be similar to what the boy felt when he was sliding down the stairwell. I think we are approaching the main chalk line, because I can see the outlines of the booths appearing through the dark. The air is fluttering against my eyelids stronger than before. I think I am faster now. I think I am close to takeoff. Now a larger step, before I let go.

The speed is highest at the end, right before the jump, the boy said. Your footsteps right beside me help, I remember he added. I hear footsteps, too. God's chair tips. He must have leaned forward too much. I am one larger step before lifting up. I don't know if God was trying to pick up another ice cube or if he was leaning in again to listen. Either way, it looks like he is trying to help clean up the mess. I don't know if he can, because he is lying down on the floor now. I think he fell. I hope he is not too hurt. I am worried, because the ground just shook and even though a lot of wind is in my ear, this is the loudest sound I heard since the beginning of the war. And there have been very loud sounds. This one was so loud, I think it made a tear in the sky that is just too big. I smell the lavender ash again. This can't be good. More of it is falling out of God's pockets as he tries to get up. An ice cube breaks underneath his hand. I think his palm is bleeding now. Red petals are falling through the echoing boom.

The street underneath me cracks. A siren. Maybe it is just the ambulance trying to help God. It can't be the border alarm, because the electricity is still out. The grownups can't catch me now. They are too late. I am about to leave the ground. Some kind of red-blue light starts circling around. I don't know if it is coming from a booth or from a car. Even though it looks mesmerizing, I think I need to get away from it. A few more steps. With each one, a memory of the long hallway again, the curtain rings, the boy sliding down the staircase, the flickering streetlight, the moon. Just jump, the boy says, while sliding down. So, I do.

The balloon lifts me up through the red and blue air. How pretty it looks. Broken red and blue pieces of light are circling around. Sometimes they hit the ground and sometimes they float up. One or two of them just brushed over my cheek. I think the grownups are trying to find me. Soon they won't be able to reach me. Soon I will be too high. Another one of the lights just managed to catch my foot. My magic slipper is dangling, but still holding on.

From up here the world is taking on a different shape. A red petal is sticking to the balloon. Maybe if I see life from a distance, everything will make just a little bit more sense. Another red petal sticks to the balloon. Must be the static. Even if I still don't understand a single thing about the world, if I see the boy, I will be okay.

I need to float a little higher up. It is hard, because the past me grabs on to my foot. She tells me she wants to come with me, because someone else lives in her room now. The future me is here, too, pulling me into the sky. I am not sure what to make of what I see.

I was hoping to see where the boy is, but instead I see me. One me is waiting inside the shelled building where the boy lives and the other is waiting in front of your door. The past and the future are happening all at once. I don't know how running across the border and lifting up is making me experience both my future and my past at the same time, but it is.

I need to lift up even more. Maybe I am not high enough to see the boy. The air against my cheek is coming from the past as I float up. I can feel the draft. Oh no. I think it is coming from the boy's open apartment door. I hear it fluttering open and closed against the wall. A stronger draft flows past my eyelids. My eyes close as more rubble falls into my eyelashes. Any time now, he will slide down the staircase railing. Any time now, I hear the past me, the one that went to his building before we left. She is still waiting.

The future me waits, too, even though she is pulling me up. I think she wants to go higher, because she wants to float past your window. The draft from the boy's open door makes your curtains move. They float up, then down, up, then down. I float a little bit farther up. I think I see you moving the curtains aside. The first time we met, you said to me that the only time you sleep with the curtains open is when there is a crescent moon in the sky. That is the only time the light is just right. Everything else is just too bright.

I hold on tighter to the balloon string, because I am ascending faster now. I can hear you glide your curtain rings across your curtain rod. Outside, it is full moon. It is full moon and the light is seeping through your window. Yet, despite the light, you move your curtain aside some more in the same moment as I float past. I don't know if you managed to see me, because I floated by so fast. I think I noticed you glance up as you leaned on your windowsill.

Maybe you are looking at the bench now. I think eventually, you will come out and take a walk. I think you will want to sit down. I think I even saw you tie the curtain closed with a shoelace to let more moonlight in. I think your elbow was resting on the windowsill as the curtain brushed against your cheek. It's the draft from the boy's old apartment. It's the draft. Part of me still wonders if you remember it. Your hair moves across your eyes.

A strand of God's hair falls over his eyes again as he bends to look at his wounded hand. I am floating farther up, the breeze is moving God's hair.

I think God may have made a new friend, regardless of everything, because the person he is sitting with moves towards him. He gently bends his knees and takes God's arm. His new friend is kneeling down now, before he sits on the heels of his shoes. Let me see your hand, he says to God and rests God's arm on his upper leg. I remember the stray dog scratching my leg in the same spot when I was on the bench. Now turn your palm up towards the ceiling, God's new friend tells him. Your hand is too blue. You need more air. You need more air. Your sleeve around your wrist is too tight. We need to unbutton it. He takes God's sleeve, stretches the buttonhole. It is now as wide as the full moon. The button slides through. The moon smiles at the bench before it hides behind a cloud. You can tell it is still there. I think you move your curtain even further aside.

God moves his head as if to reveal more of his face. I guess he trusts his new friend. Your palm is hurt. I don't know if it was the ice that broke in your hand or something more, but you need help, he says to God.

My hand is hurting, too, as I hold on tightly to the balloon. Somehow it is getting harder and harder to hold on, the closer we get to the opening in the sky. I think there is a cut in my palm, because of the boy's fluttering apartment door. The draft is just too strong. The wind around me is just too heavy. The balloon in my hand is shaking, its string is digging deeper into the skin in my palm.

The cut inside your palm is pretty deep, he says to God. But don't worry, I will take care of it. In a little bit, it won't hurt anymore, he adds and reaches into his pocket. White little flakes start falling all around me through the opening in the sky. I still smell the rubble and the burnt lavender, but something else is there, too. He is holding a piece of chalk as he pulls God's arm closer to him.

Wait a minute. One of his shoelaces is gone. I recognize his shoes. I feel his touch in my palm the second he starts drawing something over God's scars. I think he is drawing a star. It will hurt less now, he says to God. It will hurt less. He folds God's fingers in and gives God a star, just like the boy gave me mine. Wait. Is that him? I don't know. I don't even know what year it is anymore and I can't be sure anymore of anything I saw.

I have to float higher up. I have to float through the opening in the sky and then I will know if that was the boy. Maybe someone there, on the other side of the sky, will tell me what it all was.

I am getting closer to the opening. I think both God and the boy turn towards the window as the curtain in the bar moves. They are looking at the tip of a helium balloon rising up on the other side of the window. Only a little bit higher and I will know. But the draft from the boy's empty apartment moves the curtain shut. My head bumps against the red and purple lines in the sky. The glass of the bar's window makes a gentle sound. My forehead is hurting a little bit. The stray dog nudges his forehead against mine. Wait a minute. How did he get here? How did I get back to your door and where is the balloon that was in my hand? I was just on my way to the boy.

The stray dog licks my eye, brushes over my nostrils. I can smell chalk. He touches my nose with his paw. During the war, the Sarajevo Roses had a different name. We called them Paw Prints. A Sarajevo Rose appears in front of your door as I pet the dog on his head. He licks my face again. A marble rolls out from underneath his tongue. It didn't roll out the first time, but it rolls out now. I am too sleepy to catch it. It slides underneath your closed door over your uneven floor. Clop, hobble, clop. It goes on. In that, too, I saw a rhythm, unforgiveable in its beauty.

It must be the boy's. It must be the boy's.

Maybe I can lie down on the bench that appeared and fall asleep with the moon as my pillow. No one would have to worry about something happening to me, because the stray dog will stand guard. Maybe when you wake up in the morning, you will come and say hello, whether or not you are the boy. I don't know, but I taste lavender pieces in my mouth. The lavender strands are still burnt, but a little bit less burnt than before. Clop, hobble, clop, hobble, clop. The marble continues to roll along your floor. Just as it was picking up speed, the marble stops mid-roll. You are no longer looking out the window. I can barely see the top of your head now, you are almost entirely below the window line. The moonlight combs through your messy hair. I hope the reason you bent down is not because you are scared to stand so exposed at the window. But I don't think so; the night is just too beautiful for that.

It must be the boy's, I think to myself as I look up at the sky with his star in my hand.

Acknowledgements

I would like to begin by thanking George Elliott Clarke, who read the novel before anyone else (aside from my mother) and had many words of support, praise and enthusiasm. I much appreciate your engagement with helping me find a suitable home for the novel and recommending it to Michael Mirolla. On this note, I am very grateful to Michael Mirolla for believing my book is worthy enough of being included under the roof of Guernica Editions. Thank you for the care, interest and encouragement with which you welcomed me. Next, I extend my appreciation to Denise Bukowski, my agent, who helped me maximize the potential of the book with thoughtful and mindful suggestions. Many thanks to the editors Julie Roorda and Nick Popham for helping with even further refinement. I also could not have asked for a more beautiful cover image created by Nick Marinkovich and cover design created by Rafael Chimicatti. Thank you.

Last, but not least, I am beyond indebted to those dearest and closest to me for believing I could actually write a novel and for knowing how to tolerate my long periods of absence while I was writing. Reporting daily word counts to you also made me sit down with my notebook and pencil and work at it until there was a number considerable enough to mention. Thank you to the friends and strangers at Olimpico Café and Café Social in the Mile End for being around me, yet letting me write. It was the perfect balance between solitude and company to make this novel come to life. In the process, you became a kind of extended family. Thank you for the tasty cappuccinos, the words of encouragement, the timely interruptions and giving me the sense of always having another home.

About the Author

Nataša Nuhanović was born in 1984 in Zagreb, Croatia. She grew up in a mixture between Croatia, Bosnia, Germany and Canada. In 1994, her family escaped from Bosnia to Germany amidst the Bosnian war. Eventually, in 1998, her parents took her to Canada. She studied English Literature, Comparative Literature and German Literature at the University of Waterloo, University of Toronto and McGill, respectively. In 2010, Nataša published her first poetry collection, *Stray Dog Embassy*, with Mansfield Press. She continued to work in the literary field as a translator and interpreter after which she decided to venture into the medium of film. *Close the Door* is her first feature-length movie and is set to play at several festivals. *The Boy's Marble* is her debut novel.

Printed in May 2022
by Gauvin Press,
Gatineau, Québec